SY CO ARB 79

Star of
the North

By the same author

Princess of Hanover

Star of the North

A novel based on the life of Catherine the Great

HELENE LEHR

St Martin's Press   New York

© Helene Lehr 1990

All rights reserved. Printed in the United
States of America. No part of this book
may be used or reproduced in any manner
whatsoever without written permission except
in the case of critical articles or reviews.
For information, address St Martin's Press,
175 Fifth Avenue, New York, N.Y. 10010

Library of Congress Cataloging-in-Publication Data

Lehr, Helene.
     Star of the north / Helene Lehr.
          p.   cm.
     ISBN 0–312–03939–5
     1. Catherine II, Empress of Russia, 1729–1796—Fiction.   2. Soviet
Union—History—Catherine II. 1762–1796—Fiction.   I. Title
PS3562.E4417S7   1990   89–48531
813'.54—dc20   CIP

First U.S. Edition

10 9 8 7 6 5 4 3 2 1

This book is dedicated to
Sam and Stan Shindler and
Bill and Dessie Casey Whitehead

Good friends and good times
make good memories

Contents

Prologue

Only the rhythmic ticking of the jeweled clock on the marble mantel disturbed the stillness of the room as the empress studied the painting of the young girl whose likeness had been captured in delicate enameled brushstrokes.

'She's somewhat plain,' Elizabeth stated at last, addressing the man who was standing beside her.

Count Bestuzhev bent forward slightly so as better to see the painted face. He was a tall man, impeccably dressed in black trousers and a jacket of black velvet, the lapel of which sported a diamond-encircled miniature of his empress. Above a white lace jabot his face was intelligent and somber, giving him the appearance of being older than his forty-six years, an impression reinforced by traces of gray in his hair and neatly trimmed beard. He pursed his lips, then spoke.

'That she is, your Majesty,' he agreed quietly. 'But her skin is fair and unblemished. And her eyes are fine. One might even say they were quite lovely.' He straightened again and clasped his hands behind him.

Elizabeth Petrovna gazed up at him, unsmiling, and the chancellor hastened to add: 'Still, madame, it's most difficult to tell. With your Majesty's face before me even the most beautiful woman is at a disadvantage.'

The empress allowed a slight smile to play about her full red lips, but her chancellor did not return it. He had merely stated a fact. The daughter of the Great Tsar Peter was a tall, striking, handsome woman of thirty-four, who bore herself regally and with great confidence.

Elizabeth returned her attention to the portrait. Sophie Augusta Fredericka of Anhalt-Zerbst was indeed plain. The nose was somewhat long, the mouth somewhat small, and the chin was definitely pointed. However, her eyes were, as the count had noted, fine. They were not quite blue; rather, they were a peculiar shade of violet.

'How old did you say she was?' Elizabeth inquired of her chancellor, still staring at the violet eyes. An illusion of the artist's brush, she decided at last.

'She is fourteen, your Majesty.'

'Her health?'

'My reports indicate that her health is excellent,' Bestuzhev replied. 'And she suffers no deformity.'

It was a measure of Count Bestuzhev's characteristic veracity that he spoke in such a straightforward manner, for his personal choice of a wife for the grand duke Peter was certainly not the German girl whose face was now being so carefully scrutinized by the empress. Bestuzhev would have preferred his sovereign to choose the Princess of Saxony; to choose anyone, for that matter, except a Prussian.

Absently Elizabeth raised a hand and patted her hair. Its heavily powdered whiteness was in stark contrast to the black plume that decorated her coiffure. Even though the evening's banquet had ended some two hours ago, Elizabeth was still wearing her crimson velvet gown edged with Spanish lace and adorned with rubies across the tight-fitting bodice. The lavish creation was one of more than fifteen thousand that comprised her wardrobe. Satisfied that all was in place, she reached out and picked up the oval portrait.

'The girl is of good blood,' she mused. Then she tapped the portrait with a ringed finger, her manner now brisk and businesslike. 'Very well, send for her. But do it discreetly. We will make no commitment until we meet her.'

'Her family …' the count began, but Elizabeth raised her hand, interrupting him.

'Her mother only. Prince Christian is a devout Lutheran – too devout. Princess Joanna can accompany her daughter. Make certain that their retinue is small enough so as not to attract attention.' She paused, frowning in thought, then added: 'It would be preferable, we think, to have them travel incognito. At least until they reach the border. See to it that they receive papers identifying them as' – she waved a hand – 'Countess Reinbeck and daughter,' she instructed, giving the first name that came to her.

'I'll take care of everything, your Majesty,' the count replied in his quiet and deferential tone. Although he was upset with Elizabeth's decision, his expression remained bland, the narrowing of his black eyes the only outward indication of his inner dismay. Grand Duke Peter was half Romanov by birth, but he was, in Bestuzhev's opinion, all Prussian in his soul. Now the lamentable decision had been made to summon a German princess as a possible candidate for his wife. And, God help them all, a Lutheran one, at that.

After a formal bow, the count withdrew, leaving the empress alone in the room save for a servant woman who hovered at a discreet distance.

With a sigh, Elizabeth picked up the cup of wine that was never far from her reach. Sipping at the dark-red liquid, her eye again rested on the face of the German princess. She was young and, from all accounts, healthy; no doubt she would easily produce children. And that, after all, was the only reason for this union.

Children. With the thought, Elizabeth's mind fastened unwillingly upon the image of another child. A frown creased her white brow as she thought of him. Quickly she downed the wine in one long swallow.

Why did it continue to haunt her? she wondered, feeling the familiar tug of uneasiness. Would it always torment her? She shifted restlessly in the chair. How old was he now, the little tsar Ivan?

No! Elizabeth shook her head so sharply that the black plume fluttered in protest. She must never allow herself to think of the child as tsar; never that, she told herself sternly.

The wine coursed through her, relaxing her, calming her frazzled nerves. She had spared the boy's life. Surely God would forgive her for the rest. Surely He would know that she had kept her vow. She had sworn that she would never give the order for anyone's execution ... not even the living, breathing menace that hovered in the shadows of her every waking thought.

In rising anguish, Elizabeth raised a hand to cover her eyes.

And there it was: the image not even wine could dull. The image of a small child who lived his endless days walled up in the blackness of a dungeon. Alone, and without so much as a name, the boy didn't even know who he was.

But she knew.

With another, deeper sigh, Elizabeth lowered her hand and looked out of the tall narrow window. The dreamlike brilliance of the November night was slowly being eroded by approaching dawn. It was, for Empress Elizabeth Petrovna, time to retire.

After getting slowly to her feet, Elizabeth went to join her lover, Alexis Razumovsky. Once in his passionate embrace the haunting memories would be dispelled, and Elizabeth knew she would be able to sleep without fear of dreaming.

PART ONE
The Girl
1744

One

'Grand Duchess Catherine Alexeievna ...'

The former Sophie Augusta of Anhalt-Zerbst smiled at her reflection as she murmured her new name and rank. It sounded pleasant to her ear. She did a small pirouette in front of the looking glass, admiring the blue satin gown that molded her slim frame. Her breasts were, as yet, only buds, but it pleased her to see that in this last year her body was finally beginning to lose its boyish look.

Moving to the open window, Catherine inhaled deeply, enjoying the scent of roses that pervaded the June air, delighting in the color and splendor that met her eye.

These past four months had sped by with a swiftness that left her breathless. So many changes had occurred in her life since she and her mother had arrived in Moscow in the bitter cold of February that, at times, Catherine was hard-pressed to believe her good fortune. She was actually betrothed to her cousin, Grand Duke Peter Feodorovich, the heir to the throne of Russia! It followed then that she, a former German princess, would one day be empress of this vast empire.

It was a heady thought.

Just then, one of the servants approached to announce the arrival of the grand duke. Summoning a welcoming smile, Catherine turned and regarded the fifteen-year-old boy who would, within a year, become her husband. That he wasn't handsome was of no concern to her. That he preferred to be the Duke of Holstein rather than the grand duke of Russia did disturb her. Anyone who preferred a mere dukedom to an imperial crown was someone Catherine could not understand.

'What are you doing?' Peter asked. A gleam of petulance lighted his pale-blue eyes. Crossing the floor, he paused in front of her. He was not much heavier than she was and, despite the fact that his boots were fitted with one-inch heels, not much taller.

Catherine motioned toward her writing table. 'I was going to study ...'

'Bah!' He grabbed her wrist in a none too gentle manner as he all but dragged her from the room. 'That's a waste of time. There are more interesting things to do than that!'

In the corridor, he released his hold, confident that she would follow him.

Catherine sighed. She had learned much during these past four months, but there was so much more to learn. This, she knew, was her chance, perhaps her only chance. Returning to Stettin, for whatever reason, would result in her being betrothed to a minor princeling, like as not one as old as her father. At the thought, she shuddered. Somehow she would have to win Peter's affection, an affection that seemed abysmally lacking, not only for herself, but for everyone he knew. The empress led that exclusive list. Peter, Catherine had discovered, was nursing an antipathy for his aunt and benefactress that seemed without end.

'I don't think studying is a waste of time,' she murmured at last, rubbing her wrist.

His answer was an unpleasant laugh. 'It is when all you're studying is their heathen language and their heathen religion.' He glanced sideways at her, resentful that his aunt was forcing him into marriage. However, Catherine was German, as he was. There was that to be said in her favor. Despite the fact that his mother was Russian, Peter always considered himself to be a Prussian.

'If you are so dissatisfied,' Catherine went on to ask, 'why did you agree to come here?'

Peter paused so abruptly that Catherine took two more steps before she realized he had halted.

'Agree?' He stared coldly. 'You speak as if I had been given a choice. When my father died I was dragged back here against my will; just because my mother – God rest her soul – was the empress's sister.'

He began to walk again, and Catherine hurried her steps to catch up with him as he wended his way toward his apartments. On either side of the stone-walled corridors, palace guards stood still and motionless as they passed by. Though Catherine glanced at them with a tentative smile, their eyes remained fixed straight ahead. They were armed, not with muskets, but with axes. Catherine repressed a small shiver, suspecting that the lightly held weapons could be utilized with deadly efficiency when the need arose.

'Well,' she said in an effort to reason with the young man at her side, 'the empress did make you her heir. She must be fond of you.'

Peter grunted and spoke without looking at her. 'She has no love for me, nor have I any for her.'

Catherine was about to respond, but they had reached Peter's apartments.

Seeing his approach, the guards opened the door so quickly that Peter didn't even have to break his stride.

As she followed Peter into the large sitting room, Catherine eyed the toy soldiers lined up on the floor, wondering who had taken the time to outfit the little figures. They were all dressed in the blue uniform of Holstein, an exact replica of the one that Peter was now wearing. He seldom wore anything else, though the severity of the uniform did little to enhance his thin frame.

She looked up then and smiled as she saw a tall young courtier heading toward her. Of all of Peter's gentlemen, Catherine liked Leo Narishkin the best. Only a year older than Peter, Leo was nevertheless mature and intelligent – traits that Peter had yet to acquire.

'Good afternoon, Highness,' Leo said, offering Catherine a courtly bow.

'Does the sight of an ugly face intrigue you, Leo?' Peter smirked at his gentleman.

Catherine felt her cheeks flush. She knew very well that she wasn't pretty. Lord knew, even her own mother had often brought it to her attention.

Leo's engaging smile softened his own none too attractive face as he continued to regard Catherine. 'I see no ugliness, Highness,' he remarked quietly.

'Hah! Your eyes are failing you early on. It is a measure of my aunt's esteem for me that she has tied me to the least attractive princess in Europe!'

For a moment, Leo's countenance darkened, but he said nothing. He didn't consider Catherine plain at all and thought her violet eyes the most beautiful he had ever seen. Regarding the smirking face of the grand duke, Leo felt a pang of compassion for the girl who was to become his wife. For the rest of her life this lovely young princess would be tied to this dull-witted fool, he thought in despair. God help her. After offering Catherine another bow, Leo hastily left the room.

Catherine stood there, shaken. Peter, she knew, had no recourse but to marry the girl his aunt had chosen for him. Yet she had hoped to gain his affection. Obviously this was not to be. Friendship, then. Surely she could attain that.

Catching her lower lip between her teeth, Catherine watched as Peter got down on his knees. With a show of enthusiasm he began to move the wooden soldiers about the carpeted floor.

'Come on, Catherine!' he urged, looking up at her with a trace of impatience.

Only a small sigh escaped her lips as Catherine sank to the floor, trying to maneuver her hooped skirt into a more manageable position, forcing herself to join the game with an outward display of pleasure. She had long ago relinquished her dolls and found it difficult to understand why her cousin continued to play with his.

To the far side of the large, messy room, Peter's tutor, Otto Brummer, picked his teeth and observed the two young people on the floor, a preoccupied look on his heavy-featured face. He seemed neither to approve nor to disapprove of the actions of his charge. A heavily muscled Swede in his early forties, Brummer had been the only member of Peter's household to accompany him when he had been commanded to leave Holstein and come to Russia. His association with the grand duke had begun some years before when Peter's father died. Although he had been harsh and strict in his training, Brummer had been unable to instill any strength or character in his ward. He had long since given up, allowing Peter to do as he wished.

The afternoon was almost gone, having dissolved in a blur of tedium for Catherine, when Peter suddenly paused. Clasping his arms around his knees, he gave Catherine a thoughtful look.

'I've heard some rumors about your mother,' he murmured to her, his usually strident voice for once lowered.

Suddenly alert, Catherine avoided those pale eyes, aware that her heart had begun to quicken its beat. With effort, she kept her voice casual. 'Rumors? What sort of rumors?' She darted a quick glance across the room, but Brummer was occupied at the writing table, paying them no mind.

Peter hunched his thin shoulders and regarded the tips of his polished boots. 'Count Bestuzhev has uncovered some sort of correspondence. Letters of a treasonable nature,' he qualified with a meaningful nod.

Catherine just stared at him, a sinking feeling in the pit of her stomach.

Far from being condemning, however, Peter's reaction seemed to be one of rare admiration. 'Do you suppose that your mother is spying for King Frederick?' he asked, his voice still low.

A wavering breath caught in her throat. 'She would never do anything like that,' Catherine began to protest. Then she fell silent, feeling a sudden anger with her mother. She knew about the letters, but she wasn't at all certain as to their contents. What if it were true? The empress could easily send them both back home. Catherine bit her lip at the prospect. She didn't want to go home. She wanted to stay, to marry Peter, to retain her title of grand duchess.

'Well, I hope she is a spy,' Peter declared strongly, unaware of his cousin's distress. 'Someday, when I'm emperor,' he whispered, leaning forward, 'Frederick will be my greatest ally.'

Catherine ignored his last statement, her mind still on the letters. If Peter knew, she thought uneasily, it was only a matter of time before the empress learned of her mother's indiscretions. Her violet eyes sought Peter's pale ones.

'Perhaps I'll be sent away,' she lamented, blinking back hot tears. She held her breath, waiting hopefully for a word or a sign that Peter would be unhappy with her departure. His only reaction was a careless shrug. Reaching out a hand, he moved a soldier to a position more to his liking. Elbows on his knees, he cupped his chin in his hands and studied the toy army that waited mutely for his bidding.

Seeing his so obvious lack of concern, Catherine's mouth tightened imperceptibly. If she had needed proof as to Peter's regard for her, she had it now. He didn't give a damn one way or the other. For just a brief moment she was filled with an almost irresistible urge to tell him what she really thought of him, tell him how foolish and immature he was. Right now, however, the matter of the letters was by far the more pressing problem.

Leaving Peter to his games, Catherine hurriedly

returned to her apartments, determined to have a talk with her mother.

To her dismay, she discovered that the empress had already sent for Joanna. With no little apprehension as to the outcome of her own fate, Catherine settled down to wait.

Finally, thirty minutes later, Joanna returned to their apartments, handkerchief pressed to her lips, shoulders heaving with dramatic agitation. She was crying so hard that Catherine could make no sense of her words. She was about to follow her mother into the bedchamber when the page informed her that the empress commanded her immediate presence.

On trembling legs, Catherine followed the young man to where the empress was waiting, the vision of her mother's tearful face sharp in her mind. Catherine couldn't recall ever seeing Joanna weep like that.

When they reached the door the page opened it, bowed, and withdrew without so much as a word.

The empress, dressed in a green satin caftan worked entirely in gold thread, looked up from where she was seated on the divan as Catherine entered the salon known as the Lyons room. It was so named because every bit of material in it was made from the shimmering silk that was imported from Lyons.

'Come here,' Elizabeth said curtly.

Hesitantly Catherine advanced into the room, feeling a great relief when the empress indicated that she could sit down. Her legs felt as if they would no longer support her. Easing into a straight-backed chair, she clasped her hands tightly in her lap, the sound of her beating heart loud in her ears. The silence continued for an unbearable length of time, increasing her anxiety.

'Your mother is being sent home!'

The abrupt and harsh words caused Catherine to start visibly.

'It is most unfortunate that she has presumed upon our

hospitality,' Elizabeth continued tersely. 'She has taken advantage of our good will and has sought to betray us to the King of Prussia.'

Catherine's face turned even paler. Her mouth was so dry that she had to swallow before she could speak. 'I ... I don't believe my mother would do that,' she protested, close to tears.

'Believe it, Catherine Alexeievna!' the empress retorted quickly, angry at being contradicted. 'And you? Do you wish to return home with her?' Elizabeth raised a brow while she waited for a reply.

Twisting the betrothal ring on her finger, Catherine shook her head, afraid her voice would be too unsteady if she spoke. She sat stiffly in the chair, the soft light from the burning tapers doing little to warm her white face.

Elizabeth relaxed a bit and leaned back against the cushions. 'We know your departure would upset the grand duke. He has become most fond of you.'

Catherine viewed her clasped hands in her lap and made no comment. She knew exactly how much her leaving would mean to her cousin. Doubtless, she thought wryly, her departure would cause him to dance for joy.

Finally Elizabeth issued a deep sigh, her features softening as she saw the girl's evident distress. 'We know you had no part in all this. You will not be forced to pay for your mother's foolishness.' Her face hardened again. 'We will permit Princess Joanna to stay for the wedding. But immediately afterward, she must leave.'

'I understand, your Majesty,' Catherine murmured. After the wedding, the empress had said. Color crept back into her cheeks.

Shifting her weight, Elizabeth rested one elbow on the arm of the divan, her gaze turning speculative as she observed the young grand duchess. 'The grand duke is our heir, as you know, the only living male Romanov ...' She fell silent a moment, the dark specter of Ivan crossing her mind. Damn the child! she thought fiercely, clenching

her fist. Why does he still live? Why couldn't she bring
herself to get rid of him?

Uneasy, Catherine watched the play of emotion on the
older woman's face, wondering if the empress was having
second thoughts. She shivered, suddenly feeling chilled in
the warm room. If she were sent back to Stettin, it would
be in disgrace. Not only would her rank be taken from her,
but her future, as well.

Then Elizabeth gave another deep sigh. Her voice
returned to a more normal level as she continued. 'It is our
earnest wish, Catherine Alexeievna, that you marry and
have sons. The grand duke is not a ... strong person. His
health is fragile.' She leaned forward and stared hard, as if
to impress her next words on the young girl before her. 'It
is of the utmost importance that our nephew wed and
have children. Do you understand?'

'I do, your Majesty,' Catherine replied, nodding.
Although her answer was quick, children were the
farthest thing from Catherine's mind at that moment.

A feeling of weariness overcame Elizabeth and her
shoulders slumped. She wondered whether this young
girl knew that she was the last hope of the Romanov
dynasty. 'Very well,' she murmured. 'Return to your
apartments, Catherine Alexievna. We shall not speak of
this incident again.'

Despite the assurances of the empress, Catherine spent
the following weeks in a state of nervous apprehension,
expecting to be sent home at a moment's notice. Only
when the court made preparations to leave for St.
Petersburg in December did Catherine allow herself to
relax. Ordinarily the empress would have commanded
this change of residence to take place in November, but
Peter had fallen ill with the measles, and Elizabeth refused
to leave Moscow until her nephew was well enough to
travel.

On the day they finally departed for the northern city,

the sky was filled with thick pewter clouds that ambled inland from the Gulf of Finland seeking a place to deposit their burden of snow. Along the side of the well-traveled roadway, ancient elm trees restlessly stirred bare branches in mournful anticipation of the coming assault.

Catherine, together with Peter, Brummer, and her mother, sped along in the sledge in relative silence. There was usually very little silence around Peter, but today he was uncharacteristically quiet. Catherine, lost in her own musings, paid him little mind for the first hour or so. Then, happening to glance at him, her brows furrowed in quick concern. His face was flushed, and angry red spots dotted his cheeks and neck. Mindful of his recent bout with the measles, Catherine's first impression was that Peter was having a relapse.

Leaning forward, she touched him lightly on the arm. 'Peter, you don't look well at all. Are you feeling ill again?'

Roused from his half doze, Brummer sat up, cast a critical eye upon the grand duke, and gave an audible gasp of alarm. Not waiting for Peter's mumbled reply, he stuck his head out of the window and yelled at the driver to stop when they reached Khotilovo.

Less than ten minutes later the sledges drew up in front of the modest estate. Peter's face was now bright with fever, his eyes glassy and unfocused. He made no objection when Brummer picked him up in his arms and carried him inside.

Alighting from her sledge, Elizabeth gave a deep sigh, annoyed with the delay. Informed by a servant that Peter was ill, she scowled and said, 'Very well. Instruct the physicians to remain with the grand duke. He can follow when he's feeling better.'

Before the empress could get back into the sledge, Catherine came forward. 'Please, madame,' she said quickly. 'May I remain here with Peter until he's well enough to travel?'

Turning to face her, Elizabeth smiled broadly, pleased

with the request she interpreted as visible proof of the affection between the two young people. She patted the smooth cheek. 'Of course you can.'

Early the next day, Catherine hurried to Peter's room and tapped lightly on the door, waiting impatiently for a response.

When the door opened, it revealed the face of Brummer. Instead of moving aside, however, the stocky Swede just stood there, barring her way.

'The grand duke ...' Catherine began, but the tutor shook his head.

'You cannot enter, your Highness,' he said in a low voice. 'It's the pox.'

Two

The windows were tightly closed against the bitter cold of the late January day. The drapes, too, were closed. There were a mere four hours of daylight at this time of year, and now, though morning, Khotilovo was still shrouded in darkness.

Elizabeth watched in moody contemplation as the servants dressed her nephew. She had spent every waking moment of the past five weeks in this room while her nephew battled for his life. He had come close to death in those first critical days of his illness, a situation that had truly alarmed her. After that, his recovery had been fairly steady, if maddeningly slow. Yesterday, however, the physicians had informed her that the grand duke was well enough to return home.

She had already reached the palace when word had come to her that Peter was ill with the pox. Ignoring the loud protestations of her personal physician, Elizabeth had immediately returned to Khotilovo, and commanded Catherine to return to St. Petersburg. Elizabeth had never had smallpox, and while some would consider her constant attendance on her nephew to be an act of bravery, Elizabeth herself did not. The safety of her heir was paramount in her mind, and she wanted to make certain that the physicians did everything in their power to save him.

Elizabeth was growing used to Peter's face. Although it was a shame, she thought, that he had been so terribly disfigured. She had seen many people with the mark of the pox upon them, but never one as mutilated as Peter had become. But he was alive. Nothing else was of any importance.

One of the valets now stepped forward, a wig held in his hands, prepared to place it on the head of the grand duke. He halted abruptly as Peter spun around, glaring at him.

'I will not wear it!' he shouted shrilly. After raising his hand, Peter struck the hapless man. The valet bore the blow with stoic acceptance and remained standing where he was, the offending wig still in his hand.

With a quick murmur of exasperation, Elizabeth got up and came to Peter's side. 'You must wear it,' she said in an uncharacteristically cajoling voice.

Ignoring her, Peter grabbed the wig and threw it across the room. 'I look bad enough as it is,' he protested in the same loud voice that now cracked in a sob. 'Catherine will laugh when she sees me.'

Catherine, thought the empress with a quickening sense of despair, will not laugh – nor will anyone else. 'Nonsense, Peter Feodorovich,' she contradicted in a brisker tone. 'Catherine knows that you have been gravely ill, and while we admit that your face is still swollen, the white powder has helped. Why, you can hardly see the pockmarks.'

This was a gross lie, for even with a liberal application of powder the scars were still fiery and livid. Elizabeth couldn't quite repress a sigh at the sight of him. Peter's face was so swollen that his features were completely distorted. However, that would pass, she told herself, trying to quell her uneasiness. Even his hair would grow back again. But right now, she had to admit, the bald pate only added to the overall disfigurement.

'Put it on,' she urged Peter. 'You don't want Catherine to see you bald, do you?' She nodded briefly to the servant. The man approached the grand duke cautiously, expecting another outburst.

But Peter sat there in a resigned manner and allowed the

hated wig to be placed in position. It didn't help much because it was too large for his head.

Elizabeth nodded and heaved a sigh of relief. Fearful of any further display of petulance, she issued a hasty command to make ready to leave.

As they settled themselves in the sledge awhile later, Peter turned to his aunt. 'Do I really look all right?' he asked anxiously. 'Will Catherine recognize me?'

Elizabeth patted his hand in a consoling manner. 'Of course she'll recognize you. What a foolish thing to say. The swelling and discoloration will disappear in a short while, and you ... will look as you did before.'

They both fell silent. Behind them, Khotilovo receded from view and melted into the white horizon.

Meanwhile, at the imperial palace in St. Petersburg, Catherine was spending long minutes surveying her wardrobe, finally selecting a dark-green gown of heavy brocade trimmed in cream-colored lace and adorned with tiny seed pearls.

That morning, when she had received word that Peter was fully recovered and was prepared to return to court, Catherine had been filled with a relief that made her knees weak. Had Peter died, her own future would have died with him.

Catherine had barely finished dressing when a servant announced the imminent arrival of the imperial sledge. In high spirits she ran down to the front hall to greet her empress and her betrothed.

The huge brightly colored vehicle had already pulled up to the front steps. The empress, aided by a footman, stepped out, then turned and waited for her nephew. Even though the guards had opened the massive double doors to the palace, Elizabeth was standing in such a position that Catherine couldn't see Peter clearly from where she was standing on the threshold.

A moment later they both began to ascend the wide

steps. Watching their approach, Catherine felt as if the breath was being squeezed from her body.

A dark and misshapen shadow emerged from the mist and grayness of the late January afternoon. As it came closer, Catherine was gripped by a feeling of terror. The face had a cadaverous, ghastly look about it, and there was an odor of foulness that made her gasp for air.

The creature advanced toward her, its mutilated face scowling, and for the first time Catherine saw that it was Peter.

Involuntarily she took a step backward as he came closer. 'Oh, my God!' she cried out at the sight of him, pressing her hand to her lips.

Elizabeth rushed up to them both. Casting a black look at Catherine, she snapped: 'You little fool!'

Peter, for his part, was glaring at his future wife, his eyes filled with a bitterness he made no effort to conceal. He knew what he looked like. He had broken every mirror in Khotilovo in the past weeks, unable to endure the image that stared back at him.

Yet, through it all, he had thought that Catherine would understand, would put him at ease. Up until this moment, he hadn't realized just how much he had counted on her.

God damn her soul to hell! he thought fiercely, viewing her horror-struck expression. He saw all he needed to know in those bright violet eyes, and it was an expression of revulsion that he would never forgive, or forget.

A rush of anger colored Peter's face, deepening the already livid red splotches. Without speaking, he spun around and began to run in the direction of his apartments, paying no heed to the empress as she frantically called his name.

Recovering her senses, and angry at herself for her loss of control, Catherine ran after Peter. The door to his apartment was firmly bolted. Uncertain, she stood in the corridor for some minutes; then, with a sigh, returned to her own rooms. Tomorrow, she thought. Tomorrow she would set things to right.

Not until later on, however, did Catherine discover that her momentary lapse was an unforgivable error on her part, something that would actually change the course of her life.

In his bedchamber, Peter ripped off the hated wig and flung it from him. Then he threw himself on his bed. His mind sunk into heated confusion, and he felt nauseous and dizzy from the extent of his emotion.

Two days passed before Peter could be persuaded to leave his apartments. On the third night he reluctantly joined the court in the banquet hall. Seating himself beside his aunt, he cast a hard look in Catherine's direction. One day, he vowed with a savagery that left his hands trembling. One day he would make her pay.

Though Catherine offered him a soft greeting, Peter ignored it, turning his attention instead to the evening's entertainment, hearing the empress laugh heartily at the antics of several dwarfs who were teasing a large black bear. The animal roared in anger but the hall was so noisy the sound barely rose above the din.

Peter picked up his wine cup, frowned at it, then motioned for a servant to bring him a glass of vodka.

Catherine made several more attempts to draw Peter into a conversation, but it appeared that he had suddenly gone deaf. He drank steadily, almost with determination, until, finally, he slumped in his chair, snoring loudly.

With a sigh, Catherine watched as the servants carried the grand duke back to his rooms.

More than a week passed. Each day Catherine went to Peter's apartments, only to be denied entrance.

Viewing her daughter's crestfallen face, Joanna assumed a somewhat spiteful look, and her smile was little better than a sneer.

'So,' she said one day when Catherine returned from Peter's apartment, having again been refused admittance.

'You are not yet married and already you have angered the grand duke.'

'I didn't mean to ...' Catherine cried out, fresh tears scalding her eyes. 'It was such a shock. Why didn't anyone tell me?' While she still lamented her lack of control, Catherine was resentful of the fact that no one had thought to warn her of what had happened to Peter. Had she been prepared, all of this could have been avoided.

Joanna gave a demeaning snort. 'You didn't mean to,' she mimicked. 'But you have. And who are you to be offended at the sight of an ugly face? Your own is little better.' She turned away, her bearing stiff. 'It would serve you right if he refused to marry you.' She gave her daughter a sidelong glance and a cold smile. 'Perhaps neither one of us will have to wait for the marriage to take place before we return home.'

Catherine gave a gasp at her mother's words. 'Peter wouldn't refuse ...' Her voice trailed off. Of course he would, she realized in dismay. She, better than anyone else, knew how little he cared for her.

When the empress finally learned of what was happening, she sent for Catherine and together they confronted the grand duke.

The tone of the empress was at first conciliatory, as she tried to persuade her nephew to receive his betrothed when she came to visit.

Stubbornly Peter refused. 'I want no part of her!' he shouted, turning away.

'It is not what you want that matters,' Elizabeth answered, her voice rising as fast as her temper. 'It is what we want! This foolishness must cease.' She glared at them both as if they were naughty children who had earned a well-deserved reprimand. 'From this day forward,' she commanded, 'Catherine Alexeievna is to spend three hours a day in your company.' She turned to Catherine. 'You will remain here until four o'clock.'

Without further words for either of them, Elizabeth flounced from the room, scowling at anyone who had the misfortune to catch her eye.

With Elizabeth's departure, Catherine regarded Peter warily. Even silent, she could see he was furious. A hard line rimmed his lips, his nostrils were pinched and white, his fists clenched.

No matter how often Catherine tried to talk to him, plead with him, Peter refused to answer her. She might not have been in the room for all the attention he bestowed upon her.

For six straight days Peter just sat in a chair during her compulsory visit, refusing to speak or even to look at Catherine.

Elizabeth, at her wits' end, commanded Peter to speak. But when he did, only words of censure and condemnation poured forth.

In vain did Catherine try to apologize.

'You couldn't look at me!' he bellowed at her. 'Don't tell me otherwise. Even now you can't bear the sight of me.'

'That's not true,' Catherine protested, fighting back her tears. 'I was taken by surprise, that's all. I had no idea ...' She looked away and bit her lip in remorse. It seemed that whatever she said, she only made matters worse.

'Look at me!' Peter got up out of his chair. Walking to her side, he thrust his face close to hers.

Unable to help herself, Catherine drew back slightly. Laughing wildly, Peter again straightened.

'Come, Catherine,' he admonished her in a voice that fairly dripped with sarcasm. 'You must learn to look at the face of your future husband. It's part of the price you will have to pay for your crown. Oh, I know that's what you're after,' he said quickly, as she opened her mouth to contradict him. 'But that's only part of the price,' he went on maliciously, beginning to pace the room. 'The other part is the constant misery I shall cause you. Your life will be as miserable as mine.' He paused in front of her, unmoved by the sight of her tears. 'I promise you!' His body quivered with spasms of laughter mixed with sobs.

And it was a promise he kept.

Three

Spring was only weeks away, but there was no hint of its nearness in the slate-gray clouds that showered tiny white flakes upon an already accumulated winter snow.

Having just entered the drawing room, Elizabeth regarded her chancellor on this particularly bleak March afternoon, her dark eyes hard and intense. Although she had summoned him almost an hour ago, she was just now making an appearance. It had taken longer than usual for her to rouse herself from the warmth of her bed. Her head throbbed and her mouth felt as dry and dusty as the road on a hot summer day.

'Have they gotten together again?' she asked tersely, without preamble. She went to a brocade-upholstered chair and sat down heavily. In spite of the fire that blazed brightly the room had a slight chill to it. Elizabeth clutched her heavy woolen shawl closer about her shoulders as she waited for an answer.

Slowly Bestuzhev shook his head, knowing his reply would be an unwelcome one. 'No, madame. The situation is unchanged.'

'Ahh.' Elizabeth sighed in exasperation. 'The little fool. How could she have been so stupid! It will heal.' She glared up at Bestuzhev as if she expected him to take exception. 'Already there is an improvement.'

Bestuzhev, standing quietly before the chair in which the empress was seated, made no comment to this. As far as he could see, there would never be an improvement in the looks of the grand duke. True, the swelling had gone down, the livid red splotches had subsided to only a faint discoloration; even his hair was at last beginning to grow. But the grand duke would always appear loathsome. There was not so much as a square inch of his face that had been left unmarked.

Elizabeth was so absorbed in her own troublesome thoughts that she paid no mind to the silence of her chancellor. She was convinced that her nephew was acting contrary merely to irritate her.

'What do the physicians say?' she demanded at last.

'The grand duke is fully recovered, madame.'

She grunted, considering that. 'Then we will set a wedding date,' she decided with a firm nod of her head. She reached for her wine and drank heavily.

With a start, Bestuzhev noticed how tired the empress looked. For the first time, he noticed that Elizabeth was growing older. Although she was still a handsome woman, the years were beginning to take their toll. In the harsh light of day, having just gotten out of bed, she appeared markedly dissolute.

His mouth tightened with the discovery. If anything happened to this woman they would all be in the hands of the Prussian abomination, who thought more of his dolls and his toys than his duties. The thought made him cold with despair. A child was needed, another heir. If the empress lived long enough, there was the possibility that the crown could be passed directly to Peter's son.

'You are, as always, right, your Majesty,' he murmured in agreement, inclining his head.

Elizabeth nodded, then shivered, feeling chilled. Turning, she gave a sharp command for the fire to be stoked higher. Facing her chancellor again, she said: 'We will set a date in August. Five months is plenty of time for the preparations. The sooner those two are wed, the sooner there will be children, and our mind will be at rest.'

With Count Bestuzhev's departure, Elizabeth heaved

herself out of her chair and walked to the writing table. She picked up a report she had received from her ambassador in Paris and studied it with great care.

Only a few months before, the French dauphin had wed the Spanish infanta. Elizabeth's ambassador had, at her request, gone into the minutest detail of the splendid pageant that had marked the royal event.

And we shall do this, and more, Elizabeth decided, returning the document to the smooth polished surface. She set her mouth with determination and summoned her advisors.

The next five months saw seamstresses, coachmakers, jewelers, and architects scurrying frantically about. Catherine's gown was to be of silver moiré, worked in silver stitchery right down to the hem. Wine fountains were installed in the square as well as tables and benches, so that the people themselves could participate in the momentous occasion.

A week before the wedding was to take place, Catherine was in Peter's apartments for her daily visit. Brummer was at the far side of the room, seated at a table with several of Peter's gentlemen. They were drinking vodka and playing cards, occasionally bursting into raucous laughter.

Peter, as usual, was sitting in a chair, staring into space. The jacket of his blue uniform was buttoned right up to his neck.

Just looking at him made Catherine feel warm, for the August day was hot and humid. Light as it was, her own peach silk dress clung to her in a most uncomfortable manner.

On the floor, not too far from where they were sitting, stood the toy soldiers. Peter had been playing with them when she had arrived. Catching sight of her, he had scowled, sunk into his chair, and proceeded to answer her in sulky monosyllables whenever she spoke. After the first hour, they had both fallen into an uneasy silence.

Catherine sighed, toying absently with one of the

ribbons on her skirt. The wedding was scheduled to take place in less than a week. She was uncertain as to whether she was looking forward to it or not. The idea of spending the rest of her days like this was not pleasant. The alternative, that of returning to Stettin and obscurity, was equally unpalatable.

She darted an unobtrusive look at Peter. He was slouched in his chair, gazing into space with a vacant expression. His face no longer bothered her; in fact, she felt a certain compassion for her young cousin, a feeling she dared not display. She had tried it once and had been greeted with such ridicule and scorn she had fled in tears.

Turning away from Peter, her gaze fell on the wooden soldiers. Catherine pursed her lips in a thoughtful manner. It was worth a try, she mused. Nothing else had worked. She'd been unable to break through the sullen barrier that Peter had erected about himself. She felt certain that if she could, their relationship would return to its former footing.

Assuming a casual attitude, Catherine finally got up, went to where the wooden soldiers were, and sank down on the floor. Without looking at Peter, appearing in deep concentration, she began to move them about, fashioning two miniature armies, angling one group to attack the other.

For a time Peter watched her, his pale eyes dull and uninterested. It was on the tip of his tongue to command her to leave his soldiers alone. But in spite of himself, his attention was caught by what she was doing. He'd never seen that formation before. The soldiers in front of Catherine were positioned in a solid triangle.

Peter wasn't aware that he had gotten up out of his chair, but suddenly there he was, on the floor, his own eager hand directing the opposing army. What a challenge to break that triangle! he thought, his breath quickening with excitement.

He began moving his men forward. Catherine parried,

the silence between them unbroken. After almost thirty minutes had gone by she deliberately left a gap in her defenses, allowing Peter to win the game.

Straightening, he flashed her a triumphant look. 'There!' he declared loudly, eyes glittering with satisfaction. 'You're not as smart as you think you are.' He was exhilarated, feeling alive for the first time in weeks.

Catherine lowered her head. 'You're just smarter than I am, that's all,' she murmured.

He scrambled to his feet and gave a grunt with the effort. 'Well ...' He paused and looked at her as if he were giving great thought to his next words. 'I suppose you can try again tomorrow, if you want to,' he offered magnanimously.

Raising her head, Catherine smiled up at him.

The morning of August 21, 1745, finally arrived. Before the first faint pink tracings of dawn suffused the sky, Catherine was awake. Although it was not yet six o'clock, she jumped out of bed in a state of high excitement. Today was her wedding day.

While her bath was being readied, Catherine sat down to eat a light breakfast, ignoring the chattering of her ladies, pondering all the while on the ceremony that lay ahead.

Looking up, Catherine saw her mother enter the room. Joanna had apparently just gotten out of bed and wore a light silk robe over her nightdress. Her face was devoid of makeup, her dark hair hanging down her back in one thick braid. She looked drawn and tired, as if she hadn't slept the night before.

'Well, you're looking smug and satisfied with yourself,' she muttered, sitting down at the table. While a servant poured tea, Joanna nibbled on a piece of cake, waving away the offered eggs and blini.

'Why do you say that?' Catherine asked quietly, wiping her lips with the linen napkin. She hoped her mother wasn't going to make a scene on this of all days. She was nervous enough as it was. There had been harsh words between them the night before when Catherine had sought her mother's aid in an attempt to unravel the mysteries of her forthcoming wedding night. Joanna had responded in such heated tones of indignation that Catherine had quickly dropped the subject.

'Humph. You think your life will be easy from now on, don't you?' Joanna's tone was caustic and abrasive, and she couldn't quite ignore the tug of jealousy that took her appetite away. She had already been reminded by the chancellor that she would have to leave before the week was gone. She wasn't looking forward to returning to the dreary atmosphere of Stettin, to the mind-numbing conversation of her husband, to the long and boring evenings that stretched ahead of her.

Sensing the direction of her mother's thoughts, Catherine leaned forward and placed her hand on Joanna's arm. 'Mama, perhaps after a while I can convince the empress to allow you to visit me ...' She broke off as Joanna wrenched away and got to her feet.

'There is nothing you can say that will change her mind,' Joanna retorted bitterly. 'Nor will I be unhappy to leave,' she added, gathering the last of her pride. 'As for you ... Take care,' she murmured in a rare burst of maternalism. 'Take care that you never incur the displeasure of the empress. Although she has bestowed many gifts upon you, she has the power to remove them all.'

Turning abruptly, Joanna headed back to her own bedchamber to prepare herself for her daughter's wedding.

Slowly Catherine got up from the table, refusing to let her mother's words dampen her spirits. With the assistance of her ladies she undressed and sank into the perfumed warm water of her bath, feeling her taut muscles relax. Leaning back, she closed her eyes and willed the tension from her mind and body. She was still in the tub almost thirty minutes later when the empress strode into the room.

Coming forward, Elizabeth regarded Catherine with a smile. 'Stand up and let us see you,' she commanded.

Her face flushed with shy embarrassment, Catherine slowly got to her feet. After a long moment's perusal of the soft and slender form that glistened with drops of water, Elizabeth nodded her satisfaction at the displayed perfection.

'Not even my nephew will be able to resist a sight like that,' she said laughing heartily.

In his own apartments at the other end of the corridor, Peter continued to ignore any suggestions that it might be time for him to dress for his wedding. He was drilling his servants in a new military formation.

Brummer watched the little scenario for a while, then glanced nervously at the clock. 'Your Highness, it's almost time,' he ventured to say.

'I daresay they won't start until I get there,' Peter retorted, annoyed with the interruption.

'Her Majesty will be angry if you are late,' Brummer insisted, motioning the servants forward.

'Good! Maybe she'll get angry enough to send me back home,' Peter muttered, then grudgingly allowed the servants to undress him.

Brummer frowned. 'You should not speak like that. The empress ...'

Peter's laugh was muffled as his shirt was lifted over his head. 'She can do nothing to me,' he retorted. 'I'm the only heir she has ...' His face twisted with a smug look. '...unless she wants to raise Ivan up out of his cell and put his crown back on his head.'

Brummer cleared his throat and glanced about the bedchamber, his narrow close-set eyes darting about as though he expected imminent peril. 'You know it's forbidden to speak that name, Highness,' he hissed, genuinely upset by this lapse.

Laughing at his tutor's obvious discomfort, Peter replied: 'For you, Brummer, and for everyone else. But not for me.' Fully dressed now, he viewed himself in the mirror, scowling at his image. 'Blessed Jesus! I look like one of her grinning lackeys,' he complained, angered that he wasn't allowed to wear his blue uniform. When the servant brought forth the powdered wig, Peter grabbed it and flung it across the room. 'Not that! I will not wear the stupid thing!'

Still muttering to himself, the grand duke stomped from the room.

A short time after that, in the pressing heat of August, the bride and groom set out for the Kazan Cathedral.

The empress had done her planning well. The procession did indeed outrival that of the French dauphin and his Spanish bride. More than one hundred carriages followed the open barouche that held the young couple, all brand new, all brightly painted, all drawn by eight white horses of the finest breed. Noblemen in glittering attire rode on horseback at either side of the imperial carriage, disdainfully ignoring the crowd that fell to their knees with the approach of the bride and groom.

Delighted by the pomp and pageantry, Catherine turned to Peter with shining eyes that immediately clouded at his stiff bearing and unhappy expression. He tugged at the collar of his jacket, made of the same silver cloth as her dress, never once looking at her. He was staring at the crowd with a baleful eye, as if he despised each and every one of them.

Catherine took a deep breath, remained silent, and tried to tell herself that it was the heat and the fact that Peter had to dress in what he considered to be an outlandish manner that was causing his discomfort.

Finally, after a ceremony that lasted all of three hours, leaving Catherine light-headed with fatigue, they were pronounced man and wife.

Save for the required responses, Peter didn't speak to Catherine then or at the banquet that followed. He seemed morose and withdrawn.

Just after nine o'clock the empress commanded that the newlyweds be escorted to their nuptial bed.

Her head throbbing with strain, surrounded by her ladies, Catherine followed the high dignitaries as they filed from the banquet hall. Peter, who would be escorted by his own gentlemen after a decent interval of time, remained at the table.

The ducal apartments had been refurbished with an extravagant hand. The walls were of red silk and displayed jeweled icons and gold sconces. The canopied bed was hung with crimson velvet, lavishly decorated with silver and dominated by the figure of a gold eagle. The hand-carved furniture was dark walnut, massive pieces of great weight that gleamed in the candlelight.

Catherine saw none of it. All she was aware of was her determination to make her marriage work. This was, she told herself firmly, a beginning, not an end.

More nervous than she would admit, even to herself, Catherine allowed her ladies to undress her. Then she settled down in the large canopied bed. The banquet that had followed the wedding had been enormous. Although Catherine had not partaken of every one of the fifty courses that had been served, she had eaten heartily enough and was now conscious of an unsettled stomach.

Resting on silken sheets, she shivered in apprehension. She hadn't the slightest idea of what was to take place. She deplored her innocence, yet her every attempt to alleviate it in the past few days had been in vain. She had questioned her young ladies-in-waiting, only to find that they were as naive as she was. In desperation she had finally sought out her mother. But before she had even fully formed her questions, Joanna had flown into a rage. 'It's indecent even to think of such things, much less to voice them,' she had screamed, refusing to discuss it further.

Catherine propped the pillows behind her and rested back against the softness. The servants had drawn the curtains around the bed. She sat there in the semidarkness, waiting.

An hour later she was still waiting, her face flaming now with embarrassment and humiliation. Peter had decided to partake of a late-evening snack; of this she had been informed by one of her ladies. How could he do this to her? she wondered, almost in tears. From the other side of the curtains she could hear a faint murmur of voices, punctuated by an occasional laugh.

Apparently, she thought, chagrined, the delay wasn't affecting the mood of the 'witnesses.'

Too upset even to doze, Catherine lay there, alone, for yet another hour.

At last she heard Peter's loud and strident voice as he entered the room. Only moments later the curtains parted and he crawled into bed.

For a moment he sat there, having given her no more than a brief glance. Then, with a maniacal grin, he fumbled within the folds of his nightclothes and produced a few of his toy soldiers, placing them in a somewhat precarious fashion on the bed.

Catherine stared at him in disbelief, her astounded ears hearing his whispered urgings to join in with his game.

Instinctively she shrank away from her new husband. But, is he drunk? she wondered, dazed.

He was, but only slightly so. Not wishing to create a scene that would be embarrassing for them both, Catherine's numb fingers clutched at the little toy soldier thrust at her by her husband of only a few hour.. Still dazed, she began to help him place them about the coverings, grateful for the bedcurtains that shielded them from view.

That night, Catherine slept little, and when she did, she

was troubled by dreams that only further interrupted her rest. By morning her dark silken hair was tangled and matted with a cold perspiration that left her pillow damp.

In the dim light of the curtained bed she regarded her sleeping husband and wondered, crazily, whether he was a part of the nightmare that had awakened her.

A week later Catherine watched her mother's preparations for departure, torn between relief and sadness.

Outside, the day was gray and gloomy, the clouds so thick they effectively concealed steeples and seemed to bleach the land of color.

'You will write to me, Mama?' Catherine said at last when they were alone. She felt suddenly bereft and longed to discuss her marital problems. The past six nights with Peter had passed in the same fashion as had their wedding night. Catherine was confused and hurt, yet she dared not speak of it to her mother, knowing Joanna would only turn away from such a conversation.

'I will,' Joanna replied shortly, drawing on her gloves. If she noticed her daughter's pale face, she didn't comment on it, appearing lost in her own thoughts. 'But it's doubtful that the empress will allow you to receive any letters from me.' She didn't look at Catherine as she spoke.

Catherine sighed deeply. 'Why did you do it, Mama?' she asked softly. 'You must have known that your actions would jeopardize my future.'

Pausing, Joanna gave her an annoyed look that was colored by accusation. 'Your future!' The words were followed by a loud and disparaging laugh. 'What is your future compared to the mission that I was given by my king?' Her voice broke and she looked away again, her expression crestfallen. 'And I've failed,' she lamented, her voice catching in a sob. 'Not only have I failed, but the message I must deliver to Frederick will certainly cause him anger.'

Tilting her head, Catherine viewed her mother questioningly.

With only a brief glance at her, Joanna responded. 'Our ambassador is being relieved of his duties. The empress wants Baron Mardefeld formally recalled.'

Catherine put a hand to her lips in dismay. 'What was it that the king wanted you to do?'

'Count Bestuzhev ...' Joanna gave her daughter a defiant look. 'The chancellor favors Austria and England. I was to discredit him any way I could.'

Now Catherine's eyes widened in shocked surprise. The king had enjoined her mother to bring about the downfall of the Chancellor of Russia! No wonder Bestuzhev viewed her with a cold eye. Sadness vanished, leaving only relief in its wake. It was best that her mother return home, Catherine realized. If the past week had been any indication, she was in for enough problems as it was without her mother around to complicate matters further.

Four

Rain fell steadily on this late August evening, producing a thudding cadence that was monotonous and repetitive to the ear. It slanted against double-paned windows with a driving force and danced across the mighty Neva to the marshes beyond, where it became a part of the swampland.

In defiance of the relentless gloom, the crowded reception hall of the imperial palace was brightly lighted. Hundreds of candles in varied hues glowed in the overhead crystal chandeliers. The room was a vast expanse of black and white tile, its austerity offset by the many chairs upholstered in crimson velvet.

Catherine tried to contain her nervousness as she came down the stairs. She was, of late, coming to dread her meetings with the empress, who was making no effort to conceal her increasing displeasure with the wife of her nephew.

As she approached the curved entryway to the hall, Catherine took a deep breath. Only on the threshold did Peter allow her to place her hand lightly on his arm. He didn't like her to touch him.

Before the raised dais where the empress sat, aglitter with the many jewels she was wearing, Catherine and Peter paused to make obeisance. Straightening from a deep curtsy, Catherine felt chilled at the sight of the unspoken condemnation she saw reflected in the dark-blue eyes of Elizabeth. Gone was the smiling expectancy that had lasted until the celebration that had marked the first anniversary of her marriage, more than a year ago. In its place was the look she was now seeing.

Elizabeth continued to stare at Catherine for an uncomfortably long time.

'You are looking well, Catherine Alexeievna,' Elizabeth stated at last. There was no smile on her face as she spoke.

'Thank you, your Majesty,' Catherine responded in a barely audible voice. Beside her, Peter shifted his weight from one foot to the other and gave a sigh of impatience as he waited for their dismissal. His aunt's displeasure meant nothing to him.

After turning to the man seated next to her, Elizabeth tapped him on the arm with her fan, though if it was in her mind to gain his attention she need not have done so. Alexis Razumovsky seldom averted his adoring gaze from his imperial mistress.

'Alexis …?' Elizabeth's tone was deceptively casual, but strong enough to carry clearly to those in her immediate vicinity. 'Don't you find it remarkable how well the grand duchess looks this evening?' Her gaze again swung to Catherine, who felt as if she had been impaled on a shard of ice. 'She looks so … slim.' The eyes narrowed. Then, with a curt gesture of her hand, Elizabeth motioned for the ducal couple to move on.

Catherine's cheeks flushed painfully as she and Peter walked away. Nor did it help matters to see the openly curious glances that now came her way. How could she look anything other than slim? What, she wondered resentfully, would the empress say if she knew that her nights with Peter were continuing in the same manner as had their wedding night?

Catherine sighed as she sat down. Doubtless that too would be construed as her fault. Her handkerchief was damp and matted with the effects of her anxiety by the time the evening finally came to an end.

Upon reaching the relative security of her bedchamber,

Catherine allowed her maid to undress her, then she fell into bed, trembling. She longed for sleep. But it was no use. She was too upset.

The door to Peter's dressing room opened just then. Garbed in his nightclothes, he stumbled toward the bed.

Dare she make another attempt? Catherine wondered as her husband crawled in beside her.

Even with the empress's scowling face fresh in her mind, Catherine couldn't bring herself to do it. She pulled the covers up under her chin, thinking of the night some weeks ago when she had tried to speak to Peter of their obligations. He had become enraged, striking her in the face with such force that she lost her footing and fell to the floor.

After that, Catherine had made no further effort to reason with her husband. Despite the fact that she was now in her seventeenth year, she had to admit to herself that she was still uncertain as to just what it was that was expected of them. Her ignorance galled her, but she didn't know how to alleviate it. And even if she did know, Catherine had the sinking feeling that the information wouldn't change anything.

The following morning dawned just as rainy as its predecessor. Riding was out of the question. So was any other outdoor activity. Catherine spent the morning at her writing table, answering letters and penning notes in her journal.

Finally she put her writing materials aside. Feeling bored, she went into her dressing room. After removing her morning gown, she donned a rose taffeta dress with an overskirt of maroon lace trimmed in gold braid. Then she headed for the salon to join the members of the ducal court, all of whom were trying to fend off the ennui generated by the relentless rain.

Not wishing to play cards, she crossed the carpeted floor and sat down in a chair near the window, casting a resentful look at her husband as she did so. He was standing in front of the fireplace with her lady, Adela Karr.

Emitting an uproarious chuckle, Peter reached out and playfully pinched the young woman's cheek. After taking her hand, he raised it, then took a step away, facing the people in the room as if he were presenting her for their inspection.

'Have you ever seen such loveliness?' he demanded of no one in particular. Bending forward, he kissed the hand he was holding, prompting a giggle from the woman. 'Ahh … Fräulein.' He sighed dramatically. 'If you were to bestow your favors on any other save this humble servant, you would surely break his heart.' He dropped his voice to a stage whisper, accompanied by gestures that would have spurred envy in a performer of the arts. 'If it wasn't raining, I swear I would take you to the most secluded part of the garden right this minute, where I would ravish you until you cried for mercy!'

He paused, then howled in delight as Adela covered her blushing face with her hands.

Catherine shifted in her chair as she watched the little charade. She had seen this performance before. Peter, for reasons of his own, continually played the ardent suitor with her ladies.

Charlatan! Catherine thought in disgust. Peter was every bit the virgin that she was. Then, glancing around the room, she took note of the good-natured laughter that was being generated by Peter's actions. Catherine suddenly realized that no one – not even Leo Narishkin, the only man present who was not smiling and whose mouth worked with visible contempt – would believe that their grand duke was a celibate.

Restless, Catherine finally got up and walked across the room to where a cabinet and two pedestals with inlaid tops of mother-of-pearl were crammed into a corner. The furniture was new and had been delivered ten days ago. Catherine had planned to send them to Oranienbaum, but the weather of the past week had prevented her from doing so.

She was carefully inspecting the cabinet for any sign of imperfection when Peter's voice startled her.

'What are we supposed to do with all this furniture!' Regarding the new arrivals, his lip curled in scorn. 'We can hardly move about as it is.'

'I'm going to send them to Oranienbaum,' she replied, running her hand along the carved surface. 'You know I dislike moving furniture each time we take up residence there.'

'Well, it's good enough for everyone else,' he grumbled. 'Even the empress. I don't see why you insist on doing things differently.'

Catherine paid him no mind, still angry with his recent actions. Pleased with the condition of the cabinet, she now surveyed the pedestals. She had long since decided that it was foolish to drag her furniture hither and thither as did the empress each time she moved to another palace. The resulting damage offended her orderly Teutonic mind.

Putting a finger to her lips, Catherine glanced about the room, brow furrowed, wondering where to put the cabinet and pedestals until they could be sent to Oranienbaum. If the rain continued it might be a week or more until she could have them moved.

'Can I be of any assistance, your Highness?' Lieutenant Andrei Chernuishev, one of Peter's attendants, stepped forward, an eager look on his face. His blue eyes watched her closely, as they always seemed to do when she was in the room. Andrei thought the grand duchess to be the most beautiful woman he had ever seen, and he was more than a little in love with her.

Catherine gave the young man a bright smile, amused to see how his face lit up each time she looked directly at him. While his admiration for her was gratifying, Catherine could summon up no more than a casual friendship in return.

'I'm sure the servants can take of it, Andrei,' she replied

at last. Then she glanced sideways at Peter, who had returned to Adela Karr. He was standing there, head cocked, offering her what passed for a leering smile. Well, she thought angrily, two can play that game. 'But perhaps you would like to escort me to the play tonight,' she suggested softly to the lieutenant. 'The grand duke does not wish to go.'

The young man bowed, his face beaming with pleasure. 'I could have no greater honor, Highness,' he avowed with breathless enthusiasm.

Having heard the exchange, Peter turned and smirked at them both. 'You'd be doing me the favor, Andrei,' he advised quickly. 'There's nothing more boring than a Russian play – unless it's the company of the grand duchess,' he added spitefully, making a face at Catherine. She flushed and turned away.

That evening, seated beside an attentive Andrei, whose eyes were more upon her than upon the lavish production being performed by imperial command, Catherine felt herself relax. So engrossed was she that Catherine never noticed the speculative gaze of the empress as that woman viewed the young couple seated not far from her.

The very next day Catherine received a summons from Her Imperial Majesty, Elizabeth Petrovna.

When Catherine entered the sitting room she saw the empress standing by the window, the draperies of which were parted to reveal the blackness of night.

It was well past one o'clock in the morning. Despite the lateness of the hour, Elizabeth looked neither weary nor ready to retire. This didn't strike Catherine as odd. She knew that Elizabeth usually stayed up all night, preferring to sleep during the day.

Although the door to the adjoining reception room was closed, Catherine could hear sounds of laughter and music emanating from within its confines. It was in stark contrast to the scowling countenance of the empress.

Even though she was now touched by apprehension, Catherine noticed the tense lines of strain that etched Elizabeth's red lips. She was, as usual, gorgeously attired, her velvet gown the color of ripe persimmons. Small seeded pearls decorated the bodice that fit snugly across her ample bosom and hugged the still-narrow waist.

Catherine was so lost in her thoughts that when the empress at last spoke, her face fell into startled confusion.

'You understand that it is your duty to bear children, to produce an heir?' Elizabeth demanded abruptly. The voice was clear, yet it contained a spark of intensity that colored it with fear. Although none knew about it save her own personal attendants and physicians, Elizabeth had suffered a severe fainting spell only hours ago. The vision of her own mortality now lay like a malignant shadow in her mind's eye.

'Yes, your Majesty,' whispered Catherine. Her heart sank. This was the first time that Elizabeth had referred directly to the sensitive subject.

'Two years! Two years, and still there is no sign of a child.'

Elizabeth spoke with a savagery that left Catherine breathless with its implications. Miserable, she opened her mouth in an attempt to explain, but could find few words to describe what was to her inexplicable. In spite of her twenty-four months of marriage, Catherine didn't even know what a naked man looked like. Peter was always covered from neck to ankle in his nightclothes when he came to bed, disrobing in the seclusion of his personal dressing room beforehand.

Aware of Elizabeth's burning eyes upon her, Catherine took a deep breath. 'We don't ...' she started lamely. 'Peter doesn't ...' Her voice trailed off. She knew her face had flamed crimson but was powerless against the feeling of mortification that caused it.

'There is no excuse for your failure!' Elizabeth interrupted harshly, pointing an accusing finger at

Catherine. 'In my father's day, barren women were sent to the remotest nunnery, for they are of no use to anyone.' She paused and studied the grand duchess. 'Things aren't all that much different today,' she remarked idly, gratified to see the spark of dread that came into those violet eyes. 'You sleep in the same bed as your husband. If he doesn't seem attracted to you, then the fault is yours, madame. Not his!' She stepped closer, her eyes narrowing to gleaming slits. 'Perhaps your attentions are elsewhere,' she suggested softly. '...on a certain young lieutenant, for example.'

In the wavering, tentative light of the lamps, Elizabeth's beauty took on a sinister appearance to Catherine, who resisted the urge to take a step backward.

'That's not true,' she blurted out, genuinely upset by the accusation. For a moment her mind cast about frantically for the source of the unwarranted denunciation. Lieutenant? Her mouth actually gaped as she realized to whom the empress was referring. She was astounded that her public appearance with Andrei could be construed as anything other than innocent.

Elizabeth straightened to her full and imposing height. 'Andrei Chernuishev is being removed from your court.' The words were spoken with a finality that left no room for argument.

No! Catherine wanted to scream. You've got it all wrong. I was only trying to make Peter jealous. But when she said the words in her mind, Catherine realized how foolish they sounded. A man can be jealous only when he cares. The image of the glowering empress swam before her tear-filled eyes. Lowering her head, Catherine remained silent. Instinctively she knew that Elizabeth would never believe that her nephew's marriage was, after two years, still unconsummated.

Elizabeth tilted her head slightly as she regarded the grand duchess. With a sudden jolt of surprise she noted that the young and awkward German princess had somewhere along the line turned into a graceful, quite lovely young woman. Her features had settled into a delicate sort of beauty.

'We suggest that you do something about this situation, Catherine Alexeievna,' Elizabeth said at last in a softer tone. 'Pay more attention to your husband,' she counseled firmly. 'And less to handsome young lieutenants.'

'Yes, madame,' Catherine responded, wondering unhappily just what it was that she was supposed to do.

Elizabeth pursed her lips in a thoughtful manner. 'We think there are those around you who are not a good influence,' she mused slowly. 'We will make a few changes. You may return to your apartments.'

Abruptly dismissed, Catherine curtsied again. What sort of changes? she longed to ask as she left the room. But she knew that this too would have to be left unsaid.

Five

The next morning as Catherine was finishing her breakfast of sausage and blini, the doors to the ducal apartment were flung open to reveal Marie Choglokova, first cousin of the empress. After clapping her hands for attention, the woman announced in a brisk voice that the staff of the ducal household was to be replaced, by order of Her Imperial Majesty.

Catherine and Peter exchanged bewildered looks. Then, glaring at the intruder, Peter's face flushed a deep red. Throwing his napkin into his plate, he got up with a suddenness that sent his chair crashing to the floor as he stormed angrily from the room. Catherine had told him that Andrei was being relieved of his duties, but she hadn't mentioned anything about their whole staff being replaced. The thought was galling, and he gnashed his teeth in helpless fury.

There was a long moment of silence. Madame Choglokova was completely unintimidated by the grand duke's outburst. She cast a stony eye about the room, mouth tight. Slowly, one by one, servants and attendants began to file from the room.

Through it all, Catherine remained seated, her face impassive. Finally Marie Choglokova approached, the new retinue close on her heels.

In her early thirties, Marie had a certain earthy prettiness about her. She was somewhat on the plump side, although this could have been due to the fact that she was so obviously pregnant – a condition Catherine noted with an ironic smile.

In stilted tones, Marie proceeded to introduce Catherine to her new attendants. Among them was a Madame Krause, who was in her forties and who appeared distressingly sullen-looking. Anya, her new maid, looked more promising and flashed a shy smile as she dipped in a curtsy to the grand duchess.

'In the future,' Marie was explaining, 'or until such time as her Majesty sees fit, the grand duke and your Highness will remain here in St. Petersburg.'

Her astonishment now colored with dismay, Catherine listened to the rest of the restrictions that Marie recited as if from rote.

'You are not permitted to attend any banquets or other festivities, and there will be no traveling of any kind. Also,' she added, almost as an afterthought, 'her Majesty thinks it best to relieve you of your writing materials. She considers them to be an unnecessary distraction.'

Catherine moistened her lips and took a deep breath, striving for a calmness she didn't feel. Whatever changes she had expected the empress to introduce had certainly not included all of this.

'For how long?' she managed to murmur, unable to believe that Elizabeth would do this to her.

Marie offered a cold smile. 'For however long it takes, madame, for you to present the grand duke with a child.'

Catherine turned away. She didn't know whether to laugh or to cry.

'It's not all that difficult, really,' Marie went on placidly, her tone irritatingly condescending. 'I've already produced three children in four years of marriage.' Then, peering about the room with narrowed eyes, her attention focused on the book on the writing table. She viewed it with open suspicion.

'I feel certain that the empress would wish for me to continue with my studies,' Catherine exclaimed hastily, following the glance. She held herself very still, afraid to show Marie how important the books were to her. The woman seemed bent on removing every diversion she had.

'Perhaps,' Marie responded doubtfully. 'If it doesn't take up too much of your time,' she added, her eye still on the offending volume.

Catherine clamped her teeth together. How dare the woman treat her in such a patronizing manner! she fumed, rankled. 'What else is there for me to do?' The words came out in a heated rush as her temper rose.

Regarding the grand duchess with a raised brow, Madame Choglokova apparently didn't feel the need to reply to this and instead answered her with a tight smile and accusing eyes.

Before the week was gone, Peter began to fret, greatly annoyed with the unusual restrictions. In the end, he blamed his wife.

'Blessed Jesus!' he exploded a few days later. 'The witch watches me from morning until night. It's all your fault. You and your damned play. You angered my aunt, and now she treats us little better than prisoners!'

Catherine remained silent, knowing that any comment she might make would only further anger him. Something would have to be done, she thought frantically. But what?

That evening, observing Peter as he moved his toy soldiers about the bed, Catherine braced herself, then reached out and laid her hand on his wrist. The skin felt clammy, and she sternly repressed a shudder.

'Peter,' she said softly, 'you know the empress would disapprove ...'

Brows drawn down, Peter withdrew his hand in a quick movement that suggested her touch had burned his flesh.

'My aunt is perfectly aware of my feelings,' he muttered in a peevish voice, then glared at her. 'Did I ask to be married to you? Married at all?' He turned away, unwilling to look at her. It seemed to him that each time he looked directly into those violet eyes he saw revulsion. The expression had been seared into his mind.

Catherine opened her mouth to speak, then closed it again, a sigh following soon thereafter. Even with the specter of the convent hanging over her, she found herself unable to plead with her husband.

Resigned, Catherine heaved another deep sigh and settled down in an effort to find sleep.

One morning Madame Choglovkova, her head bent over the embroidery in her lap, raised her eyes unobrusively to study the grand duchess who was, as usual, reading. She compressed her mouth at the sight. Her normally thin lips disappeared, leaving only a straight line of rebuke behind. The grand duke was in the bedchamber. That, Marie thought, was where the grand duchess ought to be.

Turning slightly, Marie exchanged a knowing glance and nod with Madame Krause, seated in a nearby chair. Both women were firmly convinced that the lack of a child was the fault of the grand duchess. Marie made a mental note to include her assumptions in her next report to the empress.

One night six months after their enforced confinement began, Catherine and Peter retired to their private bedchamber after the evening game of cards. Although they were not permitted to attend outside functions, court was held every evening in much the same fashion as before.

Catherine lay in bed for a while, trying to ignore Peter's erratic snoring. He had had more than his usual share of vodka and had fallen asleep almost as soon as he put his head on the pillow.

After about an hour of tossing and turning, Catherine finally got out of bed. Without even donning a robe, she went to the door that led to the outer chamber. If she couldn't sleep, she thought to herself, she might as well read. Perhaps a good book and a cup of hot chocolate would relax her enough so that she could doze off.

Hand on the latch, she attempted to open the door – and

found that it was locked.

Disbelieving, Catherine again tugged at the handle, more forcefully. The door had been bolted from the outside. They were locked in their own bedroom!

The next night, after retiring, Catherine stood by the bedroom door, listening. Peter was in his dressing room, disrobing. Only moments after they had entered, her ears caught a faint sound as the bolt was slipped into position. A minute later she heard Madame Choglokova's murmuring voice as she addressed a servant. Then it was still.

When Peter discovered this further humiliation, he flew into a black rage and struck her. Thereafter, he did that rather frequently, but he was always careful that they were alone when he did so.

Their lives settled into tedium. Fortunately, there was still Leo Narishkin. The young man managed to provide at least some entertainment and wit. And he was an excellent chess player, a game in which Catherine could lose herself for hours at a time.

And there was Anya. Catherine was coming more and more to rely upon the young maid, who was sincerely devoted to her. Somehow, Anya managed to bring in at least one book a week, and as time passed, Catherine's collection grew. With Anya's help they stacked most of the books beneath the large canopied bed, half the space of which was taken up by Peter's wooden soldiers. Catherine no longer had to leave her room to read at night when sleep eluded her.

Spring finally settled a benevolent hand upon the land, greening it to lush productivity. For Catherine, however, there remained an aridness that seemed to have no end. She made no further attempt to dissuade Peter from his games. He, in turn, never interrupted her while she was reading.

One afternoon in late May, the empress unexpectedly sent for the grand duke.

When Peter returned a short while later, his rage was so great that his face was livid with the force of his emotions.

'She has dared do such a thing to me!' he screamed, waving his arms about. Walking with quick, furious steps, he marched into their bedchamber, muttering imprecations.

Putting her book down, Catherine got up and followed him. 'What is it? What's wrong?'

He spun around and glared at her. 'The empress has given away Schleswig. Lands that belong to me! To Holstein.' His voice cracked on a sob.

Catherine tried to stem her annoyance at what she considered to be an overreaction. 'It's just a small town,' she ventured, unable to see any cause for his upset.

'What do you know about it!' he spat. 'My aunt wants me to renounce my heritage. But I won't do it!' He slammed his fist down on a table, then backhanded a crystal vase, sending it crashing to the floor.

'Holstein is, after all, only a duchy.' Catherine tried to mollify him, ignoring his juvenile display of temper. 'And an unimportant one, at that.'

For this observation, Catherine was rewarded with a stinging slap. Gasping in anger, she stormed from the room, slamming the door behind her. Heedless of his wife's obvious state of agitation, Peter flung open the door and trailed after her, continuing with his diatribe against the empress.

'Let me tell you something! If there is any renouncing to be done, it is Russia that I shall renounce,' he declared, chin jutting out in defiance.

Sitting down in a chair, Catherine regarded him wearily, wishing he would go inside and play with his toys and leave her alone. Her cheek stung, and she rubbed at it with the palm of her hand.

'You cannot renounce it, Peter,' she said tersely, wondering why she was bothering to argue with him. 'You are the heir. There is no other.'

Pausing abruptly in his tirade, Peter's expression grew sly. He took a step closer to her. 'There's always Ivan,' he murmured, running a finger along his beardless chin. 'He wouldn't even have to be crowned. He's already a tsar.'

Looking up, Catherine caught her breath, feeling the blood drain from her face. 'What are you saying?' She glanced quickly at Madame Choglokova, but the woman appeared to be engrossed in her ubiquitous handwork. As usual, Peter was speaking to her in German. Catherine offered a quick prayer of thanks that Marie didn't understand the language.

'Ah-ha!' Peter's pale eyes glittered in malicious satisfaction, pleased with her unsettled state. He wagged a finger at her. 'You don't know as much as you think you know. He lives. I've seen him with my own eyes.'

Astounded, Catherine just stared at her husband.

'How do you think my aunt came to the throne?' Peter demanded when she made no response, annoyed that she doubted him even for a moment.

In a barely audible voice, Catherine replied: 'She is Tsar Peter's daughter ...'

Peter's laugh was shrill. 'That may be so. But it is the young son of Anna Leopoldovna who is tsar. Nor have I misjudged my tense. I say he *is* tsar. His mother may have died, but the boy still lives. My aunt could not have seized the throne without the help of her grenadiers.' He grew complacent, crossing his arms over his chest.

Catherine stared at him a moment, then asked, 'Who is Anna Leopoldovna?'

Peter frowned in annoyance, but was not surprised that she did not know of the woman who had been regent for such a short time. It was a maze of ancestry. 'When the great Tsar Peter died, he was succeeded by his wife, Catherine I. When she died, the ministers chose the daughter of Peter's half brother Ivan to replace her. Her name was also Anna.'

Catherine nodded. She knew that. Anna had reigned for

almost ten years. Catherine had assumed that it had been Elizabeth who ascended the throne upon her death.

'Well,' Peter continued, 'Anna chose as her successor, the son of her niece. That niece was Anna Leopoldovna. And it is her son who is tsar!'

Catherine ignored this. Her throat felt dry, and her heart pounded wildly at the thought that someone may have overheard the words of treason that poured so carelessly from her husband's lips.

'Where is the boy now?' she asked in a voice no more than a whisper. She darted another glance at Marie, relieved to see the placid expression.

'Schlüsselburg.'

She shivered. If the inside of that fortress was anything like the outside, then it was a grim place indeed. With a start, she saw that Marie had looked up at them, apparently having recognized the one word. The woman regarded them both suspiciously for a moment, then returned her attention to the embroidery. But Catherine had the distinct impression that she was now listening to the conversation.

She wet her lips. 'How many people know of this?' she asked at last, taking care to speak in German.

Peter gestured vaguely, beginning to lose interest. 'No one is supposed to know of it,' he replied. 'The boy doesn't even know who he is. But then, he doesn't have a name. Only a number. I will say that my aunt has her moments of humor. His number is One.' This time Peter's laugh was ugly. 'That's only fitting, isn't it?' he goaded her. 'The number-one prisoner in your precious Russia is its own sovereign!'

Before Catherine could reply, Peter walked away, returning to the bedroom and his soldiers, his laughter trailing behind him like a tattered ribbon. Sitting there, Catherine remained motionless for a long time, lost in thought.

The following morning Marie brought Catherine the

news that her father, after a brief illness, had died. The information was delivered in a dry, unemotional voice.

Already despondent, Catherine slipped into melancholy, giving way to a sorrowing grief. Tears seeped from her eyes and slid down her cheeks in a never-ending stream.

Marie watched in silence as the grand duchess wept more or less steadily throughout the day. But the following afternoon when the tears still fell, she felt compelled to speak.

'Men do not find women attractive,' she noted in her admonishing voice, 'when they have red and swollen eyes, your Highness.'

Outraged, Catherine glared at the older woman. 'Am I not to mourn my own father?' she demanded, producing fresh tears.

Marie's disapproval surfaced in the form of a frown. 'Mourn him and be done with it! I'm certain that the empress would not like to hear of your behavior.'

Biting her lip to stem the furious retort that threatened to escape, Catherine ran from the room into her bedchamber. But Peter, who was practicing his violin, spun about and ordered her to get out.

After returning to the outer chamber and Madame Choglokova once more, Catherine sank down in a chair, mouth grim. The tears had stopped, although not for the reason Marie may have supposed.

Catherine simply felt beyond them now.

Six

Catherine stood by the window that overlooked the Neva. Dressed in a morning gown of pale-blue satin, she gazed out at the unchanging scenery. She'd been looking at it now for four years. She decided she much preferred the view from Mon Plaisir or the exquisite Peterhof. Someday, she mused, watching the boats traverse the black water, she would build her own palace, and it would be furnished with the finest things Europe had to offer. There would be paintings and books and ...

She gave a deep sigh. There really was no point in daydreaming, she reflected morosely. Who knew when, or even if, she would ever be in a position to build the palace of her dreams?

Turning away from the window, Catherine shook her head slightly, finding it difficult to accept the passing time. She was almost twenty-three years old!

And yet, she thought, in a sense time had stood still. Nothing had changed. Nothing.

Walking to her writing table, she glanced down at the latest letter from her mother. Joanna was now living in Paris with her lover of the moment. The only time she wrote was to ask for money, and this letter was no exception. Catherine always sent the funds, but she was unable to answer the letter. Her writing materials had never been returned to her. She was not permitted to correspond with anyone, not even her own mother. But then, Joanna never did seem to mind this state of affairs; at least she never mentioned it when she wrote.

How right you were, Mama, Catherine thought to herself, still staring at the parchment. The gifts and the favours have been withdrawn. Even my freedom has been taken from me. I am imprisoned with a man who hates me, a man for whom I have no love.

But for how long! her mind raged. Isn't four years enough? Four years of being locked in a room at night, of being denied even the mental stimulation of an occasionally intelligent conversation?

How she longed to see a play, to ride a horse. But there was nothing; only her books. These, thank God, had saved her sanity.

Catherine picked up the letter and crumpled it in her hand. The empress has forgotten all about us, she thought in despair. She no longer remembers our existence. Perhaps this is the way I shall spend the rest of my life …

Catherine turned her mind away from that. The supposition was too depressing. And lately it seemed that she was more often than not depressed.

With an effort, Catherine arranged her face into its usual mask of acceptance. If Marie should take note of her mood, Catherine knew, it would only invite another of her lectures. Marie seemed to have an endless supply of them, each more boring than the last.

That night, as she was playing a game of chess with Leo Narishkin, it occurred to Catherine that she and Peter were not much different from the pawns she was moving so casually about the marble board.

'Checkmate!' Leo exclaimed with a broad smile of satisfaction that dissolved at the sight of her pensive face. 'If I didn't know better, I'd swear you let me win that game,' he murmured, leaning back in his chair, his homely face turning concerned. 'Do you want to play another?'

'No,' Catherine replied slowly. Still appearing preoccupied, she picked up the black queen and stared at it thoughtfully.

Leo Narishkin viewed the grand duchess for a long moment, studying the delicately chiseled features that he knew by heart. With a sigh, he picked up his wineglass and drained the contents, not for the first time wishing that he had the nerve to tell Catherine how much he loved her.

One thing held him back: He knew very well that her feeling for him was no more than friendship. Should he speak and be rejected, that threat of friendship would be irreparably damaged. That she was unhappy, he didn't need to be told. All he could do was be there, when and if she ever needed him.

As for his wife ... Leo motioned for a servant to refill his glass. He had to admit that he was reasonably content with the union that had been arranged by the empress, who had chosen one of her own ladies for him to marry. In fact, if it wasn't for the grand duchess ...

Leo now leaned forward with the intention of offering words of comfort in an effort to lighten Catherine's mood. 'Catherine ...' He broke off, hearing the page announce a new arrival. Upon recognizing the young nobleman who had just entered the salon, Leo flashed a delighted grin and went to fetch him.

'Your Highness,' Leo said formally as he returned to Catherine's side. 'I would like to present a friend of mine, Serge Saltikov. I've taken the liberty of inviting him here this evening.'

Catherine, who had gotten to her feet, now turned ... and found herself looking into the eyes of the most handsome man she had ever seen. He was tall and lean with broad shoulders and narrow hips, a physique set off to great advantage clothed as it was in tight satin breeches and matching jacket. A neatly trimmed beard accented a square jaw and high cheekbones. Dark eyes, enhanced by finely etched brows, were staring at her in such a compelling way, Catherine knew her cheeks had flushed.

'Your Highness,' Serge murmured. After taking hold of

her hand, he brought the slender tapered fingers to his lips.

Catherine resisted the sudden urge to snatch her hand away, feeling as if a flame had touched her skin. His warm breath sent a trail of fire up her arm and caused a fluttering sensation in the pit of her stomach. He was still holding her hand, pressing it tightly before he finally released it.

Leo felt his spirits plummet as he noted the reaction of the two people before him. The spark of mutual attraction had been so acute as to be almost tangible. Catherine's melancholy state had vanished as if it had never existed. Her charmingly flushed face was now animated. The curve of her white breast above the turquoise-colored velvet gown she was wearing rose and fell in a quickened fashion, as if she were trying to catch her breath.

'How is it we have never met before?' Catherine managed to ask at last. She had no idea what was happening to her. Never in her life had a man had such an effect on her.

'Serge has just returned from Paris, where he's been living this past year,' Leo put in, and couldn't resist adding: '…with his wife.'

Catherine's eyes widened slightly. Somehow she had assumed that the young man was unmarried. Without fully forming the thought in her mind, she wondered what kind of a woman would capture the attention of a man like this.

'Is your wife with you this evening?' Catherine asked. Her eyes scanned the room, but she saw no unfamiliar face among the group of courtiers that gathered in her salon each evening. Her eye rested on the staggering form of her husband, who was more than a little inebriated, and she quickly returned her attention to Serge Saltikov. She had never before compared Peter to any other man, but she found herself doing so now, much to the detriment of her husband.

'No, madame,' he answered in a deep rich voice that sent a shiver up Catherine's spine. 'My wife is in confinement at this time. She expects our first child soon.'

Again Catherine felt her face flush. She couldn't help but speculate on what exactly had taken place to produce that circumstance. She glanced toward the far end of the room at Marie, seated at one of the card tables. The woman was again pregnant. Catherine wasn't certain whether this was her sixth or seventh child, and she didn't much care. In fact, Catherine was so used to seeing Marie in that state that she seldom gave the ever-protruding belly a second thought. And she certainly hadn't ever speculated as to how Marie got pregnant. Yet here she was with a perfect stranger, wondering exactly that.

Struggling for composure, she looked up at Serge again, abashed to see a hint of amused mockery in his eyes. She moistened her lips. 'Would … you care to join us at the table, Monsieur Saltikov?'

He bowed, then extended his arm for her to take. 'It would be my pleasure, madame.'

After hesitating only a moment, Catherine placed her hand on his arm, feeling the hardness beneath soft satin. It was on the tip of her tongue to give the young nobleman permission to use her given name – as she had with Leo and a few others she considered close friends – but another look at those taunting eyes quickly changed her mind. She didn't know why, but she sensed danger for herself in this man's company. However, for the first time in four years Catherine felt so alive that her nerves tingled with pleasurable expectation.

That night Catherine found herself wishing that the snoring form beside her could magically be replaced with another man. Whether her eyes were closed or open to the darkness, she could see Serge. She had never in her life been kissed on the lips by a man, but Catherine tried to imagine it now. Her efforts brought forth the same fiery sensation that she had experienced when Serge had touched her hand.

Unable to bear the feeling of frustrated helplessness that crept over her, Catherine buried her head in her pillow and wept far into the night.

On a Friday afternoon in late March, as Catherine was in her sitting room wondering just which gown to wear that evening, a rising din from the next room caused her mouth to tighten. She didn't turn around, for she recognized the source. Peter was training his dogs again.

Anya's voice cut into her thoughts as she announced the arrival of Count Bestuzhev. Hearing that, Marie, who was as usual never far away, discreetly withdrew.

Surprised by the unexpected visit, Catherine nodded to the chancellor, noticing that he looked particularly grim today.

Bestuzhev, dressed in his usual somber attire, the diamond miniature of his empress glittering in the lapel of his brown velvet jacket, acknowledged her greeting. He darted a look at the closed bedroom door, his forehead creasing in a frown at the sounds emanating from the room. Then he faced Catherine once more.

'Forgive me if I get right to the point, Highness,' he began sternly, waving a sheaf of papers at her. 'You seem unable to extradite yourself from debt. No matter how high your allowance is raised, you still manage to exceed it.'

'My apologies, Count Bestuzhev,' said a not altogether contrite Catherine. 'There do seem to be so many expenses. And as you no doubt are aware, I do send money to my mother.'

Bestuzhev raised a thin brow. 'Commendable, your Highness,' he murmured with a trace of sarcasm. Then he fell silent as the noise from the adjoining room grew more strident. Observing the grand duchess's calm face, Bestuzhev was forced to concede a certain amount of admiration for her. How on earth she could stand living like this was beyond him. He was certain it would have driven a weaker woman mad by now.

His gaze traveled about and rested at last upon Catherine's writing table. With some surprise, he noted the works of Voltaire and Montesquieu; heavy fare, indeed, he thought to himself. He picked up another book, one dealing with the history of Russia, and now he regarded her with open curiosity.

'I'm deeply interested in the history of my country,' Catherine explained in answer to the unspoken question.

He put the book down on the table again. 'And just which country is your country, madame?' he inquired quietly, without looking at her.

'Russia is my country, Chancellor,' she replied in such a tone of conviction that Bestuzhev felt a start of astonishment. She actually means it, he thought to himself. For years now, he had thought her to be particularly clever in her studious desire to learn their ways. Suddenly he felt uncertain of his suppositions. An awkward silence fell. Bestuzhev, to his chagrin, felt uncomfortable.

At last he spoke. '... And should the day come when we are at war with Prussia?' He studied her closely, scrutinizing those violet eyes that were at once guileless and unfathomable. 'Where then will your sympathies lie?'

Catherine gave him a sharp look, and again Bestuzhev was struck by her countenance. He was well aware that there were those, Elizabeth among them, who had thought Catherine to be a plain-looking child; and in truth she had not been pretty. But for himself, Bestuzhev had long ago discerned that the unusual facial structure would, with maturity, blossom into true beauty. Time had proved him right, he thought now, bemused.

Catherine didn't immediately answer him, but instead asked bluntly: 'Will there be war, Chancellor?'

His expression became closed and distant. 'There is always that possibility,' he murmured. 'Though no one can say for certain.' Despite his words, Bestuzhev knew that the whisper of war with Prussia had already been sounded. As far as he was concerned, it was only a question of time: weeks, months, a year or two at the most.

And then what? he wondered, looking toward the closed bedroom door. He felt certain that Peter would place the whole country in Frederick's lap. They would all be under the thumb of the Prussian king.

'You need never question my allegiance, Count Bestuzhev,' Catherine remarked quietly, sensing the direction of his thoughts. 'Never assume that my ideas and feelings are the same as those of my husband. If Frederick raises his hand against us then he must be struck down!'

'It is perhaps not wise for a woman to be of a different opinion than her husband,' he suggested with a trace of a smile. 'Especially when that husband will one day wear a crown.'

'I do not apologize for my opinions,' Catherine stated firmly, raising her chin. 'Right or wrong, they are my own.'

The noise from the bedchamber grew even louder as Peter raised his voice in furious anger at someone or something; Bestuzhev was uncertain because the grand duke was speaking in German. He wondered wryly whether Peter spoke German as badly as he spoke Russian. Once more he was amazed that Catherine could live under these circumstances and retain her equilibrium.

The chancellor's wandering thoughts were captured by the grand duchess who was explaining, in faultless Russian, just why it was that she had once more exceeded her annual allowance of thirty thousand rubles. It had, his belated attention surmised, something to do with buying furniture. Perplexed, he again looked about him, this time with a keener eye. He noticed how elegantly the room was furnished. Everything appeared new ... and unscratched.

The workmanship he recognized as that of Boulle. Writing tables, cabinets, even the clocks were embellished with inlays of silver and tortoiseshell and ebony. The ducal apartments actually looked better than those of the empress, he realized with no little astonishment.

Catherine had finished her recital and was now regarding him expectantly.

On an impulse, Bestuzhev changed his mind about the lecture he had planned to deliver. 'I'll see to it that your allowance is increased, madame. But I do advise you to pay more attention to your debts,' he added quietly. 'They are getting out of hand.'

He bowed slightly, then left the room, leaving a stunned Catherine staring at the closed door. She thought she had detected a note of ... respect in his voice. But that couldn't be, she decided. With a small shrug, Catherine walked over to the table, picked up a book, and settled herself down to read.

Seven

In the corridor, Count Bestuzhev paused for a long moment, rubbing his bearded chin thoughtfully. Then he continued his journey down the hall. But he did not return to his apartments. Instead, he went to see the empress.

Having just returned from one of her frequent pilgrimages, Elizabeth's face was lined with exhaustion, her eyes rimmed with purple smudges. During these times of repentance, she was wont to fast. The Spartan combination of fasting and walking great distances from one holy shrine to the next had completely drained her energy.

'Well, what is it, Bestuzhev?' she queried testily upon his entrance. She put a hand to her forehead as if her head ached. Elizabeth walked wearily to the nearest settee and sat down heavily. She was not yet dressed and wore a yellow satin robe over her nightgown.

Coming to stand before her, Bestuzhev bowed. Her appearance no longer shocked him. He was growing used to the dissipation that seemed to age her day by day.

Bestuzhev cleared his throat. 'I've just returned from a visit with the grand duchess ...'

Elizabeth's eyes lit up and she straightened, now giving him her complete attention. 'Is she pregnant?' Bestuzhev shook his head, and her scowl returned, deepening the lines in her forehead. 'How can such a state of affairs exist?' she demanded through clenched teeth. She motioned to a hovering servant, and the woman immediately placed a glass of wine in her hand.

Bestuzhev pursed his lips and clasped his hands behind him. 'Perhaps it is not entirely the fault of the grand duchess,' he suggested mildly.

Elizabeth eyed him balefully and took a sip of wine before she answered.

'Whose fault it is really does not matter,' she exclaimed heatedly. 'Something must be done. Whatever faults exist in my nephew, he is still a Romanov. And,' she added in measured tones accompanied by a level look, 'he is still our heir!'

The chancellor was at pains to keep his thoughts from appearing on his face. That Prussian-loving imbecile, he was thinking. Yet it was true: He was the heir. God, he lamented to himself, Peter would turn them all over to Frederick without a qualm. Couldn't the empress realize that? More and more of late he found himself pondering the possibility of altering the succession. But first the grand duke had to have a son.

Struggling to regain his composure, Bestuzhev finally said: 'You are correct, madame. The grand duke is a Romanov, and he is your heir. All the more reason why he must produce sons.' He paused a moment, as if considering the problem. 'However, this he cannot accomplish unless the grand duchess bears a child,' he added in a smooth voice.

The empress gave him a sharp glance. 'Perhaps she is infertile.'

Bestuzhev raised a brow. A shadow of a smile seemed to darken rather than lighten his dour countenance. Marie Choglokov submitted her reports to him each Friday. Bestuzhev, before relaying them to the empress, took the time to listen very carefully. Over the past few months he had formed his own opinion as to the continued childless state of the grand duchess. 'I ... do not believe that her fertility has been ... put to the test, Majesty,' he said carefully.

His remark occasioned another sharp and penetrating look. 'I don't believe it. No! A man cannot plow a barren field,' she cried out, rapping the arm of the settee with her fist. 'There can be no other explanation.'

Alarm shot through Bestuzhev at her tone, for he knew very well that a barren woman – even a grand duchess – could be cast aside at any time.

'Umm ... the people, madame,' he murmured, turning grave. 'We must remember that the grand duchess is held in great esteem.'

Elizabeth made a disgusted face. 'The people, Bestuzhev, have a notoriously short memory,' she snapped. Her eyes seemed to blaze with inner fire. 'And no one can take exception with our patience. Is that not so?'

'It is endless, madame,' Bestuzhev hastily agreed. 'But again I ask: What if it isn't the fault of the grand duchess? If such is the case, a new wife for the grand duke would not solve the problem.'

Elizabeth drained her glass and thought of the weekly reports of Marie Choglokova, reports that hinted at the same concern as her chancellor. But no man could sleep beside a woman for six years and leave her untouched. Even thinking on it, she found it too incredible to accept as fact.

Yet the problems with her nephew were becoming more and more pronounced. Elizabeth, not as unaware as Bestuzhev supposed her to be, knew that despite all her efforts she had been unable to wean Peter from his Prussian ideals.

There must be a child; preferably a son. The months had grown into years, and still there was no sign of a pregnancy. There would be little point in waiting longer. Six years, she thought in rising anger, ought to be time enough for any man to produce a son and heir. Not that his wife could be held blameless. The girl was a fool! Any female her age should know by now how to arouse the passions of a man.

Bestuzhev inclined his head and stared moodily into space. 'It's too bad,' he mused idly, 'that one or the other of them couldn't be put to the test.' He shrugged. 'It does seem hopeless, I admit.'

Viewing the seemingly casual and unconcerned visage of her chancellor, Elizabeth's eyes narrowed, but she made no response.

A glum silence descended, broken only by the ticking of the jeweled clock on the mantel. The empress drank another glass of wine while Bestuzhev maintained a patient attitude. He had planted the seed, now he had to wait for it to grow and bear fruit.

'I warn you, Bestuzhev,' Elizabeth finally said slowly. 'If your suppositions are incorrect, we will find suitable lodgings for you within the deepest bowels of Schlüsselburg.' Her hold tightened on the stem of the wineglass; her whole body was rigid with the smoldering anger that flared through her.

Bestuzhev paled slightly, but he merely nodded in acquiescence. 'I would deserve no less, your Majesty,' he agreed solemnly.

After a while, Elizabeth calmed. Her measured glance fell upon her chancellor as she addressed him in clipped tones. 'Send Madame Choglokova to us,' she instructed. 'It has been some time since we visited with our cousin.'

Inclining his head, Bestuzhev withdrew. In the hall, he mopped his brow and willed his unsettled nerves to calmness. If he had made a mistake, then God help them all.

It was already early evening by the time Marie Choglokova presented herself before the empress.

She hadn't seen Elizabeth in private for more than a year now. She relayed any information she had to Chancellor Bestuzhev, who in turn passed it on to the empress. The unexpected summons caused Marie's stomach to tighten with unease. Her verbal reports were not to the liking of the empress, she knew that. Was she to be reprimanded for telling the truth?

'God knows I've done my best,' Marie muttered to herself as she walked through the corridor following the page who had been sent to fetch her.

She paused in the antechamber, taking a moment to compose herself. Her fingertips touched the powdered wig she was wearing, then fluttered nervously over the ruffles on the bodice of her pink taffeta gown.

Taking a deep breath, she entered the sitting room.

Elizabeth was already dressed for the night's festivities, a gala ball that was to precede Lent and its stringent requirements, an affair that Marie had not been invited to attend. Somewhat wistfully Marie viewed Elizabeth's ballgown of pale-blue satin. It had an overskirt of black lace trimmed at the hem with a band of floral embroidery worked in gold thread. She had, of course, never seen the dress before. The empress wore a gown only once.

Marie made a deep curtsy, then straightened. With a start of surprise, she saw that they were alone in the room. The servants, even the guards, had been dismissed.

'Sit down, Cousin,' Elizabeth said abruptly in a voice that sounded more like a command than an invitation. She motioned Marie to a nearby chair. With her movements, diamonds sparkled everywhere: in her hair, on her neck, her wrists, her fingers. She fell silent while Marie settled herself, appearing lost in thought.

The silence continued, increasing Marie's unease. She folded her trembling hands in her lap and sat very still, the beat of her heart loud in her ears.

Then the empress's dark-blue eyes regarded Marie with such an enigmatic look that the woman fidgeted nervously under the relentless gaze.

'We want to hear about the grand duchess,' Elizabeth said at last.

Marie, who made her report every Friday without fail, viewed her sovereign in wide-eyed bewilderment. 'Wh –

what is it that you wish to know, your Majesty?' she managed in a stammering voice.

'Everything,' Elizabeth stated tersely as she picked up her wine cup. 'From the moment she arises until the moment that she retires.'

Marie shifted in her chair. Over the past four years her attitude toward her charge had altered subtly, almost without her knowing it. In spite of herself, Marie had come to admire the woman who was married to the grand duke Peter. Thank God I don't have a husband like that, she had thought to herself on more than one occasion.

Aware that the dark and penetrating blue eyes had once again settled on her, Marie took a deep breath. 'The grand duchess spends most of her days reading her books,' she began hesitantly. 'This is only because the grand duke is otherwise occupied,' she added hastily at the sight of Elizabeth's quick frown.

'Doing what?' demanded Elizabeth.

'Training his dogs ... and ...'

'And what?'

'Drilling his servants in some sort of military formations.' Marie waved a hand in a helpless gesture. She herself had never been able to figure out just what it was that Peter did with his time. The strutting and marching that went on for hours on end made absolutely no sense to her.

Elizabeth's mouth had tightened until a white line rimmed her lips. She downed her wine and slammed the cup on the table with a force that caused Marie to almost jump from her chair. 'Twenty-four years old and still playing games,' she muttered in glittering exasperation. 'Go on.'

Marie swallowed, trying to ease her parched throat. 'Well, in the evening they hold court,' she continued. 'After supper they occasionally dance, but mostly they play cards.'

'Dance?' Elizabeth leaned forward in her chair, eyes brightening. 'Does the grand duke dance with his wife?'

Slowly Marie shook her head. 'Seldom, madame. Usually the young gentlemen dance with the grand duchess. I am always there, of course.' She wondered briefly if she should voice her suspicion regarding the celibacy of the ducal couple, then decided against it. Although she had hinted at it in the past weeks, the empress had never acknowledged or questioned it.

Leaning back in the chair again, Elizabeth fixed her cousin with a hard look. 'Who are the gentlemen that the grand duchess seems most attracted to?'

Marie moved uncomfortably under that cold unblinking stare. 'Leo Narishkin and his young friend Serge Saltikov seem to be the ones whose company she most enjoys. But I must tell you, your Majesty, that it is all proper,' she stressed earnestly. 'The grand duke doesn't seem to mind. In fact, he even encourages her ...' She fell silent at the look of acute annoyance that flashed across the empress's face, uncertain as to just what had caused it.

Elizabeth was indeed annoyed – by Marie's obtuseness. Did she have to spell it out, word for word? she wondered irritably. 'The two young men,' she said, her voice slow and measured. 'Narishkin and Saltikov. They are married, are they not?'

'Yes, your Majesty,' Marie affirmed with a quick nod of her head. She hoped fervently that the empress wasn't about to banish the two courtiers, knowing how much the grand duchess valued their companionship.

Elizabeth regarded her cousin steadily for a long moment before she again spoke. Noting the woman's expression, Elizabeth could see that Marie had no inkling of what she was leading up to. Damn, Elizabeth fumed silently, wondering how the woman could be so dense. 'There must be a child,' she stated flatly. 'By any means available. Do you understand, Marie Semenovna? Somehow, some way, there ... must ... be ... a ... child!'

Her lips parting slightly, Marie regarded her Sovereign Majesty with a blank expression. Then she suddenly flushed a bright pink and put a hand to her throat, feeling her pulse quicken with realization. But no, she thought, truly shocked. The empress couldn't mean that!

The empress did.

'We are of the opinion,' Elizabeth went on, toying with her now empty wine cup, 'that perhaps your vigilance has been too ... harsh.' Tilting her head, she glanced at Marie, a slow and mirthless smile hovering about her red lips.

Marie averted her eyes, finding the expression more unsettling than a frown of displeasure. Even though she now knew what the empress was suggesting – no, commanding – she couldn't quite believe it. Mother of God, she thought frantically. How on earth was she supposed to arrange a tryst of this nature without anyone learning of it? And what would happen if Catherine refused?

Hearing the empress again speak, Marie tried to calm her whirling thoughts enough to pay attention.

'It may be,' Elizabeth was speculating casually, 'that a few outings would do them both good. The grand duchess in particular,' she added meaningfully. Abruptly Elizabeth stood up, and Marie automatically stumbled to her feet. 'Return to your duties, my dear cousin. And take note of what we have said.' Elizabeth turned and, without acknowledging Marie's hasty curtsy, left the room.

Later that evening, as she seated herself in her chair at the far end of the salon, a nearly finished piece of tapestry in her lap, Marie Choglokova paid closer attention than usual to the young people about her.

The grand duke was paying court to Catherine's lady, Anna Korloff, occasionally pinching her well-rounded arm. His face held a leer that, on him, merely looked grotesque. But then, Marie thought with a slight twitching of her lips, the grand duke had few expressions that looked otherwise.

A game of whist had begun, but Catherine, as yet, had not joined it. Instead, she was standing by the window, engaged in deep conversation with Serge Saltikov. Serge was, in Marie's opinion, a very handsome young man. His dark eyes seemed to burn with sensuality. On the other hand, a cold and calculating expression would sometimes appear, one that Marie found a bit disturbing. Still, she mused fatalistically, the choice was not hers to make.

Behind the young couple, rain lined the panes of the window in continuous silvery sheets, the noise enough to completely overshadow any word they spoke.

Although she could hear nothing of their conversation, Marie continued to watch them as unobtrusively as possible, not missing the intent appraisal in the eyes of Serge Saltikov as he viewed the grand duchess. His gaze strayed to the soft swell of Catherine's breast, temptingly displayed above a white silk gown. Marie saw Catherine's face suddenly flush as she bit her lip at some remark made by the young nobleman. Glancing at the whist table, Marie noticed that Leo Narishkin was looking decidedly dejected. Although he pretended great interest in the game, his eyes kept straying to the couple by the window.

Saltikov, then, Marie decided, wondering how it could have gotten past her watchful eye. She felt a prick of annoyance. She had certainly become lax over the years. If that wasn't a look of intense interest – perhaps even love – on the grand duchess's face, then she missed her guess.

Oh, yes, indeed. And unless she was further mistaken, Saltikov was more than interested in the grand duchess. Of course, so was Narishkin. But Catherine never seemed to treat him with anything more than a casual fondness.

Finally Catherine and Saltikov joined the others. But for the rest of that evening, Marie's newly observant eye noted that the two kept glancing at one another, time and again.

Marie spent the following week observing, at last concluding that she had not been in error: The young grand duchess was falling in love with the handsome Serge Saltikov. Well, he was an aristocrat and good-looking, Marie admitted to herself. It must, however, be done with the utmost caution and discretion.

Unfortunately, there remained one very serious problem: the grand duke. Not that he would object. Marie's mouth twisted in contempt. Probably he would be relieved. But Marie now knew that the grand duke led the life of a celibate, incredible as that seemed. This Marie had ferreted out in a variety of ways, not the least of which had been talking to the grand duchess. Naturally, the poor young woman had never confirmed it in so many words. But Marie had several times asked a few carefully worded questions, and the innocence of the grand duchess had been truly astounding.

To further satisfy herself, Marie had closely interrogated the young ladies who seemed to capture the eye of the grand duke. They had all, without exception, told her that his attentions never went beyond the teasing stage.

And there was one more thing: Unlike most married women, Catherine never, ever seemed concerned when her monthly flow was late. This had happened several times. Once Marie had even thought to bring it to the attention of the empress. But Catherine had just looked at her blankly, and asked: 'Why would the empress want to know that my flow is late?' When Marie had suggested that she might be pregnant, Catherine had just smiled. 'I hardly think that is the case, Madame Choglokov,' she had murmured. When Marie had thought to probe further, the grand duchess had refused to discuss it any more.

Now, under the circumstances, Marie thought, her mind as busy as her fingers, the grand duchess couldn't possibly bring forth a child unless the grand duke could somehow be persuaded to relinquish his monkish attitude. To do otherwise would have the gravest consequences for the child, not to mention the grand duchess.

If the grand duke could be given a push to get him started, Marie reasoned, all else would fall in line.

She put her needlework aside and looked about the room in a thoughtful manner. Her eye lit on Anna Korloff, but she rejected that idea. The girl was too young. No, what was needed was an older and experienced – very experienced – woman.

With a sense of purpose, Marie got to her feet and went to find her husband. They had some plans to make; and the sooner the better.

Henceforth, her reports to the empress must be made in person, Marie decided.

But to her acute surprise, Marie was informed that the empress no longer required a report. Indeed, her Majesty insisted that she not receive one.

Eight

It was cloudy and damp on this early April afternoon. A cold mist from the river traveled about in little gray swirls that nuzzled domes and steeples and gathered in low patches that hugged the banks of the Neva, only recently freed from its winter covering of ice.

Except for the church bells the city was quiet, the markets closed, for today was a day of fasting.

In a weary gesture, Catherine passed her hand across her mouth, stifling a yawn. A pall of melancholy and irritation enveloped her. Only her books and the evening card games seemed to capture her interest. That, and the visits of Leo's friend, Serge Saltikov.

With conscious effort, Catherine turned her mind away from Serge, away from that handsome smiling face that of late was invading even her dreams. Serge was married, the father of a baby boy. She had no business thinking about him, much less dreaming about him. Yet his very presence rendered her powerless to think clearly.

Leaning back, Catherine closed her eyes for a moment, a movement that did nothing to deter Marie, who had been speaking nonstop for the past quarter hour.

Catherine felt a certain resentment over the endless litany but was unable to goad herself out of her lethargy. Her head was aching with a persistent fierceness that she was beginning to recognize; in fact, in this past year she had been seldom free from its grip. Maybe Marie was right, she mused with an inward sigh. Perhaps she was reading too much. But then there was little else to fill her days – and nothing at all to fill her nights.

In the next room, Peter's voice climbed to a shout, prompting Catherine to open her eyes again. She could hear him arguing with Emil Zeiss. He was, as usual, berating his envoy from Holstein.

A moment later the door opened. Looking frazzled, Zeiss emerged, wiping his brow with his handkerchief.

Catherine waited until the man left. Then, pursing her lips, she advanced toward the closed bedroom door.

Opening the door, she paused on the threshold, regarding her husband. Now she realized why he had insisted on receiving Emil Zeiss in the bedchamber instead of the sitting room. Dressed in his blue Holstein uniform, Peter was seated at a small table, greedily devouring a platter of boiled beef. Two of his hunting dogs hovered close by, tongues lolling in anticipation.

'Peter!' she chided in sharp annoyance. A pang of hunger shot through her, evoked by the aroma of meat. Sternly Catherine repressed the uncomfortable feeling. 'Today is a fast day.' Seated across the table from Peter was Otto Brummer. Catherine glared at him. She no longer bothered to conceal her dislike for the man. Brummer had the grace to flush, appearing sheepish.

Peter looked up at her, mouth full. 'You're not the only one to have been instructed in orthodoxy, madame.' After picking up a bone from his plate, he began to gnaw at the flesh clinging to it.

'But you shouldn't be eating that.' She came toward him, frowning at his display of gluttony. Her stomach lurched in disgust at the sight of the grease that dribbled down his chin. The meat no longer was appetizing to her.

'Devil take their church fasts,' he muttered. 'Don't you preach their heathen religion to me.'

'Their religion? It's also yours,' she commented tersely.

His expression grew more unpleasant. 'You like to conveniently forget your ancestry, don't you? Forget that you're a German.' After reaching for his vodka, he took a long draught.

'I haven't forgotten my ancestry. But neither do I ignore my responsibilities.' Catherine's voice trembled with emotion as she spoke.

Peter was grinning owlishly, still chewing noisily and with obvious relish. 'You don't fool me, madame.' His words slurred, though from the vodka or because his mouth was full of food, Catherine was uncertain. 'Others, perhaps,' he went on. 'But now me. Your show of devoutness is no more than a façade. You care no more for orthodoxy than you do for Lutheranism.'

Catherine flushed at the observation, for it was too close to the truth. 'I do my best to observe the tenets of my religion and the ways of my country.'

'Your country!' Peter spat. Finished with the bone, he flung it to the dogs. 'My God, madame, you are a fool. *Doura!*' he shouted loudly at Catherine in Russian. 'Even I know the word for fool. This is no more your country than it is mine.'

Catherine flared, eyes blazing, her patience at an end. 'We live here and will do so for the rest of our lives. You may choose to ignore that, but I shall not!'

She was about to speak further, but Peter, in no mood for more reproving words, picked up an empty bowl and threw it at her. With practiced efficiency Catherine sidestepped the hurled missile, hearing the sharp retort as it crashed harmlessly against the wall.

Clenching her teeth in fury, Catherine turned and left the room, slamming the door behind her.

Again in the outer chamber, she sank down in a chair with a great sigh. Where would it all end? she wondered in dismay. How much more of this, of Peter, could she take?

Marie, the small piece of needlework in her hands momentarily ignored, regarded the grand duchess with knowing eyes. Although the grand duke had, as usual, been screaming in his heathen language, she knew from their raised voices that there had been another argument. And *doura*, fool, she knew very well. It was time, she decided, to put her plan in motion. For the past ten days she had been waiting for just such an opportunity.

She made a show of concentrating on her handwork. 'Did you know, your Highness, that this summer will mark the seventh year of your marriage?'

Catherine glanced at her with a tired expression. 'It had not escaped my notice, Madame Choglokova,' she replied dryly.

Drawing her brows together, Marie studied the embroidery with spurious interest. 'The empress grows more displeased with the passing months, much less years, in which your Highness fails to conceive.' Her hand dipped into the enameled box that held her thread, and she carefully drew forth a bright-yellow strand.

Catherine's expression turned wary. Was this to be another lecture? she wondered unhappily.

'Not that the empress is unaware of the grand duke's … deficiencies.'

Marie was speaking in such a low voice that Catherine had to lean forward in the chair to hear her words. But she still made no comment. After a slight pause, Marie continued in the same low voice, although they were alone in the room.

'It would seem, your Highness, that you would do well to produce an heir … by whatever means are available to you.' Having rethreaded her needle, Marie plunged it again into the linen.

'What are you saying?' Catherine demanded. A flush stained her neck and crept up to her cheeks.

Marie raised her brows, but didn't raise her eyes from the piece of material that seemed to have her complete attention. 'It's no secret, least of all to me, that a certain young man,' – she raised her gaze momentarily, – 'has captured your interest.' Again the eyes returned to their task of following the nimble fingers. 'Although I must say that Serge Saltikov is handsome.'

The flush on Catherine's face turned a hot and painful crimson. Her voice emerged harsh and ragged. 'How dare you ...' She gripped the arms of her chair until her knuckles whitened, trembling with the force of her outrage. She opened her mouth to scream at this woman who had plagued her in such a relentless manner for the past four years.

But the words of recrimination just wouldn't come. Why had she been so foolish, so careless? Catherine chided herself in rising panic. Now she had given Marie the perfect weapon to use against her. Frantically she cast her mind back over the events of the past weeks, trying to pinpoint what action on her part had roused the suspicions of Madame Choglokova.

Ever since Leo had brought his friend to her court, Catherine had known she was dangerously attracted to the young nobleman. She had never before felt this way about any man.

Did she love him? That question had tormented her on more than one sleepless night. Catherine realized that she was still staring at Marie, chilled by the knowing look she was seeing.

The busy hands had ceased their labor. The older woman was regarding her with a curious intensity. But whatever Catherine may have expected Marie to say now, it certainly wasn't what followed.

'Tonight, at my house, madame,' the woman murmured, 'there is to be a small celebration. Both my husband and I would consider it an honor if you would favor us with your presence.'

Completely taken aback, Catherine's eyes grew round in shocked surprise. The habits of the past four years were so ingrained, she couldn't bring herself to trust Marie. Surely the woman would never issue such an invitation without the consent of the empress. The thought, however, didn't relax her. Rendered speechless, Catherine remained silent, her body rigid and motionless.

Marie stood up, smiling. 'Please give it some thought, madame,' she urged softly. 'I'll wager that a bit of entertainment would be most welcome.' She gathered up her embroidery and the small enameled box, then headed for the door, where she paused. 'Shall we say eleven o'clock? I will be going home then, and will return to fetch you.' Not waiting for a reply, Marie left the room.

Without being fully aware of it, Catherine's eyes sought the silver gilt timepiece on the mantel. It was just after five o'clock in the afternoon. In no little amazement she reviewed the conversation she had just had. There was no mistaking the implication. If she went to Choglokovs' house, Serge would be there. The thought, despite her fear, was intoxicating.

Then caution intruded. Try as she might, Catherine could think of no possible reason why Marie would suddenly befriend her. Therefore her invitation meant one of two things: Marie was acting at the command of the empress – or she was laying a trap.

The sort of trap that could place me in a nunnery for life, Catherine thought uneasily.

She bit her lip. If she responded to this invitation, what would happen?

Again her face flamed. She knew exactly what would happen. She leaned back in her chair. And why not? Hadn't she waited long enough?

Catherine raised her hands and massaged her temples. Lately her headaches were becoming more acute. It was as if her whole being was protesting her unnatural existence. Peter would never change, she realized. To think otherwise was to delude herself. He didn't love her, would never love her. Even the affection she had hoped with time might blossom between them had never materialized.

As for her sexless nights ... That, too, would never

change. There was no hope, as matters now stood, that Peter would ever give her a child. And Catherine had the uneasy feeling that Elizabeth would not tolerate the situation much longer.

Sighing, unable to weigh pros and cons through the throbbing headache that was tormenting her, Catherine rested her head on the back of the chair, trying to relax.

For a long time she remained quiet, staring into space, her mind curiously devoid of active thoughts. At last she turned her head and again glanced at the clock, surprised to see that it was well after eight.

Slowly she got to her feet and summoned Anya.

Nine

The house belonging to the Choglokovs was built on a small island in the middle of the Neva. While access was easy enough in winter when the river was frozen, it was necessary now, in April, to go there by boat.

While a servant rowed the short distance from the riverbank to the island, Catherine sat quietly next to Marie, trying to quell her growing nervousness.

Lifting her head, Catherine viewed the clouds that skudded across the moonless sky. The mist, especially noticeable on the river, had thickened in density. A gust of wind almost dislodged the hood of her cloak, and as she raised a hand to keep it in place Catherine wondered whether Peter would notice her absence. She doubted it. By ten o'clock he had fallen into a drunken stupor. When she had left their apartments an hour later he had been sound asleep.

By the time they reached the island the first drops of rain began to fall, and both women ran from the dock to the front steps of the modest wooden structure.

The party was in full swing when they entered. Catherine could hear sounds of inebriated hilarity rise above the wind.

No lamps were lit, and the few lighted candles that were in evidence did little to alleviate the dim shadows. Catherine recognized only a few of the young people at the gathering, not an unusual state of affairs, given the relative seclusion in which she had lived for the past four years. And, with the exception of Marie and her husband, all of them were young, in their twenties. Some were dancing, some were playing cards, and some stood in dark corners or by window embrasures, whispering and giggling. If Catherine was recognized, no one gave any indication of it. Her arrival caused not so much as a hesitation in the party atmosphere.

'Allow me to take your cloak.'

The quiet voice startled her. Turning, Catherine faced Serge Saltikov. Marie, who only a moment ago had been at her side, had moved away and was now at one of the card tables.

Serge had slipped the cloak from her shoulders and now laid it on a nearby chair. Catherine's violet eyes lingered on the darkly handsome man. How she longed to touch those dark curls.

'My beautiful Catherine,' he murmured, touching her bare arm with a caressing fingertip. His admiring glance took in the swell of her breast, delightfully displayed beneath the soft velvet of her mauve gown.

The familiar form of address momentarily shocked her, but even though she opened her mouth to speak, no words emerged. The brief physical contact had taken her breath away. Catherine felt frozen, held in place by the piercing blue eyes that were staring so compellingly into her own.

Shrill laughter from within the room broke the spell. With a disdainful look at the cavorting guests, Serge put a hand on Catherine's elbow.

'Let's go in here, where we can be alone.' He began to walk across the hall and into a small reception room.

Although Catherine allowed herself to be led, she noted archly: 'I don't recall expressing the wish to be alone with you.'

As he closed the door, Serge smiled down at her. 'Your eyes speak for you,' he said softly. He raised her hand to his lips, and his warm breath sent a flood of weakness through her. Hastily Catherine withdrew her hand.

After walking across the room, she stood before a narrow window. The brocade draperies, patterned in blue and white, had been left parted. There was little to see. Rain sheeted the glass. Beyond, all was blackness.

Catherine turned her head slightly, aware that Serge had come to stand just behind her. His booted feet had moved silently across the carpeted floor. Returning her gaze to the window, she saw his image reflected in the glass, highlighted by the brass lamp positioned on a small table not far from where she was standing.

'Is ... your wife here this evening?' Catherine clasped her hands at her waist in an effort to still their trembling, but now felt more in control of herself.

'No,' Serge whispered, placing his strong hands on her shoulders. Bending his head, his lips found the softness of her neck.

Catherine shuddered and clasped her hands even tighter. Her breath was coming so fast she felt dizzy.

With his hands still on her shoulders, Serge turned her around to face him. And then his mouth was against her own. Catherine swayed, so overcome by sensation that her legs threatened to give way. His hand moved from the small of her back to the swell of her breast. Catherine gave a gasp and pulled away from him.

'Come upstairs with me ... please,' Serge whispered to her.

She wavered, but couldn't bring herself to do it. Caution reasserted itself. Catherine moved a step away. What was she doing here? she demanded of herself. Was she prepared to throw away everything? Inexplicably, her mind went back to that day so long ago when Elizabeth had berated her for paying attention to a young lieutenant. My God, she thought wildly, that had been innocent. Her being here at this late hour could in no way be construed in such a benign way. What would the empress do if her actions on this night were discovered?

The thought was so chilling that it effectively doused

the small flame of passion that had begun to grow within Catherine.

Serge seemed to sense the sudden change in her. Issuing a sigh of resignation, he moved to a safer distance. Although his aroused state left him damnably uncomfortable, he thought it best not to rush her. He watched her for a moment, an enigmatic look on his handsome face. Then, with an almost mocking smile, he held out his arm. 'Shall we join the others, your Highness?'

The next day a courier delivered a basket of grapes with a note written in Saltikov's flourishing script.

Catherine smiled as she looked at the luscious fruit. Serge, as did all those about her, knew of her preference for fresh fruit. The enclosed note made her blush with its implications, but prudently Catherine destroyed it.

That same afternoon Marie entered Catherine's dressing room, watching as Anya curled and pinned up the luxuriant tresses of her mistress.

'Ah, your hair is so beautiful, your Highness. Such a lovely color,' Marie murmured in admiring tones. She sat down in a small velvet-upholstered chair and observed the proceedings for another moment before she again spoke. 'I've just been to see the empress,' she mentioned offhandedly, apparently not noticing the grand duchess's sudden pallor.

Hardly daring to breathe, Catherine tilted her head. 'I ... I hope you've found her Majesty in good health,' she managed faintly. Picking up a brush, she toyed with the jeweled handle. Had her absence from the palace been reported? she wondered, striving for a calmness that was almost beyond her.

But Marie's face held no hint of malice or censure. Even her usual stern expression had softened into something that approached friendliness. 'Oh, her Majesty is in good spirits,' she replied. 'And I have wonderful news, your

Highness. The empress has given her permission for you and the grand duke to join her at Peterhof.' Her smile broadened as she leaned forward expectantly.

'Peterhof?' Catherine blinked in surprise, afraid to let her hopes rise too rapidly.

Marie nodded her head and actually gave a gay laugh. 'Yes, Peterhof. We're leaving before the week is gone. The empress plans to stay through the spring and for most of the summer, as well.'

Catherine touched a wayward curl and tried to make her voice casual. 'Is … the whole court going?'

'Absolutely,' Marie affirmed strongly. She stood up, her manner brisk again. 'Well, we have no time to lose. I shall order the servants to begin the packing immediately.'

Catherine heard the efficient rustle of taffeta as Marie left the room, but she didn't turn around. For just a moment her eyes met Anya's in the mirror, then she quickly looked away.

Catherine held her face up to the sun, feeling the pleasant breeze fan her cheeks. The weeks of spring had sped by so fast she couldn't believe they were gone. Never had a spring been so sweet and exciting. She and Serge had fallen into the habit of meeting at this small secluded beach, one of many that framed the Gulf of Finland.

As they walked along, Catherine glanced up at him, still a bit surprised that no one – not even Marie – questioned her comings and goings. During those first few weeks Catherine hadn't been able to repress the need to look over her shoulder each time she and Serge met in private. She more than half expected to see Marie following her.

But no one seemed to notice or comment on her daily absence, and after a while Catherine began to relax.

They paused at the water's edge. Catherine removed her satin shoes and playfully dipped her toes into the coldness, laughing in delight.

Serge came closer, unmindful of getting his boots wet.

Reaching out, he clasped Catherine around the waist.

'Your beauty tempts a man beyond endurance ...'

Catherine wanted to step away, still a bit apprehensive of her own sensations when he touched her, but her traitorous limbs refused to obey.

'You have a glib tongue,' she said shakily, resting her hands on his broad chest and looking up into his blue eyes.

He pulled her against him, feeling the shudder that coursed through both of them. 'Catherine,' he implored in an anguished voice. 'Please don't withhold your love from me any longer. I'm only flesh and blood.'

She emitted a small whimpering sound. Although she had been fighting her feelings for this man in the past weeks, it was becoming more and more difficult for her to resist. Part of her yearned for him to pick her up and carry her to his bed, and part of her remained terrified should such an action be discovered. Once more she tried to pull away from him. But his grip was firm and he held her trapped within his arms. Ignoring her weak protest, he kissed her deeply, refusing to release her even when her hands pressed against his chest in an effort to push him from her.

The moments passed as his mouth worked against hers, forcing the soft lips to part. Catherine was now certain that she would fall to the ground if he did release his hold. Her arms crept around his neck as she returned his kiss with a hunger whose intensity almost frightened her.

When he finally raised his head, Serge gazed down at her as if he were in pain. 'Please don't torment me,' he pleaded, his breath ragged with desire. 'For weeks you've been holding me at arm's length. I cannot bear it any longer.'

Catherine, whose breath seemed to have caught in her throat, could only nod her consent.

They agreed to meet in his room. At the appointed hour, wearing the attire of a page, Catherine entered the bedchamber and was immediately swept into the strong arms of the Russian nobleman. After a lingering kiss, he picked her up and carried her to the bed.

Deftly, his kisses leaving her breathless for she knew not what, Serge helped her to undress. Then, in the light of the single candle, he removed his own clothes.

And Catherine, in spite of being married for more than seven years, gazed for the first time in delighted wonder upon the only male form she had thus far ever seen unclothed.

In the full prime of his manhood, Serge was proud of his physique, and rightly so. Catherine thought he looked like a perfectly sculpted statue come to life. After getting into bed beside her, Serge bent forward and buried his lips in the soft hollow of her neck. Catherine gasped with the contact. She felt his heart beat against her bare breast and was struck by the fact that she had never before been this close to another human being. As he fitted his body to hers, she felt the warmth of him from her head to her toes. Then his lips claimed hers, and Catherine lost the power to think, to reason. Only sensation remained.

Although she had tried many times to imagine this coming together of a man and a woman, Catherine was astonished at how far away from the truth she had been.

With much patience and ardor, Serge continued to initiate the grand duchess into the mysteries of love. His kisses were at first tender, brushing warmly against her eyelids, trailing down her cheek to the softness of her throat. Then his mouth became more insistent, causing her body to arch with a pleasure that made her nerves taut. Every part of her seemed to be on fire with the exquisite feeling.

Even the pain of that first moment didn't reach her conscious mind, so wrapped in ecstasy was she by then. With complete abandon, Catherine willingly surrendered herself to the pleasurable feelings Serge provoked, feelings she hadn't known existed.

Some time later, Serge raised himself up on an elbow and looked down at the beautiful face, the closed eyes, the lips parted with her now-quiet breathing. Flickering light from the almost gutted candle played on long slim legs and caressed the pure curve of her breast.

Serge smiled. He had long suspected Catherine's virginal state, and his senses had quickened at the thought of plucking this forbidden fruit. Lying down again, sated with his amorous endeavors, Serge wondered idly if he would have succumbed on his own. Probably not, he decided, entwining the silken tresses between his fingers. He'd been so astonished when he listened to Marie's thinly veiled invitation that he could hardly credit his good fortune. And he, like Catherine, knew the woman would never dare such a thing on her own.

Beside him, Catherine stirred. Before her eyes were fully open she reached for him. Still smiling, Serge put his arms around her and pulled her tightly against him, his body quickly responding to her murmurs of desire.

Every night for the remaining two weeks, Catherine joyfully embraced her lover, giving vent to the pent-up passions that had for so long been repressed. She was discovering a sensual side to her nature, a facet that had remained hidden all these years. She had no need to ask herself if she was in love with Serge. Such an intoxicating emotion as she felt could be no less.

On the court's last night in Peterhof Catherine returned to her apartments at two o'clock in the morning, her body still tingling from Serge's warm caresses.

She went into her dressing room, where she disrobed with the help of Anya, who always waited up for her. Then, as quietly as she was able, she crawled into bed next to Peter.

Catherine had no sooner settled herself in a comfortable position when Peter turned toward her. He ran a hand down her leg, then tugged at her nightgown, raising it to her waist.

Too shocked to even move, Catherine offered no resistance when her husband climbed on top of her. Like a dog in heat he mounted, grunting all the while as he thrust himself into her. His hands clutched at her breasts, leaving her flesh bruised and aching.

Just when Catherine thought she could bear no more of his heavy-handed pawing, Peter gave a loud yelp of pleasure and rolled off her.

During the entire performance he never spoke a word.

Afterward, Catherine lay beside her husband, stunned. And while he slept, she stared up at the ceiling, wide awake. Far from having aroused the passion she now knew she was capable of, Peter had aroused only the usual revulsion.

The white night dissolved into a pink and azure sky. While Peter still slumbered, Catherine finally got out of bed. Donning a light silk robe, she went into her dressing room.

She sat down and peered into the mirror, surprised to see that there was no change at all in her reflection. Startled by a sound, she turned, then relaxed when she saw Anya.

The maid was smiling, perfectly aware of what had taken place the night before. Few secrets can be kept from good servants. Of necessity, Anya's small room adjoined that of the grand ducal bedchamber. Peter's personal attendants occupied rooms leading off the other end of the bedchamber.

'I will take a bath this morning,' Catherine said in a low voice, her mind obviously on something other than her words.

Anya dipped in a curtsy and went to make preparations.

A while later, Catherine eased herself into the cast-iron tub. As Anya gently scrubbed her back, she began to feel the tension evaporate. A Dutch stove in the corner was stoked high, serving the dual purpose of heating the room and supporting two more pails of hot water should they be needed.

With her body relaxed, Catherine's mind mulled over her husband's unexpected actions. Why, after all these years? she wondered, feeling fresh incredulity. And why now? Now that she had Serge. She had seen little of Peter during their summer stay here at Peterhof. Like herself, he was reveling in newfound freedom. He neither questioned nor seemed interested in her whereabouts. Each night, after having spent several hours in the arms of her lover, Catherine was careful to return to her own rooms by two o'clock. Peter had always been asleep. Last night, however, he had not only been awake but had been apparently waiting for her arrival.

Of course it was for the best, she mused, in a practical frame of mind. If she did conceive, Peter would have no basis for disclaiming the child. Still, it seemed too much of a coincidence.

She motioned for Anya to get the towels. Then, resting a hand lightly on the maid's arm, she stepped out of the tub.

'But why just now?' she murmured, unaware that she had spoken aloud.

Anya laid the towel aside and held the robe in a position for Catherine to slip her arms into the sleeves. Like all of Catherine's attendants, Anya adored her mistress. All her loyalties and sympathies were with the grand duchess. It was for this reason that she now spoke, even though she knew that she had not been addressed.

'When a man has been shown to the well, Highness,' she said quietly, tying the belt of the robe, 'it is only a matter of time before he knows how to slake his thirst.'

Suddenly alert, Catherine observed her maid with sharp eyes. 'If you have something to say to me, Anya,' she commanded, 'out with it.'

A bit chagrined that she spoken so boldly, the young woman flushed. 'I'm not certain, your Highness,' she replied in a hesitant voice. 'Truly, it's just a rumor that I've heard. It may have no basis in fact.'

'Tell me,' Catherine ordered, again seating herself at the

dressing table.

Anya picked up a brush and began to apply it to her mistress's tousled hair. 'It's rumored that the grand duke has been spending a lot of time in the company of a woman named Madame Groot. And that she ...' Anya broke off and began to brush Catherine's hair with renewed vigor.

The grand duchess fixed her with a hard look. 'Go on.'

'Well, Madame Groot is a widow. She's not young ...' Anya again stopped, suddenly at a loss for words.

Catherine stared at her maid in the mirror. 'Are you saying that this woman, this Madame Groot ... seduced the grand duke?' She didn't know whether to laugh or to be angry.

'Yes, madame,' Anya responded, cheeks flaming with embarrassment.

Catherine grew thoughtful. But why should it not be so? she wondered, thinking on it. If her own life was being manipulated, then why shouldn't it happen with Peter, as well? She turned in her chair and now looked directly at Anya. 'We will not speak of this again,' she said in a quiet and calm voice.

The September evening offered rain, whipped by a brisk and chilly wind that announced the approach of fall.

In her imperial palace in Moscow the empress sat on the blue damask settee in her private salon, dressed in an extravagant gown of silver cloth. Attentively she listened to the words of her chancellor, a look of satisfaction settled firmly upon her face.

'And so she is with child?' she questioned when Bestuzhev concluded his brief report. 'You are certain?'

'I am, your Majesty,' her chancellor replied firmly.

Elizabeth turned away for a moment, concealing her inclination to probe further. No cloud of suspicion must hover over this long-awaited child.

She faced her chancellor squarely, her dark-blue eyes

level and direct. 'We are very pleased to hear this.' She gave a short nod that set the diamonds in her powdered hair to twinkle in the candlelight. 'We will send our personal congratulations to the grand duke and his wife.'

Before Bestuzhev could speak, Elizabeth waved a hand in dismissal. Then her expression settled into a solemn mask of moody contemplation as she thought of the happy event to come.

Ten

Sitting on her horse, Catherine took a deep breath of the cold and clear January air. At first glance, one would have thought that the horse was equipped with a sidesaddle. In fact, it was not. Catherine had hooked her leg over the pommel of an ordinary saddle.

Serge angled his horse closer to hers. He wore a short fur-lined jacket over heavy woolen breeches that were tucked into leather boots. He and Catherine had left the palace about thirty minutes ago and were now close to the woods that surrounded the city. The snow was firm and hard-packed on the well-traveled road, but the drifts were deep and treacherous, prompting Serge to lead his mare with a cautious hand.

Turning, Catherine regarded her lover's handsome face. If Peter was aware of her affair with Serge, he gave no indication of such knowledge. He seemed, of late, to be in uncommonly good spirits, and Catherine took pains to avoid upsetting that precarious state of affairs.

Still watching Serge, Catherine searched her mind for any feelings of guilt that might be harbored deep within its recesses, but she found only joy. It was good to be alive, to be in love. She felt complete, at peace with herself, Serge was receptive to her every whim. In his eyes she saw herself reflected as a desirable woman. It was a heady feeling.

A bit sadly, though, Catherine wondered where it would all end. She was bound to Peter for life, knew very well that her future with Serge would be limited. Best to take happiness while she could. After that one night in Peterhof, Peter had never again approached her. Now, however, she suspected that his overtures toward her ladies were carried farther than the usual horseplay in which he so frequently indulged.

Catching her glance, Serge grinned. 'Have I told you how lovely you look?' he asked softly. Reaching out, he cupped her chin, leaning forward to kiss her lips. 'Pregnancy agrees with you. Your face is as radiant as the sun.'

'That's because I feel marvelous,' Catherine exclaimed, violet eyes sparkling as she viewed the man with whom she was so much in love. 'After two days of continuous snow and sleet, it feels wonderful to be out in the air again.'

As she spoke, Catherine dismounted, slipping easily and lightly to the ground. Then she mounted the horse again, this time astride. Although the bottle-green velvet skirt of her riding habit was voluminous, Catherine always wore trousers beneath it. She detested riding sidesaddle, custom notwithstanding, and whenever she was away from prying eyes would ride astride.

Serge chuckled, watching as Catherine settled herself with confidence on the spirited white gelding.

'You know the empress would disapprove if she saw you riding like that,' he chided her, but his blue eyes twinkled beneath his fur hat.

Catherine laughed. She was, as she had said, feeling marvelous. Now in her fourth month of pregnancy, she hadn't experienced so much as one day of discomfort.

'What the empress doesn't know about, she will not disapprove of,' she replied saucily, her remark punctuated by an impish grin. Prodding her mount to a gallop, Catherine called to Serge over her shoulder. 'Come, I'll race you to the river.'

Immediately the young man responded, white teeth flashing as he smiled at her exuberance.

They had gone about a quarter of a mile when two

wolves suddenly loped from the cover of the woods, crossing directly in their path. Snarling, ears flattened, one of them nipped at the leg of the white gelding. The horse skittered and slid, then reared in fright.

Struggling to regain control, Catherine managed to hold fast as the horse lunged forward, eyes bright with panic. She dug her booted feet into the stirrups and clamped her knees as tightly as she could against the animal's heaving flesh. As if coming from a great distance, she heard Serge shouting her name and heard, too, the sound of his horse's hooves galloping in frantic pursuit. But his mare was no match for the gelding, who seemed to fly across the snowy ground as if he had suddenly sprouted wings.

Realizing that she couldn't immediately halt the panicked animal, Catherine leaned forward. Gripping the reins firmly in her gloved hands, she allowed the gelding to run at full speed. The animal surged forward, great hooves kicking up clouds of powdery snow. Cold air brushed her face and pinked her cheeks. Catherine brought her head closer to the horse's neck. She wasn't frightened, but rather exhilarated.

Finally, after many long minutes, she sensed that the horse was at last tiring. Straightening, she cautiously drew in on the reins, calling words of encouragement. She was relieved to see the animal once again responded to her commands. With a final tug, the huge gelding came to a halt, shaking his head, his heated breath leaving small clouds of steam in its wake.

She took a moment to calm her racing heart and relax her tight muscles. Then, bending forward, Catherine patted the damp neck, concerned now for the animal's welfare, knowing that in his overheated condition it was best to return him to the stables immediately. Looking down at his foreleg, she was dismayed to see the trickle of bright-red blood that stained the snow. She jumped to the ground and ran a hand over the wound, relieved to see that the injury was no more than a surface scratch.

'My God, Catherine!' Serge's frantic voice wavered hoarsely as he caught up with her. He was breathing almost as hard as the gelding. 'You had me terrified. Are you all right?'

Looking up at him, she smiled brightly. 'I'm fine,' she assured him, mounting again. 'But we'd best get back. Pagan's terribly overheated. I want his wound tended to as soon as possible.' Without waiting for a response, she nudged the horse forward and set out at a brisk canter.

After returning to the stables, Catherine gave strict orders to the groom, charging him with the welfare of the gelding. Then she and Serge walked slowly in the direction of the palace, Serge leading his mare as he walked at her side.

'Are you certain you're all right?' he asked anxiously, still shaken. He couldn't believe that she had managed to stay on the horse. It was fortunate, he thought to himself, that she had been riding astride. She most certainly would have been thrown had she been sitting sidesaddle.

Again Catherine assured him of her well-being, pleased by his show of concern.

They paused at the front steps. Catherine smiled up him. 'Will you be coming to see me tonight?' she inquired softly, resisting the urge to touch him.

'You know I'll be there,' he murmured in a caressing whisper that sent a shiver of anticipation down her spine. The warm promise in his eyes almost made her cast aside discretion and throw her arms around his neck.

Her exuberance returned in a flood of vitality that sent her running up the stairs. She had just enough time to take a bath and dress before the evening meal. Then, if all went well, she would meet Serge later, after the court retired for the night. Upon entering her apartments, Catherine smiled at Anya, seeing that the girl had anticipated her desire for a bath. The water was already warm and perfumed. About to step into the tub, Catherine faltered. A sharp pain thrust its way through her abdomen, causing her to lose her footing. Weakly she fell against Anya. Almost before it had subsided came another, stronger pain. Wrapping her arms about her stomach, Catherine doubled over in agony, causing Anya to run screaming for the physicians.

Before the night was gone Catherine knew she had lost the child. The doctors had barely completed their ministrations when the empress stormed into Catherine's room.

White-faced with anger, Elizabeth advanced slowly toward the canopied bed. Looking up, Catherine drew back as far as she was able, so certain was she that the empress planned to strike her.

'You fool!' Elizabeth screamed, glaring down at Catherine. Her features were contorted with hot emotion, lips drawn back from her teeth in something that resembled a snarl. 'Even the most ignorant serf would know better than to ride when she's pregnant.' The blue eyes fixed themselves with unswerving condemnation upon the grand duchess.

Catherine bit her lip. 'I haven't the words to tell you of my grief, your Majesty,' she managed to murmur, feeling more than apprehension. She had never seen Elizabeth in such a state. The empress was actually trembling with the force of her fury.

'Grief!' Elizabeth's voice rose to a piercing shriek. 'It's taken you eight years to conceive – eight years! And now you kill your child in a fit of foolishness.' She bent over, bringing her face so close that Catherine recoiled from the wine-filled breath. 'We warn you, madame,' she hissed in a grating voice. 'It had better not be another eight years before you produce an heir or you will spend the rest of your days staring at the walls of the remotest nunnery.'

Despite the harsh words, Catherine couldn't summon the energy to do more than nod wearily. She was greatly weakened by the loss of blood, not only from the miscarriage but from a session with the physician's scalpel, that man having insisted she be bled. The child had been a boy, and Catherine suspected that this more than anything else had caused Elizabeth's rage.

Elizabeth had straightened and was now regarding one of the physicians with a hard look. Her voice was again calm and impervious as she addressed him. 'Make certain that you tend your grand duchess with the utmost care,' she commanded. 'We would have her returned to good health as quickly as possible.'

She did not deign to look again at the ailing grand duchess and left the room without further words.

Catherine remained in bed for the next three weeks, her strength returning slowly. By the end of May she was fully recovered. The whole court then trekked to St. Petersburg, with the exception of Peter, who had decided to spend a few months at Oranienbaum.

With Serge her constant companion, the summer passed in a delightful manner. Catherine regretted the appearance of the fiery colors of autumn that heralded the return of the court to Moscow and to Peter. On that first night, he demanded his marital prerogative. Catherine submitted, gritting her teeth until it was over. Thankfully, he did not bother her again, and once more she gave herself to Serge's welcome embrace.

The Winter Carnival had barely come to an end when she discovered she was once again pregnant. The glittering whirl came to an abrupt halt. This time the empress wasn't taking any chances. Catherine was forbidden to indulge in anything more strenuous than a slow walk.

Once again monotony lay over her small court like a pall. Catherine sank into lethargy. Somehow the time passed, albeit slowly. She thought of the hours she had spent with Serge, hours that seemed to have flown by like minutes. Now Serge didn't come to see her, nor did he even write to her. While Catherine could appreciate his cautious attitude, his absence left a void that was hard to fill. Peter bothered her little. He was, it seemed, completely bewitched by one Marfa Shafirov. Catherine watched their affair with a sardonic eye.

The only break in the sameness of her day was when Emil Zeiss came to call.

She was in her fifth month of pregnancy when Herr Zeiss presented himself one day, only to be again denied audience with Peter. It was the third straight day that this had occurred. Irritated, Catherine instructed the agitated envoy to be seated in the outer chamber.

'I'll speak to the grand duke,' she said to him. Walking with purposeful strides, she entered the adjoining room, her manner quite clearly displaying her irascibility.

'Herr Zeiss is waiting to see you, Peter. You cannot send him away again.'

Peter turned and glared at her. 'Get the hell out of here and leave me alone,' he shouted, annoyed at having been interrupted. He had eight of his valets standing in a line. From the way in which they were dressed, Catherine could see that Peter had been playing soldier again. Each man was wearing a replica of the military uniform of Holstein.

She eyed her husband with open distaste. Peter stood close to the wall, observing his mock troops with critical attention. Behind him, a newly installed double-paned window gave testimony to an earlier bout of ill temper, at which time he had picked up a musket and in a fit of military fervor had blasted it to pieces. The outer surface of the window was now bespattered with wet thick drops of rain glistening fitfully in the muted glow of lamplight.

'You must see him,' she persisted, trying to control her agitation. Probably, she thought ruefully, looking at the row of men, she ought to be grateful that her husband had finally put aside his toy soldiers.

'I don't have to do anything I don't want to do!'

'You could at least speak to the man when he calls on

you,' Catherine stated in a stern voice. 'Then you would be doing at least one thing right. I'm certain that you can interrupt your games long enough to administer your precious Holstein,' she concluded with biting sarcasm.

'If you're concerned about Herr Zeiss,' Peter bellowed at her, 'then you talk to him. You make the decisions.' As Catherine glanced at him through her dark lashes, Peter caught the gleam of contempt that shone in their violet depths. It enraged him. 'There is one thing, madame,' he muttered maliciously, pale eyes narrowed to slits, 'that will give me great pleasure when the time comes for me to rule this heathen land.'

Catherine turned wary, but her violet eyes remained level and calm.

'And that will be dealing with you in the proper manner. Rest assured, madame, that is one duty I shall not shirk.'

Raising her chin slightly, Catherine refused to be intimidated by the thinly veiled threat. Her palms itched with the desire to wipe the wolfish smile from his sallow face. She had never struck Peter, not even when he raised his hand to her. She had never struck anyone in her life, but the urge to do so now was compelling.

Then she quieted and regarded her husband thoughtfully for a moment. Without speaking further, Catherine left the room. Before the door had closed, she could hear Peter issuing commands as he resumed his game.

After returning to the outer chamber, Catherine sat down at the rosewood writing table and beckoned to the envoy.

'Please come over here and sit down, Herr Zeiss,' she invited calmly. 'And bring your papers with you.' As long as Peter had given her permission, Catherine thought with resignation, there was no reason why she shouldn't try her hand at governing the small duchy.

During the coming months, Catherine became more

and more involved in the affairs of the inconsequential realm. Herr Zeiss, after his initial surprise had worn off, heaved a mighty sigh of relief. At last there was someone concerned and intelligent with whom he could discuss what were to him very important matters. He found himself looking forward to his weekly visits. Not only was the grand duchess astute, not only did she give him her full and undivided attention, she was certainly better looking than the grand duke. In fact, before too many weeks had passed, Herr Zeiss decided Catherine was quite the loveliest woman he had ever laid eyes upon. He couldn't imagine why he'd never noticed it before.

One day, only a week before her child was due, Count Bestuzhev came to see Catherine.

Of late the chancellor's behavior had puzzled Catherine; it still did, as a matter of fact. The cold dislike seemed to have warmed into something greater than tolerance, although she was at a loss to put a name to it. It was not admiration; that look she recognized well enough by now. Nor was it a liking for her. It was, rather, a watchfulness, colored by reservation.

When, only a few moments into their conversation – which, as usual, dealt with money – Bestuzhev mentioned that he was aware of her meetings with Zeiss, Catherine sighed, wondering whether this too would be denied her. To her surprise, the chancellor spoke in another vein.

'I'm pleased that you've found something with which to occupy your time, Highness.' His black eyes gazed at her with speculation.

Catherine darted a quick glance at him, uncertain as to his tone. Bestuzhev's voice could at times shimmer with sarcasm. He was, however, regarding her with total seriousness.

'I'm glad you approve, Chancellor,' she murmured at last, still in the grip of wary contemplation.

'I've heard it said that you are an able administrator,' he went on, still fixing her with intent appraisal.

She laughed softly. 'Holstein's problems are small enough.' Her face sobered. 'I must admit, though, that I do find the whole thing somewhat of a challenge,' she confessed quietly.

'If I can ever be of assistance, your Highness,' Bestuzhev offered, 'please do not hesitate to ask.' He then did an unexpected thing. Bowing low, he lifted her hand to his lips and, in a voice that was barely audible, murmured: 'Your abilities may one day benefit us all.'

With that, he took his leave. Catherine's puzzlement deepened.

That evening, after an absence of several weeks, Leo Narishkin presented himself, explaining that he had been ill.

'I hope it was nothing serious,' Catherine said to him, genuinely concerned.

He shook his head. 'It wasn't at all serious,' he replied. 'But I, least of all, would jeopardize your health, and so I thought it best to stay away until I was fully recovered.'

Catherine motioned him. 'Come, Leo. Sit with me over here. I've no desire to play cards tonight. We'll just talk.'

Leo watched with admiration as she moved toward the settee at the far end of the room. If he hadn't known of Catherine's condition, his eye would never have discerned it. The full hooped skirt completely concealed any outward sign of pregnancy.

After they had settled themselves on the cushions, Catherine turned toward her friend. 'I've not seen Serge for months,' she whispered. 'Why hasn't he come to me?'

Leo Narishkin's gentle brown eyes clouded. He knew of their affair, for Serge had often boasted of it. 'He's been advised to stay away, Catherine,' he replied quietly, longing to take hold of her hand. He loved her so dearly, but it was a love he dared not show, even to her. He wondered if it would be simpler and kinder in the long run to tell her truth. Serge had indeed been ordered to stay away. His feelings for Catherine had been no deeper than his physical desire. Serge, Leo thought in some anger, was a rogue. Unfortunately, that was part of his charm.

'Advised or not, he could have found a way,' Catherine cried out. She looked at Leo imploringly, as if he could do something about it.

Leo was tempted, but she looked so upset he didn't have the heart to tell her. 'Perhaps later on he'll come to visit you,' he offered lamely.

Catherine turned away. 'I think I shall retire early tonight, Leo. Please excuse me.' After rising quickly, she went directly to her bedchamber so that no one would see her tears.

She hadn't yet fallen asleep when the bed sagged as Peter crawled in beside her. Moving to the far side, Catherine prayed that this would be one of those nights when he would fall asleep quickly. She was in no mood for his senseless prattle or his childish games, much less his brutish attempts at passion.

In the dim light, Peter regarded his wife's swollen form. The sight filled him with disgust. For a moment he remained still. Then he leaned over her, bringing his face close to hers. In a whisper that glittered with malice, he said: 'If any ask, I should be hard-pressed to answer how it is that my wife continues to get herself with child.'

For a heart-stopping moment, Catherine didn't respond. Composing herself, she strove for a cool voice. 'If any should ask, Peter, are you prepared to say that you've not recently lain with your wife?'

At that, he muttered an angry reply and, turning on his side, was soon asleep.

But Catherine lay there for a long time, wide awake. The following morning, heralded by leaden skies that threatened rain, she went into labor.

Eleven

By late evening the child still had not been born. Outside, rain fell steadily, the monotonous sound broken only by rolling thunder and intermittent flashes of lightning

The little room where Catherine struggled to give birth was hot and airless. There were no windows, and the stove poured forth its heat without resistance. Elizabeth hovered close by, bending over now and again to peer anxiously at the proceedings.

Catherine thrashed about. The mattress, a poor one that was filled with straw and placed on the floor, felt hard and unyielding beneath her.

'Why is it taking so long?' Elizabeth complained peevishly at one point, glaring at the physicians and midwives in turn. 'The child isn't in the wrong position, is it?'

The physicians hastened to assure her that all was well. Irascible, Elizabeth sent for wine and food. If she had to wait, she might as well be comfortable, she thought in resignation.

From across the room, Peter watched his aunt with sardonic eyes, amused. Here was one situation even she couldn't control, he thought gleefully. He unbuttoned the blue jacket of his military uniform and removed it, he threw it carelessly on a nearby chair. The room was stifling, causing him to perspire in a most irritating manner.

When the food and drink arrived, Peter gratefully

applied himself to the task of filling his empty stomach, occasionally casting annoyed looks at his wife. Why did she have to keep up with that infernal screaming? The sound of it grated on his nerves. He was further annoyed that he had to spend all these hours just sitting here. It was, all in all, a wasted day.

Only one person in the overcrowded room observed the grand duchess with sympathy; that, strangely enough, was Count Bestuzhev. He, too, had removed his jacket in deference to the heat, but his white shirt was buttoned up to his neck, the lace jabot trailing neatly down the front of it. His black eyes were solemn, his face unsmiling.

Bestuzhev had reluctantly come to the conclusion that the young woman on the mattress was most probably their only hope. This was not a decision that the chancellor had reached easily; in fact, it had come slowly over the years with a sort of dawning awareness. Bestuzhev rubbed his chin as he thought of the empress's frequent fainting spells. The most recent attack had lasted almost an hour before the physicians were able to bring Elizabeth back to her senses. One day, he knew, they would be unable to do so.

His eyes toured the room and came to rest on the grand duke, who was still eating with unending appetite. The sight touched off a distant nausea, and Bestuzhev quickly averted his gaze. That, he thought to himself grimly, was their next tsar. In spite of the heated room, Bestuzhev felt a cold chill of dread course through him.

The hours passed. Elizabeth sent for more food and wine. Outside, the weather finally cleared and bright stars shone from the black sky. Through it all Catherine's travail continued without respite.

Sprawled in a chair, Peter had begun to doze when the cry of an infant, followed by the loud exclamations of his aunt, made him sit bolt upright. Curious for the first time, he ambled closer, staring at the squealing bundle held so tightly in the arms of the empress, whose face reflected a peculiar expression, one that Peter had never seen before.

The feeling that overwhelmed Elizabeth as she held the infant in her arms left her breathless with wonder. As Peter came toward her, she looked up at him, eyes shining brightly.

'A son!' she declared, emitting what sounded suspiciously like a sob. 'Peter, you have a son!'

He grinned, accepting the enthusiastic congratulations that now came his way from everyone, including Count Bestuzhev, who wore an expression of profound relief.

With a smile that held triumph and exultation, Elizabeth nodded curtly to the physicians and midwives. 'Come along,' she commanded briskly.

Still gazing with intense feeling at the newborn infant, Elizabeth led them all from the room.

Alone on the mattress, Catherine stared about her with dazed eyes. Was it over? Did she hear someone say that she had birthed a son? Or had it been just a dream? Conscious of a searing thirst that prodded insistently at her parched throat, she regarded the vacated room. Not even a servant remained.

Too helpless and too weak even to hold her head up, Catherine fell back on the soiled mattress.

Oh, dear God, just a sip of water, her mind cried out just before she lost consciousness.

When Catherine gained her senses some hours later, she found herself in her own bed. Involuntarily her body tensed for the expected onslaught of pain. Then she sighed deeply, aware that the hot and agonizing contractions she had endured for so many hours had at last come to an end.

She made a halfhearted attempt to move, but gave it up when her body painfully protested in places she hadn't known existed.

Turning her head on the pillow, Catherine glanced around the empty room, wondering how she had gotten from the mattress to the bed. She had no recollection of having been moved.

It was, she saw, still night. Only a single taper burned in solitary defiance, fending off dark shadows that nestled in the corners of the room. She was still alone, not even Anya was in evidence.

And where was her child? Frowning, Catherine strained for remembrance. A son. She had given birth to a son.

As if in confirmation, she became aware of the thundering boom of cannon salutes, coupled with the deliriously happy pealing of church bells, and she realized that the whole city was celebrating the birth of an heir.

Settling back, Catherine's mouth twisted wryly as she wondered how loud the cheers would be were it known that the heir was not the son of the grand duke. There was, she knew very well, the distinct possibility that the child was not a Romanov at all. And if that was the case, that illustrious dynasty was now at an end.

Marie's words floated through her mind, words almost assuredly first expressed by the empress herself: Have a child by whatever means are available to you.

And whose child was it? Catherine mused as she lay there, still hearing the sound of bells and cheers that drifted in through her window. Then her mouth tightened and she thought fiercely: He is mine! It is my son who will be the crown prince and, ultimately, emperor. And it is my love and guidance that will shape his life.

Closing her eyes, Catherine drifted off to sleep. Her dreams, of her son and of Serge, were pleasant.

When next she awoke, it was early morning. The bedcurtains had been drawn. For a moment she lay quietly, trying to identify the strange sounds she was hearing. The urge to close her eyes and return to sleep was almost overpowering, but the jarring scraping noises at last proved too much.

Catherine sat up weakly and parted the hangings.

Sunlight flooded the room, casting buttery yellow slashes across the carpeted floor. In no little astonishment she viewed Peter. He was standing to the side of the fireplace, his back to her, hands on his narrow hips, impatiently issuing commands to his valets. The men were moving furniture from the room and making no effort at all to be quiet about it.

'What is going on?' she demanded of her husband, annoyed that even now he could show so little consideration for her.

Turning in her direction, Peter gave her one of his nastiest smiles.

'I'm moving,' he announced cheerfully. 'Now that we have a son, there's no further reason for me to share your bed. If I have need for you, I'll summon you.'

Catherine stared at him a moment, then released her hold on the hangings, allowing them to fall back into place. She laid her head down on the pillow and remained quiet until they all had left the bedchamber.

Issuing a sigh of relief then, Catherine settled herself comfortably, thinking how marvelous it would be to once again rest alone and undisturbed.

The next time she awoke it was already midday. The curtains had been pulled back and Catherine saw Marie standing by the window. The woman had turned in her direction as soon as Catherine had moved.

'So, you have finally awakened,' Marie said, smiling brightly. Coming forward, she sat on a chair that had been placed by the bed. With the exception of a few cabinets, the rosewood writing table, and the bed itself, the chair was the only piece of furniture that remained in the room.

'What time is it?' Catherine asked. She stretched luxuriously, then plumped the pillow behind her, sitting up.

'Almost three,' Marie replied. With a hand that appeared to tremble slightly, she arranged the folds of the simple blue organdy dress she was wearing.

'Did I really have a son?' Catherine asked, smiling ruefully at her lady. She had thought that the child would have been brought to her by now. The delay was beginning to irritate her.

Marie nodded, bending forward to pat Catherine's hand. 'Indeed you did, Highness. He's such a sturdy lad. The empress is overjoyed ...' Her voice trailed away as a servant entered the room, carrying a tray of food.

Catherine viewed the blini and hot tea with appreciation. 'Where is he?' she asked as she began to eat. 'When will they bring my baby to me?'

Marie rubbed her palms together, producing a sound not unlike rustling parchment. 'Not ... for a while, your Highness,' she murmured quietly. 'A wet nurse has been found for him.' There was a slight pause before she added: 'The empress thought it wise to wait until you recover some of your strength before you went to see the child.'

Marie's dark eyes were looking everywhere except at Catherine, for she was afraid that the grand duchess would see the very real sympathy she knew must be expressed in them. It wasn't fair, she was thinking. She prayed that Catherine would let the matter rest. At least for a few days until she was stronger.

Catherine put down her fork, her violet eyes tinged with bewilderment. 'Before I go to see him?' She tilted her head. 'Where is he that I would have to go to him?'

Marie cleared her throat and viewed her hands, clasped tightly in her lap. As loyal as she was to the empress, she didn't approve of this situation at all. But someone would, she knew, have to tell the grand duchess sooner or later.

'Where is my son?' Catherine repeated, this time in a sharper tone. Uneasiness spread throughout her like wine poured on sand, but she could give no name to her troubled feeling. Sturdy, Marie had said of the child. Therefore he could not be ill. So, what then?

'The crown prince is in the apartments of the empress, your Highness,' Marie replied at last, eyes still lowered.

Catherine gave a breath of relief. Visibly relaxing, she shrugged. 'Well,' she said, picking up the fork again. 'No doubt he'll be safe enough there while I'm recuperating.

I'm certain I'll be on my feet in a matter of days. In the meantime, please see to it that the child is brought to me this afternoon.' She gave Marie a brief glance and smile. 'I've yet to see him, you know, and am most anxious to do so.' She took a sip of the hot tea and put the cup back on the tray.

Dismayed, Marie bit her lip. She had wanted to postpone the inevitable, but now saw that it would not be possible. 'I'm afraid he cannot be brought here, madame,' she whispered softly, wringing her hands. 'The child is to remain with the empress.'

Pausing, Catherine raised her brows and stared at Marie, her expression one of incomprehension. 'For how long?' she asked in a faint voice. Uneasiness returned so sharply that her stomach felt queasy with the unwanted sensation.

'He ... is to live there, Highness. Although I'm certain you'll be able to see him often,' Marie added quickly, alarmed by the look on the face of the grand duchess who had paled noticeably.

Feeling weak, Catherine leaned back on her pillow, unable to believe what she was hearing. Beneath the soft green satin of her nightgown her breasts rose and fell rapidly with her quickened breaths. Her child had been taken from her, was to live not with his mother, but with the empress! She opened her mouth to protest, but in Marie's dark and compassionate eyes Catherine saw that there was no hope of appeal. The decision had already been made.

Helpless rage welled up in her mind. Catherine began to tremble. She fought the urge to leap from her bed and burst into Elizabeth's apartments to claim what was rightfully hers. Empress or no, Elizabeth had no right to take her child away.

In a burst of furious anger, Catherine pushed the tray from her. It fell to the floor with a clatter that brought the servants running posthaste.

'So,' Catherine muttered grimly, mouth tight. 'Now I know why the empress was so anxious for me to become pregnant.' Her violet eyes darkened with realization. 'It wasn't an heir she wanted, but a child of her own!' She balled her hands into fists. 'I was to have a child for her.' Her voice rose shrilly as she glared at Marie, unmoved by the distress she was seeing. 'And she even went so far as to –'

'Hush, madame!' Marie cried out in a frantic voice. After getting up, she hastily ushered the servants out of the room.

Upon returning to Catherine's side, she sat down again, this time on the edge of the bed. She reached out, attempting to take Catherine in her arms, hoping to calm the distraught young mother.

But Catherine would have none of it. She pushed Marie away with such fierceness that the woman almost fell off the bed. With a gasp that seemed wrenched from the deepest part of her, Catherine dissolved into hot tears of frustration, continuing to strike out at Marie who sought vainly to comfort her.

Two hours later, seeing that the grand duchess couldn't seem to calm down, Marie sent for the physician.

When he arrived a short while later the physician took one look at the grand duchess and reached for his scalpel.

Marie put her fingertips to her lips, watching the silver bowl fill with blood. Catherine's face seemed to be growing paler with each passing minute. 'She is very weak,' she ventured to say.

The physician's only answer was an annoyed look. When he was through and had bound her arm with gauze, he stepped back in some alarm as Catherine again gave way to hysterical weeping. After fumbling within the depths of his bag, he handed Marie a small packet.

'Give her this with some water. It will help her to sleep. A reaction of this sort is not unusual when a woman has just given birth.'

Marie's mouth tightened, but she did as she was told, not feeling it necessary to tell the physician that Catherine's reaction had nothing to do with having just had a baby.

Later, when she was certain that Catherine was asleep, Marie gave a sigh and returned to her own room.

But the next day, Catherine's condition was unchanged. Once again she was bled. By now she was so weak both the physician and Marie began to fear for her life.

The grand duchess's debilitated condition, however, was of little concern to either her husband or the empress, who was happily planning the christening ceremony for the long-awaited heir.

Only the people mourned. When they learned that their lovely young grand duchess lay close to death, they flocked to the cathedrals to pray for her recovery, their Russian hearts saddened, for they all adored her.

The weeks passed. Catherine wept and only Anya was there to comfort her, for she refused to see Marie and would allow no one else near her.

When she wasn't thinking of her son, Catherine was thinking of Serge, hoping that he would come to visit her. But he never did.

Finally Anya told her that Serge had been sent to Sweden for a while.

The news offered little comfort. Catherine knew him well enough to know that if he had been so inclined, Serge could have sent some word to her. His absence, his lack of communication, meant only one thing: He did not, and probably had never, loved her.

Having come to that heart-rending conclusion, Catherine tossed and turned on silken sheets that felt hot from the fever of her body. Memories taunted her, some too sweet to be borne, for she knew they would never again be hers.

Serge. Oh, Serge, she thought sorrowfully. His remembered words of endearment pierced her heart like arrows, for she now realized that their love had been a sham, a bright dream that had ended with the birth of Paul Petrovich – it was her faithful Anya who informed her of the name given to her son.

When she was finally able to leave her bed, three weeks later, Catherine went no farther than the chair by the window in her sitting room. She had no desire to read. She refused to hold court; not even Leo was allowed access to her salon. She also refused to join the many festivities that were being held in celebration of the birth of the heir, ignoring Anya's continued urgings for her do so.

Catherine turned a deaf ear to everyone about her. She was waiting. And as the weeks turned into months, she continued to wait with a determination that was grim and implacable. She spent her days sick in body and in heart. She had endured much in the ten years she had come to this land. But the loss of her child and of Serge left Catherine with a dull throbbing ache that proved to be entirely out of reach of the physician's remedies.

The fairy tale was over, and Catherine was left with the hard reality of a life that seemed shattered before it had begun.

The summons came at last on a cold and snowy morning in late November, more than eight weeks after she had given birth.

Feeling as cold and as icy as the gloomy day, Catherine went to the empress's apartments to view her son for the first time since he had been born.

It was also the first time that Catherine had ever been inside Elizabeth's personal bedchamber.

She took no notice of the huge canopied bed that rested on a raised platform, nor of the sumptuous plum-colored velvet hangings that bore the double-headed eagle stitched meticulously with gold thread. She never even glanced at the walls, patterned with crimson roses and skirted with silver oak paneling that glinted in the firelight. She paid no attention to the massive richly carved furnishings, almost of all which were marred and dented from the many changes of residences.

All the windows were tightly shuttered and draped against the frosty air. Two enormous fireplaces, one at each end of the room, blazed brightly.

Catherine saw none of this and had only a vague awareness that the room seemed overheated. Her violet eyes had immediately focused on the wooden cradle placed next to the bed. Approaching slowly, she stood beside it and looked down at the heavily swaddled form of her sleeping son.

Bemused, Catherine listened as Elizabeth whispered: 'You must not touch him, nor must you pick him up.' She placed a hand on Catherine's arm, as if to forestall any disobedience. 'He's just been fed, and we do not wish to disturb his nap.' Her hand fell away and she gazed down at the child with adoring eyes. 'Isn't he beautiful?' she whispered in a now reverent tone.

Unable to speak, Catherine merely nodded. For all these weeks she had tried to imagine what her baby looked like. But the two-month-old child in the cradle was a stranger to her. She didn't feel the slightest urge to pick him up or touch him.

The two women stood there for a time, not speaking.

Finally Elizabeth tapped Catherine on the cheek with her fingertip. 'We are very pleased, Catherine Alexeievna,' she murmured in hushed tones so as not to awaken the baby. 'You must leave now. We will send word to you when it is convenient for you to visit the crown prince.'

Thus dismissed, Catherine left the imperial bedchamber, her mind emptied of conscious thought.

In the corridor, she caught sight of Count Bestuzhev. He came toward her with measured steps. The lighted torches in the wall sconces accented the hollows beneath his cheeks and brows, making him appear more somber than usual.

'Madame,' he murmured in a low greeting. 'It pleases

me greatly to see that you have recovered from your indispositions.' When she made no reply, Bestuzhev worriedly eyed her pallor, visible even in the tawny glow of torchlight. He said a quick prayer that he had not underestimated the strength and intelligence of this woman.

Turning slightly, Bestuzhev darted a cautious glance about him, making certain that no one was within earshot. 'Wherever the child is lodged,' he said quietly, eyes returning to her face, 'there can be none who can deny that it is you who are the mother of the crown prince.' He put a gentle hand on her arm. 'Nor must you ever let them forget it.'

Inclining his head, Bestuzhev stepped around her and moved away into the shadows of the serpentine corridor.

Walking slowly, Catherine continued to her own apartments, pondering the chancellor's words.

Later that afternoon, servants delivered a gift to Catherine from the empress.

Sitting at her writing table, Catherine stared at the money and precious jewels scattered carelessly on its polished surface. She had already counted the sum: one hundred thousand rubles. Payment for her innocence, her youth, and her son.

Catherine continued to stare at the coins and the glittering brilliants for a long, long time, until somewhere, deep inside her, she felt a hardening, a core of steely determination that flooded her with new strength.

The feeling and the hardness began to grow. Rather than be sad, Catherine was grateful for its existence. She knew now that she would never again give her heart to any man. From this day forward, she vowed, she would set herself a goal and never turn from it. Elizabeth couldn't live forever. It would be many years yet before her own son would be old enough to rule.

As for Peter ...

Catherine threw her head back and emitted a harsh

laugh, causing Anya to eye her with new concern.

Then, sobering, Catherine knew that her goal was not out of reach. One day the crown would rest upon her own head, and never again would anyone manipulate her life.

Carefully now, with Anya's assistance, Catherine began to dress in her most lavish gown, prepared to make her reentry into court. When she was dressed, Catherine glanced into the mirror, pleased to see how calm and serene she looked. From this day forward, she must be strong. When full power rested within her husband's hands – as it must one day – Catherine knew she would be in very real danger.

But she also knew she had several advantages over Peter, advantages that could tip the scales in her favor when the time came: her wits, her courage, her intelligence.

Weapons Catherine vowed to put to good use.

PART TWO
The Woman
1756

Twelve

The June evening was mild. A bright moon silvered the vast grounds surrounding the large timbered palace known as Oranienbaum. It was a brightly colored structure with blue and red domes and vaulted cupolas that could be seen from miles away. Nearby, a canal wended a serpentine path into the Gulf of Finland, not too far distant.

The carriage drive was lined with vehicles, and from the tall narrow windows light blazed warmly. Inside the reception hall those who had been privileged enough to receive an invitation to the ducal palace for this weekend milled about and chattered easily while they awaited the arrival of their hosts, neither one of whom had yet made an appearance. The guest list was impressive, with many high dignitaries and foreign ambassadors in attendance. Normally they would have been feted by the empress, but her Imperial Majesty was ailing, and so this duty fell to the ducal couple.

In her dressing chamber, Catherine stood quietly while Anya fastened the hooks of the pale-green silk dress she had chosen to wear this evening. At the far end of the room her ladies waited patiently; all, that is, except one. Lizbeth Vorontsova was not even in the room. Catherine had seen little of her in the past six months, but she had no need to ask where Lizbeth was. Lizbeth Vorontsova was Peter's current mistress, and the woman was seldom far from the grand duke's side.

The door suddenly flew open to reveal Peter, dressed in his evening attire, the black velvet jacket doing little to abate his sallow complexion. He glared at the group of women, who had turned anxious eyes in his direction.

'Get out!' he commanded, and waited until they scurried from the room, leaving only Anya to attend her mistress.

Seating herself at her dressing table, Catherine viewed her husband in the mirror, but only a nod of her head acknowledged his abrupt entrance.

For a moment Peter stared back at her. Then he began to pace, hands clasped behind him.

'I want to speak to you about Lizbeth,' he stated at last, his manner as abrupt as his entrance. Halting, he stood behind Catherine's chair, his pale eyes meeting hers in the mirror.

At the mention of her lady-in-waiting, Catherine's expression turned wary.

Peter waited for her to respond, fidgeting impatiently while she picked up first one, then another of the many bracelets from the jewelry box that Anya was holding before her. But Catherine made no comment.

'You must know I'm in love with her,' he continued in a voice that held a hint of a whine. 'She's all I've ever wanted.'

Masking her revulsion at the tone of his voice, which sounded more like a petulant child than a grown man, Catherine strove for an expression of interest and concern.

'You have been in love before,' she observed mildly, then nodded at Anya. 'The emeralds,' she said, and the maid immediately fastened the chosen bracelet around her wrist.

Irritated with what he considered to be her obtuseness, Peter waved an arm in exasperation. 'Can't you see that I really care for her? The others were nothing!'

Catherine's attention returned to her reflection, and she patted her unpowdered hair.

'I want you to release Lizbeth from her duties so that she can stay with me.' Peter paused a moment, watching as she fussed with her hair. As if anything she did could make her beautiful, he thought, clenching his teeth. His voice rose sharply. 'Are you listening to me?'

'Of course I am,' Catherine quickly assured him, praying he wouldn't make a scene, fully aware that Peter was quick to temper when he didn't get his way or thought he was being thwarted. Only days before, having found a rat gnawing at his cherished wooden soldiers, he had flown into a black rage. Catherine had been horrified to find the hapless rodent hanging from a tree in the gardens. It was only with repeated cajoling that she had been able to persuade her husband to remove the disgusting spectacle before their guests arrived.

Satisfied with her appearance, Catherine now stood up and smiled at Peter in an engaging manner, though her eyes had narrowed.

'Lizbeth can spend as much time with you as you like, but you know that I cannot release her from her duties without permission from the empress.' Bracing herself, she slipped her arm through his. 'Our guests are waiting,' she reminded him quietly.

Within Catherine, disdain drifted across her mind and settled into a contempt she was careful to conceal. She did, in fact, sense that this particular affair of Peter's was different from the others. That made it dangerous. Peter had taken up with her ladies before, but always had lost interest in a matter of weeks. This time, however, the affair had been going on for the better part of a year. Worse, Peter was now actually allowing the Vorontsova to spend the whole night in his bed.

Although he had frowned at her words, Peter permitted Catherine to lead him to the door.

'All right,' he conceded grudgingly, moving with sullen reluctance, his attitude leaving no doubt that he felt the subject of Lizbeth was of far more importance. 'But I'm spending the evening at Lizbeth's side,' he added obstinately as they left the room.

As they descended the wide curving stairs, Catherine continued to smile and nod pleasantly, listening in an apparently attentive manner as Peter continued to speak of his great love for his mistress.

As soon as they reached the reception room, Peter moved away from Catherine and hurried to Lizbeth Vorontsova's side.

Despite the large crowd, Catherine noted the presence of Sir Charles Hanbury-Williams, the ambassador from England. With him was an attractive young man she had never seen before. He was lean, above average in height, and from the manner in which he was dressed, Catherine knew that he was a member of the nobility.

She approached them in a swirl of pale-green silk. Her dark unpowdered hair was interwoven with diamonds that threw out glittering darts of light as she moved gracefully across the parquet floor.

'Sir Charles,' she said with a bright smile. 'We are pleased you could join us.'

The ambassador bowed and kissed the extended hand. 'The pleasure is mine, your Highness,' he replied sincerely, then motioned to the young man at his side. 'If I may, I would like to present Count Stanislaus Poniatowski, who has recently joined my staff.'

Catherine nodded a brief ackowledgment, and Sir Charles watched, amused, as Stanis was instantly captivated.

As they stood there exchanging meaningless cordialities, Sir Charles grew speculative. He had spent a great deal of time and money in an effort to change Catherine's political leanings; all to no avail. He had no doubt that Catherine, when the time came, would view England in a benevolent manner. It was the cold eye she cast on Prussia that he sought to change. If he, Sir Charles, could not accomplish this with money, perhaps Stanis could do it another way.

Sir Charles, however, was unable to discern whether the grand duchess had been impressed or attracted to the twenty-three-year-old Polish nobleman. After moving away from them, she proceeded to mingle freely and graciously among all the guests.

'She is lovely, isn't she?' he said in a low voice to the young man at his side.

Stanis nodded, thinking the description to be an understatement.

'Listen to me, Stanis,' Sir Charles went on. 'She must be won over to our side. It is imperative that we strengthen our alliance with Russia. There is no doubt in my mind that King Frederick will soon march on Saxony. I don't have to tell you that England is committed to his aid. We would do well to have Russia on our side when that day comes. The grand duchess must be persuaded to soften her attitude toward Prussia.'

Stanis looked at him and frowned. He knew very well that the empress's health was failing day by day. Soon Russia would have a new ruler. As far as he knew, that would be Peter, and he was confused that Sir Charles continued to woo Catherine with enormous gifts of money.

'I still feel you ought to ally yourself with the grand duke,' he said at last. 'He openly favors Prussia. After all, it is he who will succeed.'

The ambassador's face turned somber as he responded. 'When you meet the grand duke, you will understand. I'm convinced that if there is ever a tug of war for the crown, it will be the grand duchess who will be the victor.'

Stanis sighed and shook his head. He had always credited Sir Charles with a great deal of intelligence; in this, however, it would seem that the man had made a grave error in judgment.

'What is it that you want me to do, Sir Charles?' he asked at last.

The ambassador smiled slowly, then directed his gaze

across the room to where Peter was standing. 'As you can see, the grand duke has, well, other interests, shall we say. It might be that his wife would welcome your ... companionship. Women have been known to listen to advice under such circumstances.' He gave Stanis a long, meaningful look, then went to join his friends.

Companionship? Stanis thought, a bit startled by his employer's words, knowing full well that he was actually referring to a liaison. A relationship of that sort could take months to develop.

After a moment, Stanis began to move about the large room, pausing by the courtiers who surrounded the grand duke. His eye rested on Lizbeth Vorontsova. The current favorite was wearing a bright-yellow taffeta gown that accented her plumpness and gave an unhealthy cast to her pockmarked skin.

Stanis tried not to stare, but he couldn't help it. Why, the woman was actually squint-eyed, he thought to himself in astonishment. When she spoke, her language was that of the crudest peasant. Stanis winced at the uncultivated sounds that were emerging from her mouth. Regarding the grand duke's disfigured countenance, Stanis couldn't decide which of them was the more unattractive. Obviously the pox had visited them both, but while Lizbeth's skin was marred it had not been so deeply pitted as to distort her features, as was the case with Peter.

My God, Stanis thought, still watching the ugly pair. Putting Catherine in the company of those two was like placing a diamond on a dung heap.

Turning away, Stanis again regarded the grand duchess, hearing her pleasant laughter as she acknowledged a witticism from the French ambassador.

A footman approached, and Stanis helped himself to a glass of champagne. His eyes again sought Catherine. As if aware of his intense scrutiny, she suddenly turned toward him, a slight smile curving her lips.

Music began to play and a few of the guests were now

moving onto the dance floor. Stanis put his glass down on a nearby table, intending to request a dance from the grand duchess. Before he could reach her, however, she began to walk toward the open French doors that led to the gardens. As Stanis hurried to follow, he never saw her motion to her ladies to remain where they were.

He caught up to her on the terrace. The moon was still bright, making the night a contrast of black and white.

'May I join you, your Highness?' he asked, coming to stand at her side.

Tilting her head slightly, Catherine looked up at him. 'It would appear that you already have, Count Poniatowski,' she noted, arching a brow.

He took a step closer. 'May I … may I tell you how beautiful you are?'

Catherine's cheeks dimpled in amusement. 'A man should never request permission to offer a compliment like that, Count Poniatowski.'

Strains of music reached them, and Stanis cast a quick look inside. 'May I then request permission for a dance?' he asked quietly.

Her smile broadened as she placed her hand lightly on his arm. 'That you may do, Count Poniatowski,' she replied softly.

After returning to the reception hall, Stanis led her onto the dance floor. She was smaller, daintier than he had at first supposed her to be. She held herself so erect, her carriage so regal and proud, that she gave one the impression of being taller than she actually was.

When the music stopped, Stanis escorted her back to where her ladies were standing. He bowed upon releasing her hand.

'Never has a dance been more enjoyable, your Highness,' he murmured, straightening.

Catherine grew thoughtful as she regarded the young nobleman. She guessed, and rightly, that he was about twenty-three years old, three years younger than she was.

Normally she would not have given him a second glance. Though he was handsome enough, his features were too aristocratic, his bearing too genteel, his body lean rather than muscular. Yet there was a look in his green eyes that made her breath quicken, a look that made her want to probe further in an effort to discover its meaning.

'We also enjoyed it,' she said finally, in a voice that, to Stanis, sounded cool and distant. With a brief nod of her head, she moved away from him.

That night, in his assigned room on the second floor, Stanis stared pensively out the window. The moon was low now but cast enough light so that he could see the canal that edged the grounds of the palace.

Turning, he glanced at the bed but made no move toward it. Despite the late hour, he was too restless to sleep. He had to admit to himself that never in his life had he been so attracted to a woman as he was to Catherine.

After removing his jacket, Stanis flung it carelessly on the bed, then sat down in the nearest chair.

He had discounted all that he had heard about Catherine. In the few months that he had been in St. Petersburg, his ears had been filled with court gossip. Surely, he speculated in no little amazement, it could not be true that the grand duke spurned this woman, had actually left her untouched for all those years. He couldn't believe it. And the child; it was rumored to be a bastard. But Stanis knew very well that gossip was rampant in any court, so the rumor could or could not be true.

A sudden knock on the door interrupted his musings. A moment later it opened and a young page entered.

'Count Poniatowski?'

Stanis nodded as he got to his feet. 'Yes,' he said, walking toward the lad.

Silently the page handed him a folded piece of parchment. Moving closer to the lighted candle on the bedside table, Stanis broke the seal and read the contents. It was an invitation from the grand duchess for him to join her in her private apartments for a late supper. Stanis's hand trembled as he placed the note on the table. Hastily he grabbed his jacket and followed the page from the room, unable to credit his good fortune.

When he presented himself, it was almost one o'clock in the morning. Stanis to his chagrin, found himself nervous at the prospect of being alone with the grand duchess. As for Catherine's attitude toward Prussia – that, as well as Sir Charles, had fled his mind.

She was standing by the fireplace when he entered. His heart lurched at the sight of her. She had changed from her ballgown and was now clad in a lilac satin robe that fell softly over her rounded hips, unimpeded by hoop or stay. Stanis glanced around, surprised to see that no one else was in the room. In a corner, a table had been set for two but there was, as yet, no food in evidence.

Catherine smiled at him, amused by his so evident nervousness. She wondered whether it was his youth or herself that caused his unsettled state.

It had been two years since Serge had gone to Sweden, two years since she had felt a man's arms around her. She discounted Peter's intermittent and inadequate fumblings and was actually relieved that he was now bestowing all his amorous attention on Lizbeth.

'Are you hungry?' she asked quietly, walking slowly toward him.

Stanis took a deep breath. His collar suddenly seemed unbearably tight. 'I … No, I'm not.' She was standing so close to him that he could smell the clean scent of her hair. Casting discretion aside, he reached out and pulled her against him, kissing her with an enthusiasm that left them both breathless.

At last Catherine drew back. Taking his hand, she led him into her bedchamber.

To Catherine's delight, Stanis proved to be not only a gentle lover but an inexhaustible one, as well. The sun had long since tipped the horizon by the time he finally took his leave of her the following morning.

Before the day was gone the whole court was whispering about the new favorite of the grand duchess.

Thirteen

The July day was hot and sultry. Even the breeze from the sea failed to lighten the heavy humidity.

Count Bestuzhev, having requested an audience with the grand duchess, now walked beside her as they strolled through the relative seclusion of the lush gardens in the summer pavilion known as Mon Plaisir, nestled within the estates of Peterhof.

For some time Bestuzhev kept silent, trying to organize his thoughts. Earlier in the day he had had a serious discussion with Count Nikita Panin, tutor for the young crown prince, Paul Petrovich. Both of them had come to the conclusion that the succession would have to be changed. Panin favored a regency, and, for the time being, Bestuzhev had agreed.

And there was another problem, one that turned Bestuzhev's normally expressionless face grave and concerned. That morning he had received a report from General Apraxin, whose troops were faring badly in Prussia. It was for this reason, as well as his recent discussion with Panin, that he had sought out the grand duchess. He knew that he was placing her at risk by requesting that she put her thoughts on paper, but it was a risk he felt they both must take.

'You can well understand the feelings of General Apraxin,' Bestuzhev said finally as they strolled along the flagstone walkway. 'He's fighting Frederick's armies with great valor, but his requisitions for supplies are going unanswered.'

'And you can do nothing?' Catherine inquired, glancing at him with quick concern.

Bestuzhev shook his head, a short curt movement. 'Too many tongues speak against me, madame.'

'Perhaps if you spoke directly to the empress ...'

Again Bestuzhev shook his head. 'Whatever confidence the empress placed in me in the past has dissolved. She simply will not listen to me.' Pausing, he looked directly into the violet eyes. 'Her health is failing rapidly, your Highness. I'm not certain how much longer she will last.' He frowned and sighed deeply as he resumed walking. 'That's another thing that concerns Apraxin, and rightly so. On the day that the grand duke succeeds, he will immediately call a halt to the war. Already he speaks of it in a bold manner. I've no doubt that Frederick knows of it, too.' He grimaced as if in pain, and his voice grew stronger. 'How can Apraxin be expected to push his advantages in the face of such a situation?'

'I understand, Chancellor,' Catherine said quietly. 'Still, your suggestion that I write to him is something that requires a great deal of thought.' She gave a small laugh that held no humor. 'Can you imagine the reaction of the empress if she were to discover that I was corresponding with one of her generals?'

'Indeed, she mustn't find out about it,' Bestuzhev quickly agreed. 'That's why it must be done with the utmost caution. But the general must be made aware that someone supports him. He thinks highly of you, Highness.'

As he spoke, Bestuzhev glanced sideways at the slim figure beside him. At twenty-six Catherine was a very lovely woman.

'Some time ago,' he went on softly, walking slowly along the shaded path, 'you told me that Russia was your country. If that's true, then she needs your help now as never before.'

Catherine fell silent for some moments. Bestuzhev didn't interrupt her meditations. About them, the air was filled with the scent of lilacs and roses, and only the gentle hum of bees broke the quiet solitude.

Catherine bit her lip. 'What is it that you want me to write?' she asked at last.

Bestuzhev allowed himself one of his rare smiles, firmly convinced now that he was doing the right thing. 'Keep the letters informal,' he advised. 'But let him know that he has your support. Encourage him not only to stand firm but to push ahead.'

She looked at him, noticing the lines of weariness that etched his face. 'How will the letters reach him?'

'I've taken care of that,' he replied. 'One of my own servants will hand-carry them.' After a small hesitation, he went on to say: 'There is one other matter I wish to discuss with you, your Highness.'

They had reached a curved bench to which a huge weeping willow lent its shade. Catherine let her gaze rest upon the bright-yellow daffodils that encircled the tree, then in a graceful motion, she sat down. When she was settled, the chancellor sat beside her.

'There are those of us,' Bestuzhev began in a quiet voice, 'notably Count Panin and myself, who are not pleased with the plans for the succession.' Reaching out, he plucked a branch of the willow tree and twirled it between his thumb and forefinger.

Even though they were alone, Catherine couldn't resist glancing about them. The words the chancellor had just spoken so casually were nothing short of treason.

If he was aware of this, however, it wasn't apparent in his voice or his manner as he continued in the same quiet tones. 'It is our thought that your son should succeed and that you act as regent until he comes of age.' He hesitated a moment, then decided to say nothing of his own preferences at this time. 'We have taken the liberty of drafting a manifesto ...'

'Chancellor!' Catherine drew a sharp breath, sincerely shocked. She had no idea that such a movement was afoot. The thought of Elizabeth discovering it sent an icy chill of apprehension coursing through her. She shivered despite the sultry day. 'Do you realize what would happen if such a document fell into the wrong hands?'

'We've taken every precaution, madame.' Bestuzhev raised a hand. 'Rest assured that if it becomes necessary, I shall burn every scrap of paper that exists.'

Catherine shook her head and clasped her hands tightly in her lap. She knew the day would come when she would have to fight for her own survival. But not now, not yet. Not while Elizabeth lived.

'I do not approve,' she murmured. 'It's too soon. The empress ...'

'It can be done only while she lives, Highness,' Bestuzhev noted somberly. He flung the little willow branch to the ground. 'Afterward it will be too late.'

'The Vorontsovs and the Shuvalovs will never permit such a thing to happen,' Catherine protested. 'They're firm in their support of my husband.'

Bestuzhev nodded slowly at the observation. 'And they are the only ones, madame,' he stated flatly. 'The people themselves dislike the grand duke. They all fear that he will turn us into a province of the Prussian empire.'

'I understand your feelings, Chancellor,' Catherine said, unable to repress the sigh that followed her words. 'But you are placing both me and my son in peril by even thinking such thoughts. When the empress dies, Peter will be crowned tsar, and I ...'

'...will be only his consort, madame,' Bestuzhev pointed out, unmindful of his interruption.

She nodded slowly. 'But I may be able to check some of his inclinations.' She regarded Bestuzhev in an earnest manner. 'Even though he professes great love for Holstein, he shirks the administration of it. He leaves a great deal of it in my hands ...'

Bestuzhev shook his head. 'He'll never allow you the freedom to rule.'

Catherine fell silent, then viewed the chancellor with a puzzled look. 'Why have you chosen me?' she asked quietly, recalling the early antagonism for her he had displayed so openly.

For a moment Bestuzhev made no answer. Then he looked directly at her. 'There is no one else,' he replied simply. 'The empress will soon die. It's only a matter of time now.' His voice fell and he looked away, feeling the sadness that seemed to have become a part of him. 'I've done my best to keep the tentacles of Prussianism from invading our borders ...' He sighed with ponderous despair. 'If the grand duke succeeds, all my efforts will have been in vain.' He clamped his jaws together, staring ahead into the expanse of leafy green that met his eye.

Catherine moistened her lips. 'I ... am a Prussian,' she reminded him softly.

Again there was a long pause, and almost with an effort Bestuzhev turned to look at her. 'Are you?' he inquired in a voice no less soft than hers.

A warm pink glow, delicate as a fragile petal on a summer rose, touched her cheek. 'Only by birth,' she admitted, viewing her clasped hands in her lap. 'You are probably right when you say the empress has a short time to live.' The violet eyes were intent as they moved to his face. 'But while she lives, she is my sovereign, as well as yours. We mustn't lose sight of this, Count Bestuzhev.' She sighed deeply. 'I'm sorry ... I cannot agree to altering the succession in favor of my son.'

A regency, Catherine was thinking pensively. Oh, no, Chancellor. When and if the times comes to take such a drastic step, I will not settle for a regency.

Seeing her mouth set so firmly, Bestuzhev thought it wise to let the matter rest for now. But he decided that despite her refusal, he would still continue work on the manifesto.

'Very well, Highness,' he said at last. 'But if you change your mind, or if circumstances change it for you, then know that you have our support.' He stood up. Extending his hand politely, he assisted Catherine to her feet, after which they began to retrace their steps in the direction from which they had come.

Bestuzhev was satisfied. Momentarily he gave thought to Stanislaus Poniatowski, the young Polish nobleman in the employ of Sir Charles. He suspected that Catherine was more involved with the secretary than she let on. That, however, was none of his affair, he decided. The young man seemed besotted by the grand duchess; no doubt she was entitled to his admiration, even his love – certainly she didn't get either from her husband.

Fourteen

A few days after her discussion with Count Bestuzhev, Catherine was in her drawing room, enjoying a cup of tea and a visit with Countess Praskovia Bruce, whose plump form was encased in a red satin dress that managed to accent her ample proportions to an alarming degree. Although her features were somewhat irregular, the nose being overly prominent, her skin was white and flawless, her expression animated and pleasant.

Catherine, dressed in cool silk, sat in a chair opposite from the countess, sipping her tea and listening with amusement as Praskovia related the latest court gossip in her breathless fashion.

'Well, there they were,' Praskovia was saying with a meaningful nod, 'both in bed, naked as the day God created them, when Madame Shubin's husband came home unexpectedly. Darya was mortified. The whole court is speculating as to the identity of the man, but he –' She giggled, putting a plump hand to her lips. '–well, as I understand it, he jumped out of the window before Count Shubin could lay a hand on him.'

Putting her cup down on the table, Catherine laughed in delight. 'Am I to assume that the gentleman in question fled without his clothes?' Her eyes shone with merriment.

'It would appear so,' Praskovia responded with an answering laugh that caused her bosom to bounce up and down. 'As for Darya, she isn't saying.' She sobered somewhat and gave a deep sigh. 'I'm afraid the count took

the rod to her. I suppose we won't be seeing Madame
Shubin in court for a while, at least until her bruises heal.'
From the seat beside her, Praskovia picked up her lace fan
and began to wave it in front of her face. 'I do wish it would
rain,' she murmured, increasing the tempo of the fan. It did
nothing to lessen the sheen on her round face. 'This heat is
making me most uncomfortable.' She glanced at Catherine
and sighed. 'Although I must say, Highness, the weather
doesn't seem to bother you at all. You look as fresh as a
summer rose.'

'You're being kind, Praskovia,' Catherine demurred,
dismissing the compliment with a wave of her hand.

'Not in any way,' Praskovia protested, looking a bit
affronted. 'You're positively glowing.' Idly the countess
wondered if the rumors about the grand duchess and
Stanlislaus Poniatowski were true. Catherine really did
look radiant. She bent forward and gave a slight titter. 'In
fact, if I may say so, you look very much like a woman in
love ...'

Catherine smiled, but neither confirmed nor denied her
friend's assumption.

In the face of that enigmatic silence, Praskovia tactfully
changed the subject. 'I've heard that the tsarevich has been
in bed with a bad cold this past week.' She paused, taking a
sip of her tea, not noticing the expression on the face of the
grand duchess, whose eyes had darkened. 'I do hope he's
feeling better.'

Catherine moistened her lips and stiffened. Although
startled anger wended its way through her, she managed to
keep her face noncommittal. She hadn't seen her son in
weeks, and Praskovia's information took her by surprise.

'The crown prince is feeling much better,' she replied at
last, gratified for the calmness of her voice.

Although Praskovia continued with her gossipy chatter
for another hour, Catherine's attention was only on the
surface. Inside, she seethed with indignation and outrage.
It was intolerable to think she'd had to learn of her son's

condition from an outsider.

For the rest of that day and evening, Catherine fumed with resentment. Her son was ill, but no one had thought to tell her about it. She was unable to concentrate on cards, had no desire to dance. She sent a note to Stanis informing him that she was indisposed and would be unable to receive him that night.

Feeling depressed, in no mood for conversation, she decided to retire early. She was already in bed when she received a summons from the empress. With a sigh that bordered on annoyance, Catherine hurriedly donned her clothes again.

It was just after eleven. As she followed the page, Catherine wondered as to the nature of the forthcoming meeting. Cynically she dismissed from her mind the possibility that Elizabeth might want to relay news of Paul Petrovich.

That left only one other reason: Word of her affair with Stanis had finally reached the empress. Despite her precautions, Catherine had known it would be only a matter of time.

Her assumptions notwithstanding, a half smile played about her lips as Catherine walked slowly along the corridor. She wasn't upset and had no intention of allowing herself to be intimidated. Elizabeth might know of her relationship with Stanis, but she, Catherine, knew something that Elizabeth didn't know. It lent her confidence as she approached the imperial bedchamber.

Not having seen Elizabeth for almost six weeks, Catherine was shocked at her appearance.

Supported by numerous pillows, the empress was sitting up in bed, wearing a silk caftan embroidered with gold thread. Her face had a chalky look about it, as if white powder had been applied over a deathly pale complexion. Even though satin coverlets hid the lower half of her body, Catherine could see that she looked bloated.

Nearby, her ladies sat gossiping and stitching. Candles

burned brightly. The room had a musty smell to it.

At a small table by the window sat Ivan Shuvalov, Elizabeth's current favorite, a glass of vodka and a plate of cold chicken occupying his attention. He had not gotten up when Catherine entered. Wearing only a dressing robe, he was barefoot, his dark hair tousled. He looked as if had just gotten out of bed.

In spite of her sickly color, Elizabeth's dark-blue eyes were as sharp and penetrating as ever.

'We have been hearing rumors that do not please us, madame,' she said tersely. 'Rumors that involve you and Count Poniatowski.' Her brows dipped in a scowl. 'Is it true that he's your lover?' She stared angrily at Catherine, waiting for her to speak.

There had been a time when Catherine would have been cowed by the glowering look on her sovereign's face. That time had long since passed. Standing at the foot of the canopied bed, Catherine's face reflected only cool surprise.

'That is an unkind rumor indeed,' she replied easily. Raising her chin slightly, she gave the empress a look that was as cold as the twilight shadows on a winter's night.

Perturbed, Elizabeth averted her face from those violet eyes that were regarding her so directly. For one terrible moment she had seen the strength, the inherent determination of the young woman standing before her, and it filled her mind with unease.

Yet when she again turned toward Catherine, all she saw was the deferential expression that she was used to seeing. Elizabeth blinked slowly, relaxing again. She had, of course, been mistaken. The flickering tapers often played tricks on one's eyes.

'Well, true or not, he must be sent away,' Elizabeth muttered at last in a querulous tone. 'We cannot permit such a scandal.'

Catherine glanced sideways at Ivan Shuvalov. His robe had parted to reveal a well-muscled thigh. He was still intent on eating, not paying any attention to the conversation. Catherine's mouth compressed at the sight of him. The empress had the gall to mention lovers when her own sat in a state of near undress in full view of her ladies.

She returned her gaze to the empress. 'It's not necessary to request Count Poniatowski to leave our court, your Majesty,' she said with a lift of her brow, ignoring the quick flush of anger that stained the ashen face. 'The rumors will be laid to rest very soon, in any event.' She offered her sweetest smile. 'You see, the grand duke and I are expecting another child.'

Too astonished even to comment on such an announcement, Elizabeth could only stare at Catherine, her mouth slack.

Catherine tilted her head, the sweet smile still in place. 'How is my son, your Majesty?' she asked quietly into the void of deadly silence that had greeted her statement. 'I understand that he's been ailing lately. But as your Majesty knows, I've not seen Paul Petrovich in some weeks now.' She glanced away for a moment, lips pursed. 'I daresay the boy will be pleased to learn that he will soon have a brother or sister.'

'Paul Petrovich is well,' Elizabeth managed in a choked voice. Her fingers clutched nervously at the covers. Her eyes were wide and shocked, the veins in her neck throbbing a painful rhythm.

Catherine acknowledged the reply with a solemn nod, apparently seeing nothing unusual in the Empress's reaction. 'I'm certain that the grand duke will also be happy when he learns of the coming child,' she speculated, still regarding the empress in a disarming manner.

'He doesn't know?' Elizabeth's voice cracked on the question.

Still smiling, Catherine shook her head. 'No. I wanted you, your Majesty, to be the first one to know about it.'

For a long moment Elizabeth remained silent, unable to look away from the grand duchess. Then her eyes drifted about the large bedchamber, which was suddenly as silent as a tomb. Though their heads were still lowered over their handwork, her ladies' hands were still. The servants could have been shadows for all the noise they were making. Shuvalov had stopped eating and was now regarding Catherine with open speculation.

Aware that whatever she said now would have a direct bearing on the child, Elizabeth took a deep wavering breath and again viewed Catherine. 'This news is most welcome,' she said at last, her shaken voice gaining a modicum of strength. 'We will, for the time being, allow the other matter to rest.' She bent forward slightly, interested in spite of herself. 'When is the child due?'

'In December, your Majesty.'

'Very well. We will prepare a formal announcement.' Elizabeth's face was carefully guarded as she rested back on the soft pillows. Then, for the benefit of everyone in the room she added: 'We will send our personal congratulations to the grand duke.'

Catherine curtsied low, then began to walk toward the door. The words of the empress halted her.

'Catherine Alexeievna,' Elizabeth called out in a quiet voice that had regained its composure. 'We have said that we will let the other matter rest … but if the rumors continue, Poniatowski must be sent away.' Her ashen face was so set it appeared carved from stone.

Catherine flushed angrily, and she spun around to glare at the aged empress surrounded by satin pillows. She felt no remorse at having taken a lover, nor would she play the hypocrite and pretend that she did. Turning, she left the room, head held high.

When the door closed, Elizabeth's shoulders slumped. Wearily she put a shaking hand to her brow. Oh, God, she thought to herself. At least Serge Saltikov had been Russian, he was Orthodox. The young fool Catherine had chosen now was not only a foreigner, he was a Roman Catholic!

After struggling out of the huge canopied bed, Elizabeth stumbled to her private chapel. She ignored the objections of her frantic ladies. The sickness of her body meant nothing to her. It was trivial when compared to the sickness in her soul.

She entered the cool dimness with tears streaming down her white cheeks. The small chapel smelled heavily of incense. Jeweled icons covered the stone walls, glowing softly in the gleaming light of the icon lamps positioned beneath each picture.

On legs that trembled so badly they threatened to collapse beneath her, Elizabeth approached the velvet-draped altar. After falling to her knees on the crimson cushions, she bent her head in prayer. Within her heart lay a towering darkness, a void so black she feared that even the glorious light of God's forgiveness could not penetrate it.

Peter stared at his wife in bewilderment. 'You are to have a child?' he repeated inanely. He gaped at her, open-mouthed.

They were in her apartments. Her servants and ladies, including Lizbeth Vorontsova, were all within earshot, which was as she had planned it. Everyone – including Peter – must be made aware of the empress's acceptance of her pregnancy.

'Yes. In December,' she answered calmly enough, although her nerves were taut. One foolish word from him could result in disastrous complications. 'The empress is delighted,' she added quickly, before he could again speak. 'When I spoke to her a short while ago, her Majesty told me that she plans to send you her personal congratulations.' She took hold of Peter's thin arm and drew him outside on the balcony. Then she closed the French doors.

The air had cooled from the heat of the day, but it was still humid. Spread below them like an ethereal painting the city glowed beneath the white night.

Bewilderment had disappeared in sullenness as Peter stood there, regarding Catherine with a frown. 'How the devil –' he began, but his wife again interrupted him.

Raising her fan just high enough to conceal her lips, Catherine glanced inside. Her ladies were in a group, whispering. 'Lizbeth Vorontsova looks particularly fetching this evening,' she commented casually. 'But I'm certain you've already noticed that.' The fan fluttered slightly as her gaze returned to him. 'Though I imagine that the empress might not be too happy with all the attention you shower upon her. Especially now, when you are again to be a father.' Her eyes widened in an artless manner. 'Not that she would ever hear of it from me.'

After gathering her skirts in her hand, Catherine turned and went back into the drawing room.

Peter scowled, flushed, then followed his wife with a faltering step, fighting a savage anger that made his ears ring. God, how he hated her. But a word from her and the empress would remove Lizbeth from court. That he could never allow, because for the first time in his life he was really in love.

'My congratulations, madame,' Peter said slowly and distinctly as he entered. Before them all, he bowed. 'The news of our coming child pleases me greatly.'

Fifteen

The December air was frigid. A howling wind tore through the crooked streets of the Kremlin, scattering snow that swirled and danced in frenzied circles before it settled upon the already whitened ground.

In her apartments, Catherine sat on a divan sipping hot chocolate, only half listening to the gossipy chatter of her ladies.

Something was wrong, she was thinking to herself. But she couldn't quite put her finger on the problem. Peter had been avoiding her for months – that in itself didn't concern her. But for the past couple of weeks now, on those rare occasions when they were in the same room together, she had detected a repressed excitement in him, and each time he looked at her his pale eyes would light with something akin to triumph.

That did trouble her. Try as she might, she was unable to come up with a reason for her husband's peculiar attitude.

With a sigh, Catherine put her cup on the table and waved away a servant who had hastened forward to refill it.

As she went to lean back again, a movement from behind a screen in a corner caught her eye. The screen concealed a doorway that led to the servants' staircase. Aside from the servants, the only one who made use of it was Stanis when he came to visit her in the evening. There was, however, no reason for him to enter her apartments like this during the day. As a member of her court he need only present himself to be admitted.

Someone now peered cautiously around the screen. With a start of surprise, Catherine stared at Bestuzhev. As soon as he caught her eye, he again drew back.

Glancing around her, Catherine saw that no one else in the room had seen the chancellor's unexpected arrival.

Catherine stood up. 'Leave us,' she commanded abruptly, and waited while they all hastily departed. Walking toward the screen, she beckoned to the chancellor. He looked chilled to the bone. 'Come, sit by the fire. It's not fit for man nor beast out there.'

Bestuzhev moved slowly toward a deep-cushioned chair in front of the inviting blaze, then sat down heavily. He unbuttoned his greatcoat but did not take it off. To protect Catherine he had left the palace by the front door, waited a suitable time until he was certain he was unobserved, then entered by a side entrance, used mainly by servants.

'What's wrong?' Catherine asked quickly. Concern wended its way through her at the sight of his pallor.

Covering his eyes with his hand, Bestuzhev heaved a wavering sigh. 'General Apraxin has been recalled. He's been arrested.' He massaged his temples as if his head ached.

'But for what reason?' exclaimed Catherine. 'Only last month he enjoyed great victory.'

'He did, at that,' Bestuzhev responded with a nod. He let his hand fall to his lap. 'However, within a few days he retreated, allowing the Prussians to regain everything he had taken.'

Catherine's face blanched. Her last letter had been sent to Apraxin only five days ago. 'When ... did this happen?'

'Two weeks ago,' he replied quietly.

She eyed him sharply. 'Why haven't I been informed of this sooner?'

He shrugged, turning away from her accusing glance.

'I've just learned of it today.' His face grew bitter as he stared at the leaping flames. 'Shuvalov has convinced the empress that I'm responsible for the whole thing. They accomplished his recall without my knowledge.' He paused a moment, then gave Catherine a level look that left her chilled with apprehension. 'There's a possibility that two, perhaps three, of your letters were intercepted. I'm certain the general destroyed all the others. Do you remember what was in them?'

Feeling weak, Catherine sank into a chair. 'Not very much, really. His wife, as you know, recently gave birth to a son. I sent my congratulations, both for his new son and for his resounding victory.' Her hands worked nervously against one another.

The chancellor leaned forward. 'We don't know for certain that any letters were intercepted,' he stressed, trying to calm her.

Catherine wet her lips, then got to her feet in a restless movement. Her body felt heavy in her late pregnancy. Sitting for any length of time was uncomfortable. 'The empress is fully recovered?' she inquired after a moment, trying to sort out her whirling thoughts.

Bestuzhev made a wry face. 'She would seem to be. But her health isn't good.' Getting to his feet, he stood before her, eyes intent and searching. 'Catherine,' he said, touching her arm. 'Both Count Panin and myself are in agreement that we should go ahead with the manifesto ... immediately.'

Shocked, she just stared, wide-eyed. 'Have you lost your senses?' she exclaimed, a white hand at her throat. 'The empress must know about the letters ....' She paused, thinking of Peter's smug attitude of late. 'Of course she does,' she murmured, more to herself than to Bestuzhev. Blessed Jesus! she thought, growing frantic. She could be accused of secretly corresponding with Elizabeth's general. Bad enough, since during wartime that could be construed as treason. But a manifesto altering the succession ... 'No,' she said firmly, shaking her head and taking a step away from him.

'Listen to me,' he implored, a deep frown marring his brow. 'Despite this latest recovery, the empress grows worse day by day. She could die at any time. We must make plans now in order that we're prepared when the time comes.'

Again Catherine shook her head. 'If such a thing were ever discovered ...'

'I promise you, it will not be. If I sense any danger, I'll burn everything. You have my word on it.'

She hesitated, still uncertain. Yet she knew that Bestuzhev was right. With the death of the empress, Peter would immediately assume power. She didn't have to ask what that would mean to herself. Finally, with great misgivings, she reluctantly agreed.

She watched as Bestuzhev left in the same manner in which he had arrived. Then, feeling utterly drained, Catherine went into her bedchamber to rest until supper.

Less than a week after her meeting with Count Bestuzhev, Catherine went into labor.

Only minutes after her travail began, the room began to fill with people. Bestuzhev, looking drawn and tired, positioned himself at the far side of the room, almost as if he were disassociating himself with the event at hand.

Catherine's heart skipped a beat when Elizabeth, followed by Peter, entered her bedchamber a short while later. Elizabeth looked no better than the last time Catherine had seen her. Although her face was heavily powdered and rouged, her pallor was nevertheless noticeable.

With a sigh that sounded more like a grunt, Elizabeth sat down heavily in the chair hastily brought forth by a servant. Standing by her side, Ivan Shuvalov barely repressed a yawn.

In spite of the hot agony that coursed through her, Catherine kept an anxious eye on the empress. She saw no accusation in Elizabeth's expression, but a glance at her husband made her gasp even before the next contraction intensified it to a groan. He was watching her with that same gleam of triumph she had been noticing of late.

Then the pain gripped her, and Catherine's thoughts became hazy as one minute seemed to blur into the next.

It was late morning by the time the child finally put in an appearance.

The midwife held the naked babe up for view. 'A girl!' she announced to all witnesses.

Elizabeth frowned, then pushed herself out of her chair. 'Bring the child to us when she has been bathed,' she commanded. With no words for the grand duchess, she walked from the room, leaning most of her bulk on the supporting arm of Ivan Shuvalov.

The servants then lifted Catherine from the mattress on the floor and placed her in bed.

Coming forward, Peter bent over her, his voice only a whisper. 'Too bad your bastard wasn't a boy,' he goaded. 'The empress is not pleased, and I daresay this is not the time to anger her.'

'What?' Catherine began, but Peter began to head for the door, his laughter abrasive to all who heard it.

Despite Peter's words, however, the following week passed without incident. Catherine did not see her daughter, but she had not really expected that privilege to come about so soon.

When another week went by, Catherine began to relax. General Apraxin must have destroyed all her letters, or the empress certainly would have mentioned it by now.

Her relief, however, was short-lived. As soon as she saw Leo Narishkin enter her sitting room, she knew from the distraught look in his eye that something was terribly wrong.

Without offering a greeting, Leo drew her away from her gossiping ladies. 'Bestuzhev has been arrested,' he whispered.

Catherine paled, aware that her heart began to thud painfully in her breast. 'Where is he?'

'For now he's merely under guard in his apartments. But by tomorrow he could be sent to Schlüsselburg.' He darted a quick glance across the room at the chattering women. 'Can we speak in private?'

She gave a short nod. Striving to keep her voice calm, she dismissed not only her ladies, but the servants, as well.

When they were all gone, she faced Leo. 'Did you manage to speak to Count Bestuzhev? Did he have a message for me?' She broke off, unable to voice her fears. If the empress had had the chancellor's apartments searched and had uncovered the manifesto, then she was lost. The darkest cell in the most distant convent would be her future home.

Leo took her hand and felt it trembling and cold within his own. 'He said to tell you that he kept his promise.' And then, though they were alone, his voice sank to the merest whisper. 'I was with him when he burned everything.'

Catherine's eyes widened. 'You knew?' she breathed. Although she never doubted Leo's friendship or support, he was, when all was said and done, a member of Peter's entourage. She had never even considered the idea that he might be in alliance with the chancellor.

Leo's nod was solemn. 'Knew, and was in agreement. I've been with the grand duke for many years. He's as unfit to rule as is the meanest serf.'

Catherine wavered and made no resistance when Leo put an arm around her. 'There's more,' he said gently. 'The empress is planning to dismiss part of your staff, as well as those she considers too sympathetic to you. Sir Charles has been sent back to England. He's already on his way.' He paused a moment, then continued. 'Poniatowski, too, has been ordered to leave.'

'Stanis,' she murmured sorrowfully, not recognizing the pained expression that crept across Leo Narishkin's face.

She clenched her fists. 'I must see the empress, Leo. It's my only hope. The Shuvalovs won't rest until I, too, am in prison.'

Leo sighed in a dejected manner. 'I don't see how you can get to her. I suppose you could send a message requesting an audience ...'

Catherine shook her head. 'No. Even if it reached her she would probably deny it.' She drew away from the protective circle of his arm, her brow furrowing in thought, trying to gather her wits about her. 'The empress must, of her own accord, send for me,' she mused. 'But you're right, Leo. On second thought, I will send a message to her.'

He cocked his head to one side, concerned at the thought that she might be placing herself in further jeopardy. 'Take care, Catherine,' he cautioned earnestly.

She smiled up at him, composed once more. 'You're a true friend, Leo,' she said softly, resting a hand on his arm. 'But I don't plan to write any harsh words.' She became pensive. 'I'm simply going to request that the empress send me away.'

'What?' Leo again reached for her, putting his hands on her slim shoulders. 'You can't do that! Where would she send you?'

'Home,' Catherine replied quickly. 'She is ridding her court of all my friends; doubtless I will be doing her Majesty a favor by also leaving.'

Leo's frown deepened. 'Your plan is good ... as far it goes.' He sounded doubtful. 'When she receives a message like that, she will most certainly send for you. But what will you do if she grants your request?'

'You were never a true gambler, Leo,' she chided him, patting his arm. 'Go now. It's not wise for you to be here at this time.'

Leo held her gaze a moment longer, his expression still doubtful. Then he gave her a short bow and departed without further words.

When the door closed, Catherine sat herself down at her writing table and penned the letter. She then gave it to a page and with hurried steps went into her bedchamber.

Somehow, some way, she knew she would have to evoke Elizabeth's sympathy.

How?

Chewing on her thumbnail, Catherine paced the room, her skirt swirling about her with each turn she took. She could, she thought, fall to her knees, weeping. No ... no, that might irritate the empress.

Her thoughts still in a quandary, Catherine absently glanced at her reflection as she passed the mirror. Pausing, she stared intently at the green brocade gown she was wearing. It was richly embellished with embroidery that had been stitched with silver thread. A costly emerald necklace encircled her slim throat, and in her hair a diamond coronet threw out tiny darts of light. She looked every inch the grand duchess.

Yes ...

Catherine began to smile. The empress would be expecting to see the grand duchess. What if she could be reminded instead of the young and innocent fourteen-year-old girl she had first seen so many years ago? Memories rushed at Catherine: Elizabeth had been so beautiful at that time that Catherine had been dumbfounded with the splendour she had displayed. As any woman would, Elizabeth had seen and been affected by the so-obvious admiration of the young girl from Stettin.

'Anya!'

The maid hurried forward and began to assist Catherine as she removed her gown and the underlying hoop that made it flare out on either side of her waist.

Then, with much care, Catherine dressed in a gray wool dress and took off all of her jewelry except for her wedding ring. While of infinitely better material, the dress was not unlike the one she had worn when she and

Elizabeth had first met so many years ago. Finally, waving Anya away, her movements feverish, Catherine removed all the pins from her hair, after which she fashioned it into the simple coiffure that she had worn as a girl.

After once again scrutinizing her appearance in the mirror, Catherine returned to the outer chamber. The room was pervaded by the warm gold light from the candles and the blazing fire, but it seemed cold to Catherine. Sitting down on the divan, she clasped her hands in her lap. A stillness came over her as she waited.

Her mouth was set in a tight grim line as she watched the silver gilt clock. It was now just past nine in the evening. Her mouth grew even tighter as the hands moved relentlessly and with a maddening slowness toward midnight.

Sixteen

It was past one o'clock in the morning before the page finally returned with the summons. His youthful face was solemn, almost sad, for he was a great admirer of the beautiful grand duchess. By now the whole court knew that Catherine was in serious trouble. When the empress was displeased, she took no pains to hide that fact.

Taking a deep breath, Catherine rose and followed the scarlet-and-gold-clad young man as he led her to the empress. She walked along the dimly lit corridor, wondering if this was to be her last night of freedom. It was not inconceivable that her return trip would be made under guard.

Determinedly Catherine cleared her mind of that terrifying thought.

The sitting room to which she was led by the page was not overly large. It was a bit less ostentatious than the others that comprised the imperial apartments. The walls were a pale ivory with gilded wainscoting and almost completely covered with jeweled icons. The painted faces stared sadly.

Upon entering, Catherine glanced about, then quickly caught her breath in dismay as she saw that the empress was not alone. Almost in unison, Peter and Count Alexander Shuvalov turned to face her. Seated in a large and comfortable chair, the empress stared at her in stony silence from beneath flattened brows.

Catherine clasped her hands loosely in front of her.

Now, of all times, she must keep a cool head, she told herself sternly. If things went wrong she could be sent home, be buried in the darkest dungeon, or be banished to a nunnery for life. None of the choices particularly appealed to her.

Advancing toward them, Catherine made a deliberate effort to control her rising uneasiness, determined that whatever Peter and Shuvalov saw in her face, it would not be fear. If Peter was her enemy, Shuvalov was even more so. He was avid in his support of the grand duke.

Pausing before Elizabeth, Catherine hesitated only briefly, then sank to her knees. 'Your Majesty,' she breathed in a quiet voice.

Elizabeth eyed her coldly. She had forsaken her normally extravagant attire and was wearing a simple caftan of blue silk. The once-beautiful dark-blue eyes were more bloodshot than usual. Catherine felt a pang of hope. It was obvious that the empress had had a great deal of wine to drink. When she was inebriated, she grew overly sentimental.

'You wish to return home?' Elizabeth demanded abruptly, still eyeing her in an unfriendly manner.

Catherine answered with a solemn nod. 'I can see that you are displeased with me,' she whispered.

Elizabeth gestured, appearing irritated. 'Get up,' she said. 'Get up off your knees.'

Slowly Catherine did as she was told.

Peter was regarding her with a smile filled with contempt. Look at her, he thought to himself. Standing there, plain and ugly. She looked no better now than when he had first seen her. Fool! She hadn't even taken the time to arrange her hair in a fashionable manner.

From the table beside her, Elizabeth now picked up a packet of letters from a gold bowl. Catherine felt the blood drain from her face. For a moment she thought she might faint. She inhaled deeply in an effort to ward off the sudden attack of dizziness.

Three. That much she could see. There was nothing in those letters that could be construed as damning to herself – except of course for the fact that she had penned them without permission. As for the manifesto ... A small part of her began to relax. They could not possibly have that document. If they did, she would be under guard by now.

'These are yours.' Elizabeth waved the letters, fixing Catherine with an angry stare. 'Who gave you leave to busy yourself with our military affairs! How dare you write to our general while he was on the field of battle!' The voice rose to a shriek, causing Peter to smirk at Catherine. He was enjoying himself and her discomfort.

Catherine straightened, regarding the empress with as much coolness as she could muster under the circumstances. 'If your Majesty has read those letters,' she murmured, 'then she knows how innocent they are.'

Alexander Shuvalov suddenly stepped forward from the shadows, his gaunt face set in a menacing scowl. Catherine eyed him warily. Like Ivan Shuvalov, Alexander was tall, but not nearly as handsome or as well muscled as his kinsman.

'These,' Shuvalov said, motioning to the letters still clutched in the hand of Elizabeth, 'may be as you say, innocent, your Highness. 'But we know that there are others not so innocent.'

Catherine threw him a short look of contempt. If there were, she thought to herself, you would have already thrust them under my nose. She raised her head and the firelight played about her shining tresses.

'There are no other letters, Count Shuvalov,' she contradicted quietly, pleased that her voice remained steady, 'for none other were written. Not by me.'

His eyes grew hooded. 'Perhaps, madame, there were other letters,' he suggested slyly. 'Letters containing secret instructions to the general.' He emitted a scornful laugh. 'Surely Apraxin didn't take it upon himself to leave the field of victory.'

Catherine wasn't in the least bit fooled by the soft voice. 'Do you accuse me of treason, Count Shuvalov?' she demanded haughtily.

Shuvalov gave a careless shrug, a bored expression on his gaunt face. To his side, Peter stood somewhat stiffly, his pale eyes glittering with anticipation. He couldn't wait to be rid of his wife. Once she was found guilty, he was thinking smugly, then he could marry Lizbeth, something he wanted more than anything else in the world.

Catherine again faced Elizabeth, dismayed to see that her attitude was still fierce and unforgiving. 'I am falsely accused, your Majesty,' she said earnestly. 'I swear to you that never, never did I in any way send orders or instructions to General Apraxin, nor to anyone else for that matter.' This was true, and Catherine hoped fervently that the veracity of her statement was reflected in her voice. 'My crime, if it be so called, was to congratulate a friend on the birth of a healthy son.'

In the light from the single candelabra on the table, Elizabeth regarded the grand duchess for long moments. Although she wasn't aware of being nudged in that direction by Catherine's appearance, the years seemed to fall away, one by one, and she suddenly recalled the fourteen-year-old girl she had first seen more than fifteen years ago. So young, she thought sadly. They had both been so young on that long-ago February evening.

With an abrupt change of subject, Elizabeth asked: 'Why do you want to return home?'

'Because the love I feel for you as sovereign and aunt will not bear the thought of your displeasure,' Catherine replied simply.

'We are not displeased with you,' Elizabeth responded in a softer tone. She shifted her weight uncomfortably, wishing she could lay her weary body down in bed. 'Let us say that we are … disappointed to learn of your foolish act.'

Sensing capitulation on his aunt's part, Peter gave a cry

of rage. 'She's not to be trusted!' he shouted in a venomous voice. 'Can't you see that?' He held his body rigid, hands clenched at his side, his breath coming hard.

Briefly Elizabeth glanced at the disfigured face of her nephew. Her dislike made her grit her teeth.

Peter was glaring at Catherine with absolute hatred. 'How can you trust a woman who betrays her own husband?' When he again looked at his aunt, his eyes appeared wild. 'Send her back home if she wants to go. She's of no use to me. She's a harlot! A harlot who has more lovers than she has sense!' He pointed a trembling finger at his wife, who stood quietly, eyes lowered. Only the faintest tinge of pink colored her cheeks and indicated that she might have heard his words.

Elizabeth gave the grand duke a sharp look. Her hands gripped the arms of her chair as if she were ready to spring up and physically attack him.

'Be quiet, you prattling idiot! We do not want to hear another word from you.' She relaxed a bit and her face grew thoughtful. 'Leave us alone.' She looked in turn at Peter and Shuvalov. After a small hesitation, they reluctantly withdrew.

Peter's mouth had once again run away with his brain, Catherine realized, still keeping her eyes lowered. If there was one thing guaranteed to send Elizabeth into a fit of fury, it was for someone to cast aspersions on the paternity of the children.

When they were alone, Elizabeth turned to Catherine with a sigh. 'Somehow we cannot believe that you would behave traitorously to your empress.'

'Nor to my country, Majesty,' Catherine interjected firmly and with great sincerity.

For the first time, Elizabeth laughed, even if it was short and quick. 'Yes,' she mused, rubbing her chin with her fingertips. 'I do believe that you actually regard Russia as your country.' Then she grew somber again. 'For this we forgive you much, Catherine Alexeievna.' Her sigh seemed to come from the depths of her soul.

Catherine repressed a shudder. She was safe ... for now. But for how long? Once again Elizabeth's protection lay about her like warm fur cloak, but Catherine knew very well that that security would be withdrawn when the empress died.

Elizabeth reached for her wine and took a long draught before she continued. 'In any event, Bestuzhev is being exiled. We no longer trust him. General Apraxin will stand trial for treason. As for you ...' she observed Catherine for a long moment. 'Count Poniatowski must leave this court.' She raised a ringed hand as Catherine opened her mouth to speak. 'We will hear no argument,' she said firmly. 'He is leaving tomorrow. You will not see him again, not even to say good-bye. Do you understand!'

Catherine bowed her head in a docile manner. 'Yes, your Majesty,' she whispered, resigned. Though her love for Stanis had never reached the depth of feeling she had felt for Serge, she was sincerely fond of the Polish nobleman and knew she would miss him.

'We will speak no more of your returning home,' Elizabeth went on. 'Your place is here.' Her gaze became speculative. 'How long has it been since you have seen your son?'

Catherine thought. The answer gave her a jolt of surprise. 'It has been ... almost three months.'

Elizabeth pursed her lips. 'From now on you will be permitted to visit him once every week.' She turned away, staring moodily into the shadows that wavered just beyond the flickering firelight. 'My nephew is a fool,' she muttered shortly. 'He doesn't realize that his careless words can do harm to the children.' Her eyes narrowed as they again rested upon the grand duchess. 'You understand that Paul Petrovich must be protected?'

'I do, your Majesty.' Catherine's heart lifted at the thought of being able to see her son more often.

'And you know that I love the child as if he were my

own,' she whispered. She moved her hands in a desperate manner. 'I wish to God that I could live long enough to see him grown ...' Her voice broke.

'Please don't speak like that ...' Impulsively Catherine sank to her knees and put her head in Elizabeth's lap.

The room was silent for many moments. Neither woman moved.

'Catherine Alexeievna ...'

Catherine raised her head and looked up at the older woman, wondering at the sound of her voice. It appeared to have come from a great distance.

'There is grave danger in store for you when I am no longer here to protect you,' Elizabeth murmured, dropping all formality.

Still on her knees, Catherine reached for one of Elizabeth's puffy hands and brought it against the side of her face. 'I know that, Little Mother,' she whispered.

'Your husband will kill you if he can,' Elizabeth continued in the same curiously distant tone.

'I know that, too.' Tears slipped from her eyes and fell on the hand pressed to her cheek.

'You must be strong. Not only for your sake, but for your son's, as well.' Elizabeth looked down into the beautiful face and sighed deeply. 'I'm weary, Catherine Alexeievna. Each night I see Death lurking in the shadows, waiting. I fear to close my eyes against its presence lest it creep closer. But despite my vigilance it will soon have its way with me.'

Catherine again buried her head in Elizabeth's lap. The sound of her weeping was muffled as she clung to the woman who had had more of an impact on her life than any other living person; the woman she respected, feared, hated ... and loved.

When he left his aunt's chambers, Peter went directly to his own apartments where Lizbeth Vorontsova was waiting. His face was a mask of fury as he related the recent events.

'She's like a viper, that one,' he shouted. 'She weaves a

path of deceit and treachery, yet she manages to worm her way out of it time and again.'

Lizbeth poured him a glass of wine and tried to calm him down, but he paid her no mind.

'At least my aunt is getting rid of the Polish nobleman. She's sending him away. She told me that she would.' Peter downed the wine and Lizbeth quickly filled the glass again. 'Not that that will stop her,' he raged on. 'But I tell you this: Not even at my aunt's insistence will I accept another one of her bastards!' He flung the glass against the wall where it shattered into a spray of shards, leaving blood-red streaks in its wake.

'One day soon you will be tsar,' Lizbeth consoled soothingly in her somewhat nasal voice. She stroked his brow with a gentle hand. 'Then you'll be able to do anything you want to do.'

He looked at her for a moment without speaking. Then his face grew sly and sinister. 'And one of the first things I will do as tsar is divorce her. I will send her to a convent for the rest of her life!'

Lizbeth smiled in pleasure at these revelations.

Warming to the subject, Peter continued to elaborate to his mistress on what the fates held in store for his wife. They spoke far into the night.

Seventeen

The months passed. Bestuzhev had departed for the northern provinces, leaving in the dead of night so that none would witness his disgrace. The fate of General Apraxin was never decided because he never came to trial. The day before it was to begin the old general died, his heart no longer able to withstand his shame.

On this October evening, having been seated at one of the tables in the salon, Catherine got up, feeling too restless to play another game of whist.

One of Peter's gentlemen gave her a warm smile as she walked across the room. Catherine turned away, aware that Peter was watching her. She knew that if she so much as smiled at a man it would provoke a cutting remark from him. Since the night of her meeting with Elizabeth, she and Peter had come to an uneasy truce. However, truce or no, she could sense a waiting, a watching in her husband that left her greatly disquieted.

Catherine paused by the window, viewing the scene it framed in bemused wonder. Two days ago a fierce storm had descended. While it had begun as rain on the first day, that quickly changed to snow on the second. After the rain and snow the temperature had dipped well below freezing, and tonight a pale moon had risen upon a city that glittered beneath an iced coating. Everything seemed made of glass.

Leo had come to stand at her side.

'My wife tells me that the empress has taken to her bed

again,' he said to her in a low voice. 'Her hold on life weakens daily.' He sounded worried, and Catherine knew it was her own safety that caused his concern.

She turned to look at Peter. He was seated on a divan in the corner of the room, Lizbeth at his side. They were gazing into each other's eyes with a moon-struck expression.

'She's been ill before,' Catherine murmured, hiding her unease.

Leo gave a great sigh and downed the vodka in the glass he was holding. 'I only hope to God the war ends before her Majesty succumbs.' He viewed his empty glass thoughtfully, then flashed Catherine a quick look. 'You know, Frederick has been anticipating our every move. It's uncanny! Our regiments seem unable to take him by surprise.'

Catherine again looked out the window but made no reply. She knew that Peter was sending every available scrap of information to Frederick. At least once a week he met privately with Keith, the English ambassador who had replaced Sir Charles. Although Catherine deplored her husband's actions, she said nothing; not to Peter or to anyone else. It would be foolhardy, she knew, to antagonize him at this point. Peter was waiting for only one thing: his aunt's death. And from Leo's grave face it appeared that that could happen at any time.

Catherine raised a hand to her forehead, aware that her head was aching. The strain of these past months was beginning to tell.

After making her excuses to Leo, Catherine retired to her room and to her lonely bed.

The next afternoon, just as Catherine was about to leave the palace for a visit with Countess Praskovia Bruce, she heard voices and laughter coming from Peter's adjoining room. As she passed by the open door, she was surprised to hear Peter call to her.

Entering, she paused abruptly on the threshold,

viewing Count Schwerin in startled astonishment. The Prussian officer was seated across the table from Peter, eating and drinking as if his presence was a most ordinary thing.

Behind the count's chair stood a lieutenant, but Catherine suspected that the surveillance was no more than perfunctory. Further taken aback, she heard Peter invite her in a jocular tone to join them.

'I think not,' she replied, making an effort to control her anger.

'Oh, come on, Catherine,' he insisted, motioning her forward. 'Count Schwerin has been telling me of his many victories against the Russians.'

Catherine raised a brow. 'He must have lost at least one battle,' she noted in a dry voice.

The prisoner – for that's what he was, a prisoner of war – stared at her with eyes that were frankly admiring. He was a stocky man with a broad chest that terminated in a paunch. Leaning back in his chair, he grinned at her.

Peter, however, wasn't in the least amused. 'I will not allow you to slight a guest at my table!' His words were rapid and edged with the hint of hysteria that always seemed to accompany his rages.

The harsh words continued, but Catherine's eyes were again drawn to the lieutenant, who was still standing stiffly behind the prisoner's chair. She could see by his stance that he was outraged. Glancing at his insignia, Catherine noted that he was a member of the elite Ismailovsky Guard. He was a giant of a man. Not even his heavy jacket hid his broad shoulders and powerful arms. His features were so regular that to call him handsome would have been an understatement. His black eyes were staring at her in an almost imploring way, and Catherine found herself unable to look away.

At last, breathless from his tirade, Peter finally fell silent. But he continued to glare at Catherine furiously, unaware that she had been paying no attention to him.

'Again I must refuse your offer, your Highness. I do not dine with the enemies of my country.' Catherine spoke slowly, her quiet tone in sharp contrast with her husband's shrill voice. A brief look at the handsome lieutenant told her that he, at least, appreciated her remarks. His chest swelled as he took a deep breath of satisfaction.

Before Peter could speak further, she turned and left the room.

Toward the end of that week the skies cleared and the sun, in a defiant blaze, melted the early snow. Relieved by the break in the weather, Catherine headed for the stables.

Dressed in riding breeches, her jacket trimmed in gray velvet, Catherine was waiting for the groom when the lieutenant, whose name she now knew to be Gregory Orlov, approached her and bowed.

'Where is your prisoner, Lieutenant Orlov?' she asked him with a smile. 'Surely you didn't allow him to escape?'

The lieutenant's handsome face was unsmiling as he replied. 'He's well watched, your Highness. Though I suspect he has little desire to escape,' he added with evident bitterness. 'His life here has been made … most comfortable.'

She nodded, a slight frown creasing her brow. 'I don't approve, but there is little I can do about it.'

'But you've done much, Highness,' he contradicted earnestly. 'And the Ismailovsky regiment know of your courage and your patriotism. And your beauty, as well.'

'Thank you, Lieutenant,' she murmured. Though she appeared distant and casual, underneath this spurious façade, Catherine was aware that her heart was pounding. Not since she had first laid eyes on Serge had a man so captured her imagination.

Gregory was still staring so openly that Catherine flushed, annoyed with herself for doing so. Fortunately, the timely return of the groom excused her from making any further comment.

Ignoring the man, Gregory quickly stepped forward. He extended his cupped hands to assist Catherine in mounting. Then he reached out and caressed the horse's neck, his dark eyes fastened on Catherine. He had related the incident with the Prussian prisoner to his fellow officers. They, like himself, had been impressed by the grand duchess's courage. For some time before Catherine's entrance on that day, Gregory had stood behind Schwerin's chair, feeling the outrage boil within his chest until he was certain he would do something foolish. He longed to take his sword and slit the grand duke's scrawny throat as he continued to prattle incessantly in German, treating his prisoner as if he were an honored guest instead of a hated enemy.

Finally Gregory handed the reins to Catherine. Staring at his powerful hands, Catherine hesitated a moment before her own slim hand reached for the bridle strap.

'I offer you my life, should you ever need it.' Gregory bowed again and stood there, watching her in silence.

Catherine met his glance a moment longer, then spurred the horse forward. In only minutes she had managed to put Lieutenant Orlov from her mind, knowing full well that Peter was waiting for her to make just such a mistake.

After returning from her ride, Catherine went to her apartments to dress for her weekly journey to Peterhof to visit her son. Perhaps, if the empress permitted, she might also visit her daughter, Anne. Catherine dismissed that thought as unlikely, however, because the child was still in the imperial bedchamber.

In the apartments of the tsarevich, which were not too far distant from those of the empress, Count Nikita Panin listened intently to Paul Petrovich as he recited a part of his gospels. They were seated by the bow windows that overlooked the rear gardens.

'Well done, your Highness,' Panin said when the little

tsarevich at last concluded. 'Now you must put on your jacket. Your lady mother will be here shortly to visit you.' He closed the book of gospels and, getting up, returned it to its proper place on the bookshelf.

The boy's face fell into a pout, and his blue eyes shone with quick tears. 'We would rather play in the courtyard,' he stated plaintively. 'The servants have constructed a small slide for us.'

Panin turned and regarded his royal pupil sternly. 'The grand duchess visits only once a week. You must make her feel welcome.' He frowned, knowing that Paul never looked forward to his mother's visits and generally fidgeted the whole time he was in her presence.

Issuing an audible sigh of resignation, Paul Petrovich ran into his bedchamber. Going to his window, he stared down at the road. It was just as white with snow as the surrounding landscape, but it had been tamped down so that the sledges could easily glide across its length.

He was looking for *her* sledge, hoping all the while that something – anything – would keep her from her weekly visit. These weekly visits were something new, a change in his routine that was most unwelcome. He had even complained to the empress, who usually granted his every wish. This time, however, she had only sighed and told him that it was for the best.

The grand duchess was his mother. Paul had often been told that – mostly by his tutor. Yet it was to the empress that he ran when he was upset or joyful. It was into her lap that he climbed when he was weary and wanted to be held. The empress was his mother, if not in name then in fact, and Paul greatly resented it when he was told otherwise.

His eye caught a movement in the distance, and Paul frowned as he saw the sledge. It was *her*! She didn't love him; he knew that. He didn't know how he knew, but Paul knew it with a certainty that was as forceful as if she had told him so.

In the outer chamber, Panin sank into a chair to await the grand duchess's arrival. As he waited, his brow creased in thought.

The empress had been ailing again this past week. It wasn't common knowledge, but Panin knew of it because he brought the tsarevich in to visit her several times each day. What would happen to Paul when she died? he wondered uneasily.

If only the boy could be crowned, Panin thought to himself for perhaps the hundredth time. The grand duchess would make a perfect regent until her son came of age. Of course he and Bestuzhev had already discussed this possibility before, but with the chancellor's dismissal and subsequent exile to the far northern provinces, the idea had been laid to rest. Panin had concluded, however, after many hours of studying the issues, that Paul's future depended, not upon his father, but upon his mother.

Not for the first time his mind dealt upon Paul's birth. He'd often wondered whether there was any truth to the occasional rumors that the grand duke had not fathered the tsarevich. The boy didn't look like the grand duke, but Panin dismissed that as inconsequential; who knew what Peter's face would look like now, had he not been so disfigured as a youth?

Panin had finally decided, mostly because he wanted to believe it, that Peter was in fact the boy's father.

As for the little girl that was another matter. There was little doubt in his mind that the child was a bastard, despite the empress's acceptance.

The announced arrival of the grand duchess put an end to Panin's mental wanderings, and he immediately rose and bowed, watching as she handed her fur cloak to a servant.

'The tsarevich will be here in just a moment, your Highness.' Panin's dark eyes regarded Catherine deferentially as he spoke.

The grand duchess nodded briefly. After walking across

the carpeted floor, she sat down in a large comfortable chair. 'Please feel free to sit, Count Panin.'

'Thank you, madame,' Panin murmured, sitting down in a chair close by. He had a great respect for the grand duchess, although he suspected that under the generally congenial manner lay a hard core of shrewdness. This, however, in no way detracted from his respect.

'How is the tsarevich doing with his lessons?' Catherine inquired after a moment.

'Very well, madame,' Panin replied with satisfaction. 'He can recite a part of his gospels by heart, and we have begun lessons in history just this week.' He smiled, transforming his round face in a pleasant way. 'Of course, I'm afraid that the tsarevich would rather play than study. He's a high-spirited lad.' He turned, seeing Paul enter the room. He got up, went to the boy, and took a small hand in his own and led the tsarevich to his mother.

Bowing from the waist, the young tsarevich regarded Catherine somberly. 'We are pleased to see you, your Highness,' he stated formally.

Catherine observed the grave little face, and the smile that came to her lips was hesitant. Each time she saw the boy, she was struck anew by her lack of feeling for him. At times she actually had to keep reminding herself that this was her son.

'Well ...' she said with false brightness. 'So you are about to begin lessons in history ...'

Paul stood there in silence, making no reply.

'Your mother is waiting for an answer, Paul Petrovich!' Panin spoke sharply, again dismayed by the lack of feeling between the crown prince and the grand duchess.

Turning, Paul flashed his tutor a sullen look. He was not afraid of any reprimand. The empress – the only adult he did love – would never allow it.

'Your Highness ...' Panin's tone now held a warning.

With a sigh, Paul finally responded to his mother. While he could count on no physical chastisement, it was not beyond Panin to refuse to let him go outside to play.

At last it was over. Count Panin escorted a relieved Catherine to the waiting sledge that would take her back to Oranienbaum.

She was actually in the sledge when a guard came running at top speed to inform her that empress wished to see her immediately. Puzzled, Catherine followed the guard as he led her to Elizabeth's bedchamber. She had seen little of the empress in these past months, and the summons was unexpected.

Her puzzlement turned to shock when, upon entering, she found Elizabeth crying hysterically, resisting the efforts of Countess Shuvalov, who was trying to calm her mistress. Although Elizabeth tried to tell her what happened, she was unable to speak coherently, and it was a servant who at last, and with regret, informed Catherine of the death of her ten-month-old daughter, Anne.

'It happened less than an hour ago,' the servant concluded, and was herself in tears.

Stunned, Catherine just stood there for long moments, at a loss for words. At last Elizabeth's sobs quieted and she gained control of herself once more. Patting the edge of the bed, she beckoned to Catherine.

'Come, sit beside me.' She sniffed and put a silk handkerchief to her nose. Her eyes were red and swollen.

For a time neither woman spoke. Then Elizabeth said: 'You have our sympathy. The physician didn't at first think it serious, but she died only hours after being stricken with fever. I myself was with her at the end.'

Catherine looked away, ashamed of herself for feeling so little emotion, while the empress seemed truly saddened. But the child, even more so than Paul, was as a stranger to her. She had never held it, never nursed it, never pressed the small warm body against her own.

Elizabeth studied Catherine for a moment. 'I'm getting old, Catherine Alexeievna,' she said in a tired voice, and when Catherine demurred, Elizabeth raised a hand. 'It's true. I no longer fool myself. The time will come when I am no longer here. Paul is still a child. He has never known anything but my love and adoration.' Fresh tears welled in her eyes.

'Do you think that I would treat my child in any other manner?' Catherine inquired with some asperity.

Elizabeth shook her head slowly. 'It's not you I worry about. You will never harm the boy, I know that. But when I die, Peter will be tsar.' She regarded Catherine steadily, her eyes still misted. 'It's not only Paul who will be in danger then,' she said softly. 'But you, as well.'

Catherine paled, but in truth she was already aware of that observation.

Turning, Elizabeth looked directly at Catherine, then reached for the slim hand. 'I'm gravely ill, as your own eyes can tell you. But you mustn't mention it to anyone. Do you understand me?'

Catherine nodded slowly, and looked down at the hand that held her own. It was puffy and the skin felt dry and parched. 'I will not speak of it, your Majesty,' she replied in a quiet voice.

Elizabeth released her hand. 'They'll all know soon enough,' she said bitterly. Again the blue eyes searched Catherine's face. 'Peter especially must not learn of how ill I am.' Her face crumpled into anguish. 'I've no doubt but that he would immediately send word to the Prussians.' She gave a short and harsh laugh. 'How Frederick would love to learn that I am nearing –' She paused, unable to speak the word. Thoroughly exhausted, she sank back on the pillows and closed her eyes, her lips moving in fervent prayer.

Thus dismissed, Catherine got up. With slow steps she again made her way to the waiting sledge.

After her daughter's funeral, Catherine continued with the usual round of winter festivities that were fast becoming meaningless to her. Time and again she encountered Lieutenant Orlov, and each time she was more drawn to his darkly handsome face and thoroughly masculine manner. Although she realized the danger of any involvement, it was becoming more and more difficult to turn her mind and thoughts away from him.

To her close friend, Countess Praskovia Bruce, Catherine finally confided her attraction for the lieutenant. On hearing that, the countess giggled in delight, then proceeded to inform the grand duchess of the many tales of the lieutenant's courage and bravado, not all of which occurred on the battlefield.

Finally Praskovia paused and studied Catherine thoughtfully for a moment. 'You know, Highness,' she said carefully, 'I've been thinking of planning a supper party for tomorrow evening. Nothing elaborate, you understand. Only a few close friends.' She raised her brow and looked at Catherine as if just struck with a new thought. 'Might we count on your presence, madame? You know how much the count and I enjoy your company.'

Catherine gave her friend a sidelong glance and a conspiratorial grin. 'I'd be delighted to join you, Praskovia.'

The following evening, just before eight o'clock, Catherine arrived at the dacha of Countess Bruce, an imposing three-story structure, unusual from its neighbors in that it was made of stone instead of timber.

The supper party was indeed small. Aside from the grand duchess, the only other guest was Lieutenant Gregory Orlov.

Catherine didn't return to her apartments until the gray light of morning had put in an appearance.

During the months that followed, it was noted that the grand duchess and the countess became the closest of friends, and it was not unusual to see the ducal carriage in front of her dacha several times a week.

Eighteen

The sound of harnesses and trappings drifted lightly across the frigid air as the sledge moved easily over the frozen ground.

Catherine tucked the fur robes closer about her body, her movements tense with her thoughts. Even though more than an hour had passed, she was still shaken from her visit with Paul. Of course, she probably should not have spoken to the boy as sharply as she did. Still and all, she hadn't expected him to shout at her as if she were one of his servants. The boy was obviously spoiled. Even Panin couldn't control him.

Sighing deeply, Catherine tried not to think about the weekly encounter, feeling emotionally drained from the experience.

A short while later, Catherine peered outside, relieved to see the domed and terraced dacha that lay nestled within a clearing surrounded by a stand of tall pine trees.

For the past six months now she had been stopping at the home of Prince Dashkov on her return trip from Peterhof. It was not, however, the prince that she called on, but rather his vivacious wife, Princess Eketerina Dashkova. Although only nineteen, Eketerina had been married for almost five years and had two children of her own.

At those times when Catherine was feeling melancholy, Katrina always managed to lift her spirits. She was young, intelligent, and her gay manner was infectious.

She was also the younger sister of Lizbeth Vorontsova. For this reason, Catherine had at first approached their friendship with reservations. But no two people could have been more opposite in looks or disposition than Lizbeth and Katrina, and over the months, their friendship had grown.

Her arrival had been noted. As Catherine got out of the sledge, the front door opened.

The princess greeted her with a broad smile that revealed white teeth. 'I am so glad to see you, your Highness,' she said. 'Please come into the other room. It's much warmer in there.'

Catherine followed her young friend. The drawing room was warm, the fire blazed high. Between two settees a low mosaic-topped table held a pot of steaming chocolate and a gleaming silver bowl filled with freshly made pastries.

Dressed in a soft blue wool dress, Katrina watched as Catherine settled herself on one of the divans. 'You've just come from Peterhof?' she asked, pouring the chocolate into a gold-bordered porcelain cup.

Catherine nodded as she removed her fur cloak. After accepting the cup, she sipped at the hot, rich liquid.

'Did you enjoy your visit with the tsarevich?' Katrina asked when Catherine made no immediate response.

'Time seems only to separate me from my son,' Catherine said at last with a sigh, setting the cup down on the table. Her violet eyes darkened. I'm beginning to dread these weekly visits,' she confessed.

'Did anything go wrong?'

Catherine gave a small shrug. 'Just about everything that could,' she said ruefully. 'When I entered Paul's apartments he was on the floor … playing with toy soldiers.'

She paused, seeing in her mind's eye the angry face of the small boy as he glared at her in much the same way as did Peter. For the first time in more than five years,

Catherine found herself wondering about Paul Petrovich's father. The child was beginning to resemble Peter in a most extraordinary way. Was it possible? she speculated, truly mystified. Was it possible that Peter had actually fathered Paul Petrovich?

'I'm afraid I protested rather sharply,' Catherine went on. 'The boy became angry. Unfortunately, I then became quite insistent.' She took a deep breath. 'In the end, he ran from the room in tears. Even Panin couldn't persuade him to return.'

'He's so young,' Katrina observed. Then she sighed, for she knew of the same insane obsession with toy soldiers that had for so long gripped the grand duke. Leaning forward, she patted Catherine's hand. 'I know that in time he'll understand.'

'I hope you're right,' Catherine murmured.

Katrina tilted her small head. 'Did you see the empress?' she asked quietly, pouring herself a cup of chocolate and adding more to Catherine's cup.

Catherine shook her head as she reached for a pastry. After taking a bite, she said: 'Her Majesty seems to be indisposed again. Or so I was informed,' she added quickly, mindful of her promise to Elizabeth. 'It could be that she just didn't want to receive me.'

Observing the grand duchess as she spoke, Katrina was struck by the fact that Catherine looked more than upset. 'You look tired, madame,' she said impulsively. 'Perhaps you should consider taking the waters.'

'I'm fine. Really,' Catherine assured, momentarily avoiding Katrina's probing eye.

Although if what she suspected was true, she wouldn't be fine for very long, Catherine thought in resignation. Having finished the pastry, she again reached for her cup, holding it between her hands, feeling the warmth on her skin. She saw that Katrina was still staring at her. It made her uneasy. She decided it was time to change the subject.

'The latest reports of the war are most encouraging,' she

said brightly. 'I've heard that the army is just outside of Berlin.'

Katrina immediately relaxed, her attention diverted. 'Frederick has his back against the wall,' she noted with enthusiasm. Then her pretty face clouded. 'Yet all he has to do is hold on until ...'

Catherine looked away and gave a slow nod of agreement, knowing that Katrina was referring to the empress's death. She replaced the cup on the table once more. 'Frederick may win this war by default,' she conceded.

Staring at Catherine with suddenly intent eyes, Katrina's mouth hardened. Like everyone else, she knew that when the empress died, the grand duke would most likely surrender to Frederick. The thought, to her, was intolerable. 'It needn't be so, madame,' she said quietly. 'On more than one occasion in our past history the crown has not gone to the chosen successor. If you were to –'

In a quick motion, Catherine stood up. This was not the first time that Katrina had spoken along such lines. More than once Catherine had indicated that she disapproved of such words, but Katrina persisted nonetheless. They all seem to think it would be so easy, Catherine thought with some annoyance as she reached for her cloak. Did they expect her to simply walk up to Peter and remove the crown from his head?

'I must be going,' she said shortly, ignoring Katrina's dismayed face.

Obediently the princess followed her to the front door where she stood watching in moody resignation as Catherine entered the waiting sledge and sped from view.

Back at Oranienbaum, Catherine disrobed and lay down on the bed, intending to nap. She had fallen into a light doze when the rustle of brocade caused her to open her eyes. In some surprise she stared at Lizbeth Vorontsova, wondering what could have lured her from Peter's side.

Lizbeth was standing at the foot of the bed, her narrow-set eyes lit by a gleam of triumph. Beside her, Anya's face was so pale she appeared to be on the verge of swooning.

Catherine sat up, pulling the quilt to just under her breast. 'How dare you disturb me!' she demanded of Lizbeth.

'Forgive me, your Highness,' Lizbeth simpered, not in the least bit apologetic. 'The grand duke and I are on our way to Peterhof. We've received word that the empress is gravely ill. It's said she cannot last the night.'

With a sly smile, Lizbeth dipped in a curtsy that was more a mockery than an obeisance. Without waiting for Catherine to speak, she turned and flounced from the room.

Catherine looked at Anya. 'Make preparations for our return to Peterhof,' she instructed. She took a moment to inhale deeply, conscious of her pounding heart. Then she got to her feet and walked toward the pier mirror. With an unusually critical eye, she regarded the reflection she saw.

For the past five months she had managed to keep anyone from learning about her affair with Gregory Orlov. Anya, of course, knew. So did Countess Bruce. Catherine had gone to great lengths in order to keep anyone else from finding out about it, knowing the danger to herself should their affair become known to Peter. Not even Katrina Dashkova was aware of the clandestine relationship.

Still staring at her reflection, Catherine clasped her arms about her stomach. But how would it be possible for her to keep this a secret? she wondered frantically.

Never, never would Peter accept this child as his own. Not that she had planned to tell him, or anyone else for that matter. Just this past week Countess Bruce, her only confidante aside from her faithful Anya, had told her that she had been successful in locating a couple who would adopt the child as soon as it was born.

'Madame?'

Catherine turned and regarded Anya's concerned face.

'I'm all right,' she said quietly. 'Does it show?' she asked, again looking into the mirror.

'No, your Highness.' Despite the assurance, Anya's face didn't clear. 'But in a few weeks …'

'Let's take one day at a time, my dear Anya,' Catherine interrupted quickly.

'But you'll be at the palace,' the young woman exclaimed. A note of panic crept into her voice. 'If the empress is as ill as they say, then your Highness will be required to wait with the others. God forgive me, madame, if the empress died now, today, the funeral would take weeks!' She put her hand to her mouth, but the gesture couldn't contain the sob that erupted.

Catherine patted the shoulder of the young woman. 'My hooped skirts will conceal everything … at least for the next few months. I need hide myself only for the last few weeks.' Once more her eyes sought the looking glass. Her face looked pale and tired. Perhaps a bit of rouge … More important, her waist was still narrow, her abdomen flat. She turned sideways, then bit her lip. It was almost flat.

Anya let herself be calmed, but inwardly she had grave misgivings. The squint-eyed Vorontsova had nosed about on more than one occasion, asking questions as to her mistress's 'indispositions' as if she had a right to know. Anya wasn't entirely certain that the woman was doing that on her own either. It was possible that the grand duke had sent her to pry. But Anya was one step ahead of them both. She had been deliberately careless with her own soiled linens during these past three months; and she sincerely doubted that anyone even suspected that Catherine's monthly flow had ceased.

Yet a protruding belly was not so easily hidden …

Shaking her head, Anya walked to the wardrobe. After gathering several dresses in her arms, she laid them on the bed, then looked at her mistress with worried eyes while she waited for a selection to be made. She knew that no one, not even the grand duke, would strike out at the grand duchess as long as the empress lived. Anya would let her thoughts go no further. God would provide; He always did.

With Anya's assistance, Catherine dressed with more than usual care. First the corset, then the wide hoop that was the foundation of all her gowns. Over this, Anya fastened an underskirt of white satin. Finally, over that, a dress of gray woolen material. The neck was high and the sleeves long, for the December day offered temperatures well below freezing. Catherine slipped her feet into short fur-lined boots. Then Anya draped a sable cloak around her shoulders.

Finally Anya picked up the matching sable muff, offering it to her mistress with a hand that trembled.

Reaching out, Catherine patted the smooth and rosy cheek. 'Calm yourself, Anya,' she said. 'Everything will be all right.'

Turning, Catherine made her way downstairs and out into the gloomy afternoon. Anya, together with the rest of her attendants and ladies, was to follow shortly. Peter, she knew, had already gone ahead in his own sledge, the Vorontsova close by his side.

Catherine settled herself on the cushioned seat, pulling the robe across her lap. With a mittened hand she drew the collar of the cloak over her face until only her eyes were visible.

Four horses drew the vehicle swiftly over the frozen countryside. It had begun to snow again. The only sound other than plodding hooves was the gay jingle of the bells on leather trappings. Catherine concentrated on the pleasant intonation, refusing the troublesome thoughts that clamored to gain entrance to her conscious mind.

In less than an hour they reached Peterhof.

Catherine went to her apartments only long enough to

deposit her outer wraps, then immediately made her way to the empress's bedchamber.

This time, she saw, the empress was indeed fatally ill.

The bloated, dropsical figure stirred, moaned, then fell silent again. There was, Catherine thought with saddened amazement, nothing left of the once-beautiful and vibrant Elizabeth Petrovna. There was only this almost obscene caricature that already had the waxy look of death upon its face.

Catherine moved closer. Although Elizabeth's eyes were open, it was obvious that she recognized no one.

Catching her lower lip between her teeth, Catherine turned her head and regarded Peter. He was standing on the other side of the bed. A half smile decorated his sallow face as he watched his aunt with avid interest. Sickened by his display of poorly repressed elation, Catherine averted her eyes.

One by one, the doctors moved to the far end of the large bedchamber, the slump of their shoulders more eloquent than any words could be.

A few minutes later they were all ushered out of the room to wait in the antechamber. Only Chancellor Vorontsov remained as the priests began to perform their final ministrations. Vorontsov, who had replaced Bestuzhev, was an obese man who stood perhaps an inch or so over five feet. He was Lizbeth's uncle and, Catherine well knew, no friend of hers.

Vast as it was, the antechamber seemed hot and airless. All the windows were tightly shuttered and draped. Two fireplaces blazed high. Catherine, in her woolen gown, felt faint. She put a hand to her throat and took a deep breath, aware that Katrina was heading toward her. The princess's pretty face reflected deep concern.

'Are you feeling ill, Highness?' she whispered, peering intently into Catherine's pale face.

'No, no,' Catherine managed. 'It's just such a shock.' She sat down and tried to control her reeling senses, thankful that Princess Dashkova fell silent.

The next hour passed slowly. Catherine longed to leave the room, to step outside for a breath of fresh air, but she forced herself to sit quietly. It was not easy to do. The heat was making her nauseous. At last the door was flung open and Chancellor Vorontsov emerged. Looking neither right nor left, he walked directly to Peter and bent a knee.

'Your Imperial Majesty,' he intoned respectully. Then he straightened again, a gleam of satisfaction in his eye as he officially informed them all of the death of Elizabeth Petrovna.

From his position across the room, Count Panin regarded Catherine with a pained expression as Peter let out a short loud yelp of glee.

'Now we'll set things to right!' he announced shrilly to them all. Turning abruptly, never once looking at his wife, Peter headed for the door. Most of the people in the room hurried to follow him, eager to be the first to offer their allegiance. Only Panin, Katrina, and Prince Dashkov remained.

After hesitating for only the briefest moment, Count Panin walked slowly across the room. Bowing before Catherine, he said simply: 'Your Majesty.'

Catherine couldn't prevent a rueful smile as she placed her hand on his extended arm and allowed him to escort her from the room.

In the corridor, her ladies were waiting. As soon as they saw her they dipped in a deep curtsy, then followed her as she made her way back to her apartments, where she dismissed them.

Anya had arrived from Oranienbaum, and the rooms were now warmed by blazing fires, the bed turned down invitingly.

Feeling more weary than she had ever felt in her life, Catherine undressed and crawled into bed. In only minutes she fell fast asleep.

A shrill voice from the adjoining room awakened her

some hours later. Quickly Catherine got out of bed. After donning a voluminous caftan, she went to the outer chamber to see Katrina Dashkova. The princess, wearing a long fur cloak that reached to her ankles, looked distraught as she confronted Anya.

'I don't care if her Majesty is asleep! You must awaken her! It's imperative that I speak to her immediately!'

'Katrina!' Catherine exclaimed at the sight of her friend. 'What are you doing here? It's after midnight.'

'I must speak to you, your Majesty. Alone.' Katrina looked to be on the verge of tears.

'Come inside,' Catherine said, fighting down her unease. She returned to her bedchamber, Katrina close on her heels.

Catherine sat down, but Katrina just stood there, trembling visibly, though with fear or anger Catherine was unable to determine.

'The tsar and my sister are at my home,' Katrina began with a sense of urgency. 'They've been there for hours. Your Majesty, he is publicly speaking of marrying Lizbeth. It's all he talked about all night long. You must do something!' Her words tumbled over one another in her haste, emerging in a breathless rush.

Feeling dismay in the pit of her stomach, Catherine put a hand to her throat. 'There ... there is nothing I can do, Katrina.' So soon, she was thinking in despair. She hadn't expected Peter to act so soon.

'There has got to be something you can do. Something I can do. Just tell me,' the girl pleaded, wringing her hands.

Slowly Catherine shook her head. She felt numb with the feeling of helplessness that crept over her. But in spite of her inner turmoil, Catherine couldn't prevent the wry smile that found its way to her lips, though it certainly held no humor. She could just imagine what everyone would think if she were to lead a revolt, her belly swollen with an illegitimate child. It was, she realized, a blessing in disguise that her husband's attention was, at this critical time, elsewhere than on his wife.

Katrina's dark eyes shimmered with tears. Weakly she sat down on the edge of the bed, staring at Catherine. Why did she just sit there, as if nothing untoward had happened? 'My God, madame!' she cried out. 'Do you want to spend the rest of your life in a nun's cell?'

Catherine made no immediate reply. She needed time desperately. The coronation! She took a deep breath as she thought of that. Peter wouldn't be so foolish as to act before his position was made official. And the preparations for that event would take months. Months ...

'We will do nothing, my dear Katrina,' she said at last, making her tone firm. 'And we urge you to take no action in our behalf.' She watched the princess with worried eyes and prayed that the headstrong young woman heeded her words.

'The time is not right,' Catherine concluded, grimly amused by her own words.

Nineteen

The day was bleak and gray, almost as if it, too, mourned the passing of Empress Elizabeth Petrovna. The people wept and grieved over the death of their revered Little Mother. Only a few were aware of the banquet planned by their new tsar in celebration of her demise.

One evening, while continuous revelry occupied the court, a highly agitated Panin managed to visit Catherine, who had been feigning illness in order to absent herself from the ill-timed festivities.

'The tsar has ended the war!' he reported in a choked voice, looking severely shaken. He plucked a handkerchief from the pocket of his green velvet jacket and mopped his face. Though the late December day was brittle with cold, Panin's round face was shining with perspiration. 'But that's not the worst of it,' he went on. 'The tsar has not only sent word to Frederick that all his lost lands will be returned to him, he has apologized for taking them in the first place!' He stuffed the handkerchief back in his pocket, sighing deeply.

Even though she had not seen Peter since the night Elizabeth had died, the news was not all that much of a surprise to Catherine. 'Sit down, Count Panin,' she said, motioning for the servant to bring brandy.

But the man made no move. He was now regarding her with an intent look, and even before he spoke Catherine knew what he was going to say.

'Madame, if only you would allow us to act in your

behalf ...'

She raised a hand to silence him. Again the feeling of helpless frustration washed over her. Although Peter had made no move to divorce her, she realized all too well that her respite was temporary. She knew her response would further dismay Panin, but having no recourse, she said: 'I can do nothing.'

Panin expelled a long breath of resignation. 'Then will your Majesty at least consider leaving St. Petersburg and going to Oranienbaum?' he implored. 'It's dangerous for you to be here at this time.'

Catherine didn't need to be reminded of that. There was no doubt in her mind now that she would have to fight Peter for the crown, perhaps for her very life. Although Panin wanted to saddle her with a regency, she wasn't about to place that crown on anyone else's head but her own. To that end, one of the first things she would have to do would be to make herself visible to the people. Obviously that could not be accomplished from Oranienbaum.

Her violet eyes were level and somber as Catherine regarded the tutor. 'Whatever our relationship was in these past years, her Majesty always extended her protection to me when it was most needed. I will not leave St. Petersburg until after the funeral.'

Panin appeared about to press the issue, but a look at her face told him any argument would be useless. Appearing dejected, he bowed low, then backed out of the room.

After going into her bedchamber, Catherine summoned Anya to help her dress. She chose a plain black velvet gown. High-necked and longed-sleeved, its austereness was unrelieved by so much as a ruffle of lace. Disdaining all jewelry except her wedding ring, Catherine draped a black veil over her head, then went downstairs to the state room to pay her last respects to the former empress.

It was crowded. A long and endless queue of people

walked slowly by the catafalque, which had been draped in gold cloth and surrounded by jeweled candelabrum.

Upon approaching the coffin, Catherine paused only briefly, then sank to her knees, staring at the dead empress. Elizabeth once again looked beautiful. Gone was the bloated, pasty look, and in its place the skin was as smooth and serene as marble. The Royal Embalmer had done his work well.

Catherine raised her eyes to the ermined canopy. Above it, the gold two-headed eagle glinted softly in the reflected light of the scented tapers. She bowed her head and prayed.

Toward the end of the day Catherine went back to her apartments. But the following morning she returned again to the catafalque, dressed in the same simple black gown.

And the people saw, and they took note. They were profoundly touched by the tears of the beautiful tsarina as she knelt before the coffin for hours at a time. She was there when the doors opened to admit the daily mourners, and she was still there when the day came to an end.

Other eyes, too, were watching the tsarina. Two members of the Imperial Guard in full dress uniform stood stiffly at attention, one at the head of the coffin, the other at the foot. They were relieved every hour, when two new guards took up the vigil. They each, in turn, stood motionless, observing their new tsarina with mounting respect. More than one of them spent the allotted hour blinking in a fierce determination to quell his rising emotion.

In their quarters, the men compared their observations. Then, with hard and bitter eyes, they related that not once – not once – did the new tsar pay his respects to their departed Little Mother.

One day Panin went to the state room. From an alcove he watched as the simple people filed by. In only a few minutes he noticed that their eyes were more upon the kneeling Catherine than upon their dead empress.

For just a moment Panin's eyes rested on the body of Elizabeth. He wasn't sorry she was gone; he only wished that it had happened sooner. These past months had been nothing short of a nightmare as far as he was concerned. As death had drawn nearer, Elizabeth had sought to hold it at bay with increasing bouts of debauchery. Panin had been more and more reluctant to bring Paul to her apartments. She would pray for hours on end, then would rip her clothes off and insist that Shuvalov make love to her at once, regardless of who was in the room.

Then there were the hallucinations that had plagued her during the last weeks. More than once Panin had come upon her while she was conversing with an empty chair. To her, of course, it was not empty, but rather it held a holy spirit who spoke words only she could hear.

Panin's attention was now caught by an old woman who had stepped apart from the crowd of people. Her head wrapped in a scarf, she hesitantly approached Catherine, who was still kneeling, head bowed in prayer. Prostrating herself, the old woman reverently touched the hem of Catherine's black velvet gown, her eyes filling with tears that slipped silently down her wrinkled face.

Panin watched for another hour or so. The scene was repeated time and again. At last, a thoughtful look on his face, he returned to his apartments. Perhaps, he mused, taking heart from what he had witnessed, there might still be hope for a regency.

On the eleventh day the casket was finally sealed. With much pomp it was then carried to Kazan Cathedral for the funeral services, all members of the court following at a sedate pace.

Again Panin noted that the eyes of the people followed Catherine.

They were halfway to the cathedral when a short burst of shrill laughter assaulted Panin's ears. Oh, God! he thought, unable to believe what he was seeing. Peter had stepped out of the procession line. Hands on his hips, he was cavorting through the street, his booted feet tapping out a gleeful dance to a rhythm accompanied by music only he could hear.

The crowd was so stunned that for a moment there was absolute silence.

Panin himself was so appalled by this insulting behavior that without realizing it he plowed right into a priest who had paused in front of him. The man didn't even notice. His hands were covering his face, and from the convulsive movement of his thin shoulders, Panin knew the priest was sobbing.

As well we might all, Panin thought with a deep sigh.

Peter had gotten back into line now, but was still walking with a jaunty step as the procession continued on to the cathedral.

Faces were bleak as the people watched the crude antics of their tsar. Once more their eyes focused on Catherine, who, walking slowly, head bowed, gave no outward sign of having noticed anything amiss. Men and women alike were staring at her as if she were a living symbol of their Russian spirit.

Panin slowed his steps as he heard the whispered murmurs from the crowd.

'He is mad!'

'No. He gloats ...'

'He plans to turn us all into Prussians ...'

'Long live our new Little Mother ...'

'...God grant us her Imperial grace.'

Panin's heart lifted as he moved on. There was no doubt now in his mind that, with Catherine's help, Paul Petrovich could be crowned. From what he'd just seen and heard, there should be no difficulty in persuading the people to accept Catherine as regent.

Some weeks later, now in her fourth month of pregnancy, Catherine went to the dacha of Praskovia Bruce and into the waiting arms of Gregory Orlov.

After the fire of their ardor had been temporarily

quenched, Gregory raised himself up on one elbow and stared down at the face of his beloved mistress. They were in a little-used bedroom on the second floor. Countess Bruce, as usual, had discreetly absented herself, obstensibly to pay a social call.

Heavy brocade draperies were drawn tightly against the bright afternoon sun, leaving the spacious room soft and shadowy.

'Catherine, we must make plans, and we must do it now!' Absently Gregory curled strands of her hair about his fingers as he spoke. She had, he'd often thought, the most beautiful hair of any woman he'd ever known.

Catherine answered him with a lazy smile. Her body content, she was in little frame of mind to dwell upon serious matters. When she was with Gregory her problems seemed remote, and she was happy to have it so.

'Listen to me, my darling,' he whispered, kissing her brow. 'Day after day that dolt of a husband of yours flaunts the Vorontsova. He speaks openly of making her his wife.'

'And if he sends me to Siberia, will you come with me?' she asked in a teasing voice.

'It's no matter for joking!' he growled. After pulling away from her embrace, he sat on the edge of the bed, giving no thought to the fact that he was naked. 'The people are with you, Catherine,' he said. A note of urgency crept into his voice. 'It was bad enough when he halted the war and almost fell into the arms of Frederick. But now he's tampering with the church. The people are enraged, as well they might be. They see the statues of their saints being removed from the cathedrals. Now the fool wants the priests to shave their beards. He's trying to Lutheranize the church!' He sounded outraged.

After getting abruplty to his feet, Gregory walked across the room. On a table a copper samovar held hot tea. He reached instead for the silver decanter beside it, poured himself a generous vodka, and quickly drank it.

Watching his movements, Catherine admired the broad

muscled back and long, firmly muscled legs. What a magnificent animal he is, she thought to herself. He was unlike any man she'd ever known. When they were alone like this she allowed him to assert himself without restraint; she enjoyed playing the part of an ordinary woman. But as much as she admired and wanted Gregory Orlov, she had long ago decided that she would never allow him to have complete control over her. No man would ever have that privilege again.

Coming back to the bed, Gregory stared down at her. 'Say the word, my darling Catherine, and my fellow soldiers will place you on the throne.'

Catherine sat up, unheeding of the silk sheet as it fell away to reveal her perfect breasts. In the dim light, her hair tousled about her shoulders, Catherine looked much younger than her thirty years.

'And what makes you think that the soldiers will follow me?' she asked solemnly. 'I'm no more a Russian than is Peter.'

Gregory took hold of her shoulders, his black eyes so intense they seemed to burn from his face. 'You are a Russian, Catherine! Never again say otherwise. Besides, your son is Russian by birth.' He released her. Her nearness made his head swim, and he wanted no such diversion at this time. 'My brothers have not been idle these past weeks. They've uncovered more support for you and your son than we ever dreamed possible. Alexei works night and day in your behalf,' he said of his youngest brother.

She lay down again, now in a contemplative mood. 'The Shuvalovs and the Vorontsovs support Peter,' she noted slowly. 'The two most powerful families in court. Oh, I know,' she went on quickly, seeing the look on his face. 'The combined support of the Guard is more powerful.' She leaned toward him, resting her hand on his thigh, feeling it tighten beneath her light caress. 'But that's just it, Gregory. The Ismailovsky Regiment is but one. What of the others?'

'We'll get them all,' he insisted, putting his own hand on

top of hers. 'I promise you, Catherine. But we must make plans now. We cannot act on the spur of the moment,' he explained in a voice more patient than he felt. 'Even if I were to give the word now, today, it would take more than two weeks for us to organize.'

Catherine sighed. Reaching up, she trailed her fingertips across his furred chest. 'I'm afraid I can't help you with any plans right now, my dearest Gregory.' Her voice fell to a whisper. 'You see, I'm going to have a child. Your child.'

After his first flush of surprised pleasure wore off, Gregory's face turned white. He clutched at her hand so tightly, she winced. 'My God, Catherine, no one must know. If I've placed you in any danger, my life would not be worth living.'

'It will be all right,' she said in an effort to calm him, hiding her own deep fears.

He frowned. 'Is there any chance, any at all, that it's his?' he asked at last.

She shook her head. 'None. Peter's so enamoured of the Vorontsova, he hasn't come near me in over a year.'

'Then we must act quickly!' He began to get up.

'No, no,' she protested, grabbing his arm. 'We must do nothing at all. The danger is not so great, really,' she went on after he again sat on the bed. 'When I'm dressed, my skirts hide everything. I'm going to stay in my apartments as much as possible. I've already spoken to Countess Bruce and we've made arrangements.'

'But when the babe is born? What then?' Gregory looked doubtful. How could she manage to keep such a thing a secret? he was thinking.

Catherine looked away. 'I need only one woman to attend me.' Then she returned her gaze to him and saw his uncertain expression. 'This will not be the first child that I've had,' she reminded him.

'Blessed Jesus!' he exclaimed fiercely. 'It's madness to wait. There's no telling what that German dog will do if he finds out.' He clasped her to him. 'I swear I'll kill him if he so much as harms a hair on your head.'

She laughed in delight, feeling the tension leave her. Then she sobered, seeing that he spoke in all seriousness. 'An act like that would cost you your own head, my love.'

'Which I would give up gladly to protect you.' He pushed her back against the pillow. Bending closer, he kissed her willing lips.

For the following months, as they had both agreed, Gregory prudently stayed away. So, too, did most members of the court, for they could see that a cloud of imperial disapproval had fallen over the tsarina.

Princess Dashkova was, however, the exception. Not only was she infuriated because Catherine was being virtually ignored, she was outraged by the fact that Peter was speaking of war with Denmark, a country that had for years been an ally of Russia. For Katrina, there was only one solution to all their ills: Oust the tsar and put Catherine in his place.

After one particularly exhausting session with the insistent Dashkova, Catherine sat in quiet contemplation for almost an hour. The time had come, she realized, for her to seclude herself.

Getting up, Catherine allowed Anya to help her disrobe. Wearing nothing more than a satin shirt, she viewed her burgeoning image in the looking glass. Without her hooped skirt it was quite evident that she was far along in her pregnancy.

'We can delay no longer,' she said, turning to Anya's worried face. 'Let's get on with it.'

'Yes, madame' came the swift, somewhat breathless reply.

With Anya's help, Catherine disrobed, put on her nightclothes, and got into bed. When she had settled herself, Anya set about bandaging her ankle, after which she carefully positioned a pillow beneath Catherine's foot.

More pillows were placed on either side of Catherine, and when Anya finally draped a satin coverlet over the swollen form of her mistress, all evidence of her pregnancy seemed to have disappeared.

The days dragged by. Only when visitors were more than insistent did Anya admit them into Catherine's bedchamber.

Fortunately, aside from Panin, Leo Narishkin, and Princess Dashkova, there weren't too many. To recognize the tsarina was to incur the wrath of the tsar, who was now acting as if the Vorontsova was his lawful wife.

At last there came a day when the familiar pain began. Catherine immediately sent for Praskovia Bruce. A short time later, her face taut and concerned, the countess entered the tsarina's apartments.

Anya led her into Catherine's personal bedchamber and promptly locked the door. One look and Praskovia could see that Catherine was well along in her labor. With a grim nod to Anya, she set about aiding her tsarina in her travail.

This time there wasn't even a mattress. Anya had prudently rolled back the gray-and-rose Persian rug. No more than a thin blanket separated Catherine from the hardwood floor.

Anya stoked the fire high and tried to control her terror. The guards would stop anyone at the door … except the tsar himself. The thought provoked a moan, and the countess eyed her sharply.

'Hush!'

Chagrined, Anya pressed her lips together. She was ashamed that she could act so cowardly in the face of Catherine's bravery.

Through the late afternoon and early evening, Countess Bruce and Anya worked side by side, the countess watching the clock with worried eyes as the hours seemed to slip by one by one with no sign of the child being born. God help them all, she thought frantically, if any complications arose. Whether she sent for a physician or not, the end result would be disastrous for the tsarina.

Catherine had her teeth clamped together and her mouth pressed tight, not allowing even the smallest outcry to pass her lips as, one by one, the hours passed.

'What time is it?' she said through gritted teeth at one point.

'It's past one, madame.' Praskovia's calm voice belied her growing fear. They desperately needed the darkness of night to aid them in carrying out the rest of their plan. Many hours of thought had gone into its conception. However, as difficult as it had at first appeared, the problem had finally been solved.

Just outside the window waited one of Praskovia's most trusted lackeys, one whose full sympathies were with the tsarina. At the appropriate time, Praskovia would signal him from the window, after which he would immediately return to his own house – and set it aflame. Since his residence practically bordered the palace, it would create a very useful diversion.

But for maximum effect, it had to be dark for the plan to work.

At last, just after four o'clock, Praskovia could see that it would be only minutes now. She picked up a candle, stepped to the fire to light it, then walked to the window, where she gave the prearranged signal.

Less than a quarter of an hour had passed when Praskovia heard the alarm sounded. Covered by the sound of the guards' running feet as they sped through the corridors in answer to the strident clanging of bells, Catherine's second son took his first breath of life.

Acting quickly, Praskovia swaddled the infant in a fur robe. 'Have you selected a name, your Majesty?' she whispered to Catherine.

Catherine produced a weak smile. 'Call him Alexis Gregorovich Bobrinsky,' she answered.

As Praskovia turned away, Catherine's heart twisted in anguish. 'Wait!' she cried out. 'Please ... let me hold him.'

Praskovia hesitated, already hearing the commotion generated by the fire. 'Your Majesty ...' she began, but Catherine raised her arms, reaching for her child.

'I must hold my baby, if only for a moment.'

Praskovia put the small bundle into the waiting arms. Still on the floor, Catherine clutched her son close to her breast. Bending forward, she placed her lips on the petal-soft cheek.

Turning on her heel, Anya ran from the room to the outer chamber. Cautiously she opened the door, then peered into the corridor, relieved to see that it was deserted. Quickly she made her way back to the bedchamber again and spoke to the countess, who was now wringing her hands.

'The guards are gone. There is no one about.'

'Your Majesty ...' Praskovia implored, growing frantic with the delay. If anyone saw her walking through the corridors carrying a newborn infant in her arms ... Praskovia shuddered at the thought of what the consequences would be.

Reluctantly Catherine relinquished her son and watched as Praskovia spirited him from the room. Outside the April sky was turning pearly gray, but all eyes were fastened on the red-and-yellow flames that leapt high into the air, threatening the palace itself.

Moving quickly, Anya gently sponged her mistress's weary body, then helped her back into bed.

'Three times,' Catherine murmured, a sob in her voice, and Anya bent toward her solicitously. 'Three times I have borne a child.' Catherine looked at Anya with tears in her eyes. 'But yet I am childless!'

Then, utterly exhausted, she fell asleep.

Twenty

As he stomped through the halls of the newly completed Winter Palace, Peter's body was contorted with fury. A few paces behind him, Chancellor Vorontsov hurried to keep up with him, his short black satin cape billowing about him like the wings of a wounded bird.

'Please, your Majesty, I beg you to use restraint at this time.'

Vorontsov's voice was breathless with his exertion and the fast pace set by the tsar. They were on their way to the tsarina's apartments. Unhappily for the chancellor's labored breath, the apartments were on the other side of the palace. In view of the fact that the Winter Palace contained over one thousand rooms, the journey wasn't a short one. The chancellor had lost his breath when they had raced down the exquisite staircase of Carrara marble that led from the tsar's personal chambers to the corridors that served the rest of the rooms on the second floor, and he had not regained it since.

'The harlot knows of our *ukaze* against private chapels!' Peter raged without a break in his stride. 'We shall see to it that the disobedient slut is sent to Suzdal,' he screamed without turning to the man behind him. 'Once in a dark cell of the nunnery, she can pray to her heart's content.'

Vorontsov gasped, running a few steps to catch up. He was clearly distressed by his tsar's ill-controlled anger, knowing full well that the time was not yet right to move against the tsarina. Her support was too great at this time.

The week before, the whole court had moved into the Winter Palace, a truly monumental structure sprawled beneath a roofline of ornamental vases, interspersed with more than one hundred fifty gold statues. The apartments assigned to the tsarina had contained no private chapel, which in itself was of no concern to Vorontsov or to anyone else. The tsar had forbidden their use. But the tsarina, upon learning of this omission in her new residence, had foolishly given orders to have a chapel constructed. When the tsar had learned of her blatant disobedience, he had flown into one of his predictable rages. Even the Vorontsova hadn't been able to calm him down.

'Remember Shuvalov's advice, sire,' Vorontsov tried again. He was walking so fast that he turned his ankle, causing him to clutch at the stone wall for support. He winced but kept on going.

'Shuvalov is as cautious as an old woman walking on ice!' The description was delivered with clipped precision through tight lips.

Approaching the carved double doors at the end of the corridor, Peter made an impatient gesture to the guard, who immediately flung them open.

'How dare you!' he bellowed loudly as he caught sight of Catherine emerging from her dressing room, a startled look on her face. She had apparently just gotten out of her bath and was attired in a rose satin robe, her damp hair tumbling loosely about her shoulders.

Catherine came to an abrupt halt at the sight of the two men who had entered unannounced. Behind her, Anya pressed a hand to her lips, her face pale with fright.

Peter shouted the words again, not bothering to explain the reason for his agitation.

Slowly Catherine dipped in a curtsy, then regarded her husband warily. She recognized the look on his face all too well, but was uncertain as to what had caused the provocation.

'I'm sorry, sire,' she whispered. 'I don't understand …'

Hands on his narrow hips, Peter walked around her while she stood very still. His booted feet made sharp staccato sounds on the tiled floor as he paced with measured steps. At last he halted, facing her again, arms folded across his chest.

'We have forbidden the use of private chapels, madame,' he murmured in a soft and menacing tone. 'Surely you are not so isolated that you are unaware of our wishes in this matter.' He inclined his head, peering at her from beneath lowered brows.

Catherine blinked, startled by his words. 'I could not imagine that you would deny me the solace of a chapel,' she replied, truly amazed at his unbridled reaction.

His nostrils pinched and whitened as his mouth curled. 'You are no more privileged than any other of our subjects,' he stated nastily. 'We have ordered the work stopped!' His eyes narrowed as he brought his face close to hers. Catherine moved her head slightly, as if she found the very smell of him offensive. 'And do not dare presume to order otherwise, madame,' he warned her in the same tone.

Involuntarily Catherine took a step back, feeling his hatred in an almost physical way. She hadn't seen Peter for more than six weeks now, but it was quite obvious that his attitude toward her had not softened. Her strength had returned quickly after the birth of her child two weeks ago, a situation for which she was immensely grateful, for only six days after the event Peter had commanded that the court be moved here. She shuddered to think what might have happened had the command been received a week earlier.

Shifting her weight uneasily, Catherine became aware that Peter was staring at her in a peculiar, intent manner.

Peter was, in fact, about to order her arrest. He tingled with the anticipation of such a move. But the words of his trusted advisor, Alexander Shuvalov, rang in his unwilling

ears: 'Do nothing, sire, until after your coronation. There
will be none who will dare raise their voice then.'

Still looking at his wife, Peter's lips twitched. He was
sorely tempted to ignore this counsel, wise as it may have
been. For more years than he could remember he had
wanted to rid himself of her hated presence. The
restriction – short as it would be – rankled.

Though she wasn't aware of it, Catherine's cautious and
outwardly subservient attitude saved her. In spite of his
heated anger, Peter was gratified to see her recoil.

'I'm sorry if I upset you, sire,' she murmured in a quiet
voice, lowering her eyes. 'I apologize for my thoughtless
behavior.' The words stuck in her throat, producing a
pang of nausea that caused her to take a deep wavering
breath. She clasped her hands tightly at her waist, fighting
to control her nervousness, knowing that one wrong
move now would be the end of her. She hadn't meant for
her simple order to produce such dire results.

Watching her, Peter's pale eyes gleamed malevolently.
Perhaps he would wait before giving the order for her
arrest. It warmed his heart to see her cringe. It might be an
amusing diversion to play cat and mouse for a while. His
chest swelled. No longer was this woman beyond his
reach.

'The convent awaits you, madame,' he finally informed
her slowly, 'should you ever again disobey the commands
of your tsar.' A smile crept up his sallow cheeks. Reaching
out, he idly fingered a strand of her hair. 'It would be a
shame to shave it all off,' he mused, cocking his head at
her sharply indrawn breath. 'I wonder what you would
look like bald.'

Before she could respond, he turned and walked from
the room, looking smug and satisfied. Vorontsov, relief
etching his chubby face, quickly followed.

With their departure, Catherine collapsed into the
nearest chair, waving Anya away.

Soon, she thought. She would have to act soon. Her

hands clenched into fists as she thought of Peter's threats. A nunnery! She'd see him in hell before she allowed that to happen to her. She would have to leave here. Perhaps, with distance between them, Peter would forget about her for a while. Then she could make her plans.

Raising her head, she motioned to the ever-present Anya.

'Pack our things,' she commanded. 'Tomorrow we are going to Mon Plaisir.'

Anya dipped in curtsy. 'For how long, madame?'

Catherine's smile was cold. 'For however long it takes, my dear Anya.'

The maid took a few steps away, then turned toward Catherine again. 'The banquet is tomorrow evening, your Majesty ...' For the past week, the palace had hummed with the preparations taking place for the huge affair.

Catherine shrugged. 'The tsar never notices my absences. There is no reason why he should do otherwise on this occasion.'

By the following afternoon the trunks were packed, and Anya directed the servants to place them in the carriage.

The June afternoon was pleasant and sunny, but still cool enough to wear an outer wrap.

Catherine had already donned her cloak when the command was issued: The tsarina would, and must, attend the evening banquet, by direct order of the tsar.

It was Gregory himself who delivered the message, having intercepted the courier in the hallway. Impulsively he urged Catherine to refuse to attend.

'There's no way that I can disobey a direct command, you know that,' she replied tiredly, removing her cloak. Her voice was calm, giving lie to the threads of uneasiness that wound about her already taut nerves. This was the first time that Peter had commanded her attendance at any function. She knew very well it wasn't her company he sought.

'Then plead illness,' Gregory implored, growing

desperate. 'Catherine, I grow more concerned for your welfare each day, each hour!'

Again Catherine read the command, dismay darkening her eyes. 'There must be some reason, some particular reason why he's so insistent.' She shook her head. 'I dare not even pretend illness ...'

'Then tell me when you're ready, and we'll act,' Gregory whispered. 'You cannot delay much longer.'

Catherine turned away from him, still upset with the pending evening ahead. She put a hand to her temple, her head was throbbing. 'Please, Gregory. I cannot discuss this now. It's not a step to be taken lightly. I need time ...'
How correct was Gregory in his assumption that the guards would support her? she wondered frantically.

'How much time do you think you have?' he asked roughly.

Catherine was about to make a reply when Princess Dashkova burst into the room. She was already dressed for the evening, her slim body attired in a crimson satin gown that sparkled from the reflected light of hundreds of tiny diamonds cleverly sewn into a pattern of roses. Her black hair was heavily powdered and intricately woven into a pompador that soared almost six inches above her head.

Coming closer, Katrina glanced briefly at Gregory Orlov, but did not otherwise acknowledge his presence. She disliked him intensely, but she knew that he was a firm supporter of the tsarina; for this, she tolerated him. She was unaware of the close relationship between her royal mistress and the lieutenant, and knew only that Orlov was boorish and without grace or culture.

Though Katrina wasn't aware of it, Gregory heartily returned this dislike. In spite of her delicate form, he found her most unfeminine, saw nothing at all attractive in the small-boned, vivid features, which he likened to a hawk.

'Your Majesty, forgive the intrusion,' Katrina said in her

breathless manner. 'But there is something you must know.'

'What is it?' Catherine asked quickly, taking a step toward the young woman.

Again the princess looked at Gregory, annoyed to see that he was apparently not to be dismissed. A quick frown marred the smooth brow as she continued. 'The tsar plans to bestow upon Lizbeth the Order of St. Catherine. He will do this tonight, at the banquet.'

Gregory's face flushed a deep crimson. 'That's impossible,' he growled in outrage, staring at Katrina. 'The Order of St. Catherine cannot be given to other than a princess or a grand duchess.'

Katrina eyed him coolly, offended that he had the audacity to address her. She wrinkled her nose, finding his odor of masculinity repulsive. 'Nevertheless, Lieutenant. Tonight it will be given to my sister.' She turned to Catherine, her face falling into grave consternation. 'There's a rumor that the tsar will command you, your Majesty, to personally pin it on. My sister has bragged about such an event taking place.'

Gregory clenched his fists. Only the sight of Catherine's white face prevented him from giving vent to his fury.

So this, Catherine was thinking, was the reason for the unexpected command. Peter wanted to humiliate her publicly.

'He may not go through with it,' Katrina said hastily, alarmed by Catherine's ashen color. 'After all, there will be better than five hundred people there tonight, important people.'

'What better time?' Catherine murmured dully. She swayed slightly, and Gregory quickly put his arms around her, assisting her to a nearby chair.

Frantic, Katrina took hold of Catherine's hand, chafing it between her own. Then she glared hotly at the hovering Gregory. 'Get out! I will care for her Majesty. You have no business being here.'

Gregory was about to protest, but Catherine gave him an imploring look. 'Yes, please go,' she said softly.

Casting a black look at the princess, Gregory strode from the room, determined to gather his forces while there was still time.

After emerging into the moon-filled night a short time later, Gregory crossed the square to where his horse was tethered. The animal nickered affectionately at the sight of his master. Gregory patted the stallion's rump, then mounted.

The carriage drive that led to the palace was crowded with vehicles. Gregory could hear sounds of laughter and jovial greetings as the guests hailed one another.

Moodily he watched the scene for a moment. Then, his teeth bared in a cry of rage, he dug his booted feet into the stallion's sides, spurring the animal to a gallop.

Instead of returning to his quarters, Gregory headed for the compound that housed the Preobrazhensky Guard. Beneath the brilliance of a full moon the road stretched before him like a white satin ribbon. His pulse pounded in rhythm with the stallion's hooves. He would have given anything to be at Catherine's side this evening. The fact that she needed his protection and he was unable to give it drove him into a frenzy. He could not, would not, wait any longer. With or without her permission, he was prepared to act.

He was breathless, the stallion winded when they finally arrived almost thirty minutes later. Though prodded by an irresistible urge for haste, Gregory had taken the precaution of slowing the horse to an easy canter, then allowing him to walk for the last half mile.

It being a Saturday night, most of the men had been given leave to enter the city or to otherwise occupy themselves. The compound was deserted, the barracks empty and forlorn.

Gregory identified himself to the guard at the gate and was immediately admitted. He led the stallion to a trough and dismounted, tying the reins to a wooden post.

He headed for the officers' quarters to seek out his brother, Alexei, who was a captain. Alexei would know what to do. Of Gregory's four brothers, Alexei was the one gifted with both intelligence and shrewdness. He was neither impulsive nor foolhardy.

Upon entering the long rectangular room, Gregory saw his brother at a table, deeply involved in a card game. Like the four men with him, Alexei had removed his jacket and had his shirt sleeves rolled up to the elbow. From the look of them, Gregory surmised they were prepared to play all night.

Ignoring the growls and curses that came his way when he interrupted the game, Gregory drew Alexei aside. Though some two inches shorter than Gregory, Alexei had the same rugged countenance as his brother.

Both young men walked to the far side of the barracks and sat down on one of the cots.

In a hoarse whisper that adequately conveyed his agitated state, Gregory explained the evening's events. He didn't have to explain his relationship with Catherine. That, Alexei already knew.

'I tell you, Alexei,' Gregory said heatedly, 'that German dog will kill her. We must act. How much support have you uncovered?'

Alexei's dark eyes were somber as he replied. Having the rank of captain, he had the freedom to come and go as he pleased and had been diligently at work these past weeks, ferreting out who was in favor of the tsarina.

'Every man I've spoken to will lay his life at her feet. Passek is helping me,' he said of a fellow officer. 'Between the two of us we've covered a great deal of ground. The regiments of Ismailkovsky and Preobrazhensky are for the tsarina. However, none dare speak of it as yet.'

'They will have to do so soon,' Gregory muttered. He ran a hand through his dark and tousled hair. 'What about the Semonovsky Regiment?' he inquired, turning toward his brother.

Alexei shrugged his broad shoulders. 'Here, I'm not certain, not just yet anyway. Passek has some friends in that regiment, close ones. He'll find out.'

Alexei got to his feet and stood there looking down at his brother. 'I'll send word to Passek tonight. If all goes well, we can move in about two weeks' time.'

Gregory jumped up, looking distraught. 'That's too long,' he cried out. 'It must be sooner than that.'

Seeing the dismay on his brother's face, Alexei clasped Gregory to him in a fierce bear hug.

'Don't fret,' he said. 'Nothing will happen to the tsarina. Not while we have the breath with which to fight.'

Twenty-One

Her face pale and taut, Catherine allowed her servants to dress her for the banquet. Katrina hovered solicitiously nearby. Too nervous to sit still, she kept pacing about the room, returning to Catherine's side every minute or so, as if she might be of some assistance.

Catherine chose a gown of soft blue velvet with a tight bodice and a wide hooped skirt trimmed with bows of silver lace.

Almost apologetically, Anya opened Catherine's jewel case and held it out for her inspection. It held only two necklaces, neither one of which was particularly impressive. Peter had confiscated almost all of Catherine's gems and presented them to Lizbeth.

Catherine sighed as she viewed the contents. 'The sapphire pendant,' she murmured.

Fury etched Katrina's face as Anya fastened the simple gold chain around Catherine's neck. 'It will never do,' she blurted out. 'Take mine ...' Her hand went to the diamonds at her throat, but Catherine shook her head.

'If the Vorontsova saw it, it would most likely wind up in her jewelry box.' She got to her feet. 'Katrina, it might be wise for you to go ahead without me.'

'No!' Katrina's answer was quick, and she raised her chin defiantly. 'I would consider it an honor if you will allow me to walk at your side, your Majesty.'

Catherine smiled and nodded. 'Thanks to you,' she said quietly as they began to leave the room, 'I am at least prepared for any insult my husband may think to confer on me.'

Accompanied by her ladies and Princess Dashkova, Catherine made her way slowly downstairs.

The great hall was brilliantly lighted by better than two thousand candles that blazed in the crystal chandeliers. As Katrina had noted, many important personages were in attendance this night. Ambassadors and other dignitaries mingled with the highest of the aristocracy.

A flare of panic coursed through Catherine as she entered. Glancing toward the imperial table, she saw Lizbeth beside Peter. Obviously she was not to be seated next to her husband, Catherine thought to herself, concealing her uneasiness as best she could.

She hesitated uncertainly on the threshold. A hush had fallen over the assemblage as everyone turned in her direction. After a long and painful moment, Chancellor Vorontsov approached her, a trace of a smile on his fleshy lips. Catherine did not return it. After extending his arm, he led her slowly across the room. As they passed in front of the raised dais upon which the tsar sat in a velvet-draped chair, the chancellor paused, allowing Catherine to dip in curtsy.

When she straightened, Catherine looked at her husband and repressed a shudder at the dark enmity she saw reflected in those pale eyes. Beside him, Lizbeth Vorontsova, dressed sumptuously and begemmed with the imperial jewels, had no more than glanced at Catherine with a brief condescending look, quickly turning away as if she were affronted by the beauty she saw and could never hope to attain.

Catherine's violet eyes darkened at the sight of Lizbeth's necklace, and she was conscious of the plain gold chain around her own neck. Angry words rushed into her throat, but she swallowed them.

Not yet. Not yet, her mind cautioned. Gems did not make a tsarina. That was something the simple Vorontsova would have to learn.

Finally Chancellor Vorontsov moved forward, leading Catherine to her chair … at the far end of the table.

It was a measure of the esteem in which Catherine was held that most eyes in the hall were averted, unwilling to witness this petty act of humiliation thrust upon her.

The Vorontsovs and the Shuvalovs were the exception. Both clans stared openly, avidly, enjoying the spectacle before them.

General Burhard von Munnich was also viewing Catherine. Munnich, who had spent twenty years in exile and who had been recalled by Peter, was firm in his support of his tsar. But the aging general's expression was more thoughtful than unfriendly. Despite his loyalty, he disapproved of the tsar's actions on this night. Moreover, he had been quick to note that most of the court, and even most of the visiting personages, appeared sympathetic to the tsarina; a few even appeared angry. It was a sight that made him uncomfortable, but he didn't know why.

The meal progressed in a more or less usual manner. Somehow Leo Narishkin managed during the course of the evening to position himself at Catherine's side. Even more so than usual, she appreciated his familiar and comforting presence.

Peter, she saw, was drinking heavily. Time and again he reached for Lizbeth, kissing her on the lips and murmuring endearments that were audible to everyone within earshot.

Thanks to Katrina, Catherine was able to steel herself for the coming event. When at last Peter got to his feet, she wasn't surprised by his actions, only relieved, because he himself pinned the Order on Lizbeth's bodice. He glanced about him, his pale eyes seeming to command the polite applause that followed his action. But he never once looked at his wife.

At Catherine's side, Leo was struggling with his emotions. The treatment accorded the tsarina this night caused his throat to constrict in helpless rage.

Not far from where Catherine was seated, Count Panin was also sitting quietly, his grim mouth and narrowed eyes appearing glued in place.

But as it turned out, Katrina did not know all, for what Peter did next took everyone by surprise.

'We raise our glass in honor of the imperial family!' Peter's voice, thickened with wine and slurred by vodka, nonetheless rang out in strident tones.

As if one, the assemblage rose, their glasses held high. Catherine, still seated and with a gracious smile fixed upon her numb lips, acknowedged the toast with a slight nod of her head.

Suddenly the tsar flushed a deep crimson, accenting his disfigured features. His brows drew together in a fierce frown. Seeing this, everyone fell into an uneasy silence.

He glared at Catherine. 'Is there good reason, madame, why you do not show the respect due the imperial family?' he demanded harshly.

Catherine gave him a level look. 'In what way have I been remiss, your Majesty?'

'You remain seated, madame.' Peter's low voice was silver with sarcasm. He fixed her with a menacing scowl. 'How can this be? Why do you not rise in honor of our imperial family?' Catherine made as if to reply, but Peter's voice again rang out. 'Stand up!' he shouted at her. 'You do not remain seated as if you were a part of our imperial family.'

With great dignity, Catherine got to her feet, but could not prevent the tears that sprang to her eyes at this public humiliation. They were not the tears of a wounded pride, but rather the result of a heated fury that made her pulse beat faster. And to think, she thought bitterly, that all these months she had been turning aside the support of her friends. No more! her mind raged. With this final insult, Peter had forfeited any consideration on her part.

'I *am* of the imperial family,' she retorted in a clear voice. Although she had been about to speak further, she fell silent at the look on her husband's face. He appeared angry enough to commit murder. In a swift and savage motion that startled those close to him, Peter swept his arm across the table, sending the gold dishes clattering to the floor.

'No greater fool lives than you, madame!' he bellowed in a voice choked with fury. '*Doura!* You can never again lay claim to such a distinction.'

The hall was silent, not even the servants dared move. Count Panin had turned the color of fresh milk, an appalled look in his eyes. Leo, in dumb anguish, felt his own face flame in outrage. And, to varying degrees, the whole assemblage reflected the twin emotions of shock and anger.

Catherine paid no mind to the white, horrified sea of faces that swam before her eyes. In a slow and delicate motion, she curtsied to her husband. 'I beg your indulgence, your Majesty.' Her low voice was clear. Only a few caught the note of desperation in it. 'I request permission to retire.'

'Granted!'

With great effort at self-control, Catherine walked from the hall with measured steps, her eyes fixed straight ahead of her. Katrina made as if to follow her, but was detained by her husband's firm hand on her arm.

Watching Catherine's receding figure, Peter smiled thinly. When she passed over the threshold, he burst into a loud laughter that ran hollowly through the otherwise silent hall, and his sallow face glowed with a feverish exultation that was matched in the expression of his mistress.

Catherine fled back to her rooms, her violet eyes haunted by visions she did not yet want to look upon: divorce or death. She had been sentenced to one or the other – and in public.

Her face was implacable as she reached the relative security of her bedchamber. Only then did she falter. She had held herself so rigid, so tight in these past hours that her muscles protested with the slightest movement on her part. Exhausted, Catherine collapsed on the bed, too filled with despair and anger even to cry.

Reports of the public humiliation of the tsarina traveled swiftly throughout the court. Nevertheless, Gregory didn't learn of it until the following morning, when Katrina hurried to his quarters to impart the news. Her dislike had been momentarily buried beneath her concern for Catherine's safety.

Upon hearing of what had taken place, Gregory's anger was so great that Alexei had to forcibly restrain him, lest he do something foolish enough to cause his own death.

'Your brother is right,' said an agitated Katrina, watching him struggle with Alexei. 'You can be of no use to her in Schlüsselburg. Or in your grave!'

'What does he plan to do?' Alexei asked her, still keeping Gregory in a firm grip. Although his voice was calm enough, his eyes glowed with the same fierce savagery as did his brother's.

Katrina made a helpless gesture. 'The very least will be the convent. The trouble is, we don't know which one. If he spirits her away, we may never find her again.'

'I'll kill that German dog!' cried an anguished Gregory, still struggling against his brother's relentless grip.

'She'll be avenged,' Alexei said to him, tightening his hold until Gregory had to gasp for breath. 'But for now, we must act. Swiftly.' When he was certain that Gregory was in control of himself once more, he looked at Princess Dashkova, whose white face was framed beneath the hood of her cloak. 'How much time do we have?'

'None,' Katrina replied shortly. 'The tsar has commanded her to retire to Peterhof. She leaves this morning. From there …' She put a hand to her lips, unable to voice her fears.

'Can you get to her before she leaves the palace?' Alexei

inquired.

Katrina's brow wrinkled in thought. 'I think so. The prince and I plan to leave for home this morning. I will insist on saying good-bye to her.'

'We need at least ten days,' said Gregory, looking at his brother for confirmation. But it was Katrina who answered him.

'Too long,' she stated flatly, glaring at them both. 'In the seclusion of Peterhof she could be killed or sent away before anyone knew of it! Three days. You must do something within that time.'

Again Alexei reached for his brother, seeing his face turn an alarming shade of scarlet, but Gregory's voice was steady and cold as he spoke. 'Tell her that we'll act with all due haste. If she senses imminent danger, tell her to send Anya to me and I'll come immediately.'

'Anya will not be allowed to accompany the tsarina,' Katrina said with a sigh. Then she brightened. 'Mon Plaisir! Why didn't I think of it before? If I can persuade the tsarina to stay at Mon Plaisir, she would have the advantage of time should any danger threaten. And she would still be on the estates of Peterhof and therefore not in violation of the imperial command. She can see the palace from there. If the guards arrive unexpectedly, she'll have time to mount a horse and ride away.'

'Good,' Alexei responded with a nod. 'I know where the summer pavilion is located; the seclusion is perfect. When we have everything settled here, we'll get word to her.' He faced Gregory. 'I'll find Passek. We begin at once.'

Nodding to each other, the three conspirators went their separate ways.

But as it turned out, they didn't have days at all; they had only hours.

Twenty-Two

At the pavilion known as Mon Plaisir, Catherine stood on the terrace just outside her bedchamber. The shingled beach that led from the edge of the terrace to the waterline gleamed a pale ivory. As she gazed out upon the waters of the Gulf of Finland, Catherine thought that she would never tire of the glowing white nights peculiar to this area in the summer months. In the half twilight of the June night the water appeared black. Shimmering silver slashes danced along its surface and rippled outward toward the horizon.

Turning to her left, Catherine could see the extended wing of the pavilion that housed the chapel. Its diadem of five golden cupolas glinted dully in the suffused light.

A sigh escaped her lips as her eye traveled the familiar sight. She had no doubt that Peter would be further angered when he discovered that she had disobeyed his order to remain at Peterhof. Although, in truth, she was close enough that were she to walk to the front side of the pavilion she would be able to see the splendid palace. She knew that Peter had gone to Oranienbaum, probably with Lizbeth. Catherine could imagine how they plotted her fate.

She lowered her head slightly, and her expressions altered subtly. In the silvery glow it appeared grim and resolute. But, my husband, she thought to herself, you are not the only one to plot.

For a moment, wistfully, she wished that Gregory could

be here with her. But that could not be, not tonight nor for many nights to come. He could help her with her battle, but in the end Catherine knew she would have to stand alone.

The alternative, for her, was unthinkable. She had no intention of spending the rest of her life in a nunnery. She shuddered, thinking of it, and pulled her robe closer about her shoulders. The convent, save for those who voluntarily entered it, was akin to being buried alive. She would rather be dead if it came to that.

For now, however, there was nothing she could do but wait.

In the grip of this somewhat fatalistic conclusion, Catherine turned and went inside. She had already dismissed the servant woman she had brought with her, and so she was completely alone. A rather unusual occurrence, yet she found the solitude comforting at this time.

After entering her bedchamber, Catherine removed her satin robe and crawled into bed, not bothering to close the French doors that led out onto the terrace. She liked to awaken to the sounds of the early dawn.

Settling herself between silken sheets, she stared up at the ceiling, her eye absently tracing the outline of the birds and flowers painted on its surface. Although the hour was late it was not dark, and in the soft glow of the white night the charming pastel colors seemed luminous.

Finally she turned on her side. Her thoughts drifted over the years, and for the first time in more than a decade she found herself thinking about Stettin. Probably the gray-stoned castle that used to be her home was now occupied by someone, but she had no idea who that might be. Her father had been dead many years. Her mother had died in Paris the year before in her lover's house. With Joanna's death, all ties to her past had been broken.

She didn't think that she had slept, but suddenly, with a sharp nudge of surprise, Catherine found herself looking up into the anxious and drawn face of Alexei Orlov, who was viewing her intently. She hadn't heard him enter the room. The jacket of his uniform was unbuttoned, appearing hastily donned. He wore no hat and his hair was as tousled as if he had just gotten out of bed.

'It's time,' he said simply and in a low voice.

Dazed, Catherine just stared up at him.

Alexei reached out a hand and gently touched her bare shoulder. 'Passek is under guard. We must move fast.'

'What is it you want me to do?' Catherine shook her head, trying to rid herself of the insidious clutch of sleep that fogged her brain.

'You must show yourself to the guards. They will be your strength.'

Momentarily confused and disoriented, Catherine raised her hand to brush aside the dark strands of hair from her forehead. 'Has something happened?' she asked, growing alarmed.

Alexei withdrew his hand and his mouth was hard as he replied. 'Yes. I'll explain everything once we're on our way. There's no time to lose. Gregory has already gone to the compound to alert the men.'

Then she was wide awake. She gave a curt nod and quickly got out of bed, giving no thought to her state of dishabille before the captain, who was not so preoccupied that he didn't notice how lovely she was. He envied his brother.

After walking behind a screen, Catherine began to dress in a hurried fashion, trying to focus her attention on the ordeal that lay ahead. She couldn't help thinking that everything was moving too fast. She'd had no time to plan. Mother of God, she thought worriedly, she didn't even know the number of her supporters.

Her breath coming more rapidly, Catherine slipped into a black velvet gown, its stark simplicity glaringly innocent of any adornment. Just as hurriedly as she had dressed, Catherine now ran a brush through her hair, allowing it to float loosely about her shoulders. Moments later she stood before Alexei, seeing his nod of approval.

In the carriage, Alexei quickly informed her of the recent events. Passek, that fool, he reported angrily, had had more than his share of vodka.

'He has betrayed us?' Catherine gasped, a hand to her throat.

'No, no.' Alexei shook his head. 'It was his insulting words against the tsar that caused his arrest. But that leaves little to the imagination. By now everyone knows there's a faction planning to set you on the throne.'

Alexei fell silent, not wishing to alarm her further. He snapped the reins sharply, prodding the horses to a faster pace. It had been more than two hours since Passek's arrest, time enough for word to have reached Peter. Knowing this, Alexei resisted the impulse to turn around, but his ears were alert for any sound of pursuit.

After the short exchange of words, they spoke no more. Catherine clung to the side of the rocking carriage as it sped through the miles to Ismailov. She was surprised at herself; she now felt resigned, almost detached. Ahead lay victory – or imprisonment and certain death. In spite of that she felt a lifting of her spirits, as if a great weight had been removed from her shoulders. Much better to act, she told herself firmly, than to sit and wait for fate to play the final card.

Just outside the military compound they came upon a lone figure, and with a cry of relief Catherine welcomed Gregory into the carriage. While Alexei had gone to fetch Catherine, Gregory had been busy alerting the regiments.

A short time later they entered Ismailov. In some astonishment, Catherine viewed the masses of men gathered in the yard. Despite their number, no sound broke the stillness.

The carriage rolled to a stop. Without hesitating, Catherine stepped out, suddenly confident and determined. About her, the silence was palpable.

Thousands of eyes were focused on the slim and beautiful young woman as she came slowly forward. The early dawn dusted her sable hair with a coronet of light and gave an alabaster glow to her smooth skin.

Catherine let her violet eyes scan the crowd of soldiers. She knew she must not falter, must display no lack of courage. They would accept her – or they would kill her.

Finally she paused in their midst. 'I come to you for sanctuary,' she said simply, extending her hands out to them.

The silence lasted only a moment longer, then erupted into an ear-shattering din as a roar emerged from them all.

'*Vivat!*' they yelled, shouting their hurrahs, and not a few wept for joy. The men, without exception, gazed at their beautiful tsarina with adoring eyes, each of them prepared to lay his life at her feet.

Captain Cyril Razumovsky stepped forward. With tears streaming down his cheeks, he bent on one knee before her, touching the hem of her simple black gown.

'You need only lead us, your Majesty,' he said in a voice choked with emotion. 'We will follow to our death, if need be.'

After getting to his feet, Razumovsky stepped aside as a priest approached Catherine. Raising the large silver crucifix, his face reflecting the same emotion as the men about him, he offered a solemn blessing.

Captain Razumovsky assisted Catherine back into the carriage, now driven by Gregory at a more sedate pace because the priest was walking in front of the horses. Behind them, the whole regiment fell into line, their step buoyant, their bearing proud.

Just outside of St. Petersburg they were hailed by the Semonovsky Guards, who joined their comrades with the same display of enthusiasm.

News of the coup spread like fire through dry tinder. By the time they actually entered the city a short while later, Nevsky Prospect was so crowded with cheering, shouting citizens that the carriage could move no faster than a crawl.

At the sight of the wildly ebullient citizenry, Catherine's earlier compusure began to give way to a muted excitement that heightened her color and gave a sparkle to her violet eyes. She felt the love of the people embrace her like the passionate arms of an ardent lover and gave herself up entirely to the feeling it generated within her.

His voice joining the cheers, Gregory drove directly to Kazan Cathedral. Standing in the doorway, crucifix in hand, the archbishop watched the approaching carriage with tears in his eyes, profoundly relieved that the sinful stains of encroaching Lutheranism would at last be halted.

Minutes later Catherine entered the cool dimness of the cathedral, which was oddly silent in view of the hundreds of people who were crammed within its sanctified walls. Outside the crowd no longer cheered. Even the bells were momentarily hushed.

With a slow and dignified step, her head held high, Catherine approached the jeweled inconostasis where the archbishop was waiting to receive her. By his side stood a crimson-robed priest holding a censer. Slowly the man swung the silver vessel back and forth, imbuing the air with the pungent smell of incense.

Catherine kept her eyes fixed straight ahead. Upon reaching the altar, she knelt before the archbishop and bowed her head.

To the side of the altar, Panin, with the child Paul held in his arms, watched Catherine with a passive face that belied the amazement and dismay that coursed through him. She was taking the crown not only from the head of her husband but from her son, as well. He thought of the rumors of the imprisoned Tsar Ivan. It was said that he was still alive. If that was true, he reflected dourly, then two tsars lived. And one tsarevich, a crown prince, whom he now held to his breast.

The archbishop's voice droned on, the only sound to break the unnatural stillness.

Panin heard the solemn words in the grip of a
desolation so great he felt bowed with the weight of the
disturbing sensation. He had known for weeks now that
such a coup could occur with a minimum of turmoil and
bloodshed. But he had misread one important facet of the
discontent that had been steadily building up ever since
Peter came to power. It wasn't the rightful successor that
the people wanted to take the place of their hated tsar; it
was the foreign woman who had so blinded them with her
charisma that they were all willing to overlook her origins!

Panin saw the archbishop anoint Catherine, then place
the crown upon her head. He thought: They are actually
doing it. They are actually crowning this German woman!
He clutched the tsarevich tighter and longed to speak out.
But as he glanced at the faces of the people about him,
Panin knew that he could not. They would tear any
dissenter limb from limb.

The sudden sound of the bells jolted him, and Panin
realized that it was over. Catherine was now Empress and
Autocrat of all Russia.

Still carrying the sleepy tsarevich in his arms, Panin
resignedly followed with the rest as they made their way
from the cathedral to the palace. The cheering noise,
combined with the bells, was deafening.

Once inside the palace, Catherine made her way to the
throne room. After seating herself on the ermine-draped
chair, she proceeded to acknowledge those members of
the court who stepped forward to swear their allegiance.
With a touch of cynicism, which she carefully concealed,
Catherine noted that the Vorontsovs were among the first
to take the oath.

By now Paul had awakened sufficiently to be set on his
feet where he stood wide-eyed, watching the unusual
proceedings. A few moments later he understood all he
needed to know.

Panin finally came forward. Bending a knee, he took the
oath along with the others. If his eyes held a hint of

condemnation, Catherine chose not to see it as she graciously acknowledged his declaration.

But Paul hung back. His brow furrowed, and his lips drew down as he studied his mother with angry eyes.

To the startled dismay of them all, the child stepped up to the dais. He was still in his nightclothes, his small feet shod in satin slippers, for upon learning of the coup, Panin had immediately roused the boy from bed in the desperate hope that the people would opt for their rightful crown prince.

Staring unblinkingly at the new empress, Paul said: 'Where is my father? Where is the tsar?'

Quickly Panin took hold of the child's hand, then regarded Catherine's pale face with a beseeching look. 'His Highness is weary, your Majesty, and all this must be confusing to him.'

But Paul, though only eight years old, was not confused. He wrenched his hand from his tutor's grip, his mouth set obstinately. He would, he thought to himself, remember this day. His mother would never have his allegiance.

Looking down into the face of her son, Catherine saw a cold, unrelenting hatred. Several emotions coursed through her as she viewed the boy in silence, but she drove them all from her mind. Not even her own son would mar this day, she decided, turning away from those accusing eyes.

She still had not spoken, and Panin, with a look at her face, hastily led the protesting tsarevich to the next room.

An hour later Catherine left the throne room to change her clothes. When she reappeared a short while later, she was wearing the uniform of the Preobrazhensky Guard. So proud was her bearing that another great cheer erupted from the onlookers when they caught sight of her.

'A long life to our Little Mother!'

'*Vivat!*'

As she left the palace and proceeded down to the

square, Panin, still clutching Paul's hand, went out onto the balcony. From this vantage point he could see Catherine as she mounted astride a white horse, sitting the animal as easily and as confidently as any soldier could hope to do.

The huge square was filled with troops, but now it was strangely quiet. In the midst of the reverent silence, the newly proclaimed empress solemnly led her horse in a great circle as she rode around her regiments.

At the sight of her actions a cold, thin smile stretched Panin's lips. He had always suspected that Catherine's interest in history was exaggerated. But he now saw that she had done her homework well. The act she was performing was as old as the cossacks and hussars. The meaning was clear, to him and to everyone witnessing it: She was publicly displaying her intent to take command.

With a feeling of urgency, Panin's eager eye searched the crowded square. Now would be the time for anyone to take exception. His ears strained, but the silence remained unbroken until Catherine returned to the point from which she had started. Then it was shattered as thousands upon thousands of voices were lifted in a tremendous roar of affirmation that rose even above the sound of the pealing bells.

'What does it all mean, Panin?' Paul Petrovich demanded of his tutor. Although he addressed the man standing beside him, Paul kept his eyes on the slim woman astride the horse.

Panin held the small hand tightly in his own. 'It means that your mother now rules Russia,' he replied simply, still viewing the scene below.

Tilting his head, Paul stared up at him, his bearing stiff and rigid and uncompromising. 'And what of the tsar? Where is he?'

Nikita Panin gazed somberly at the child, but he made no answer.

Twenty-Three

Nine miles away, in Oranienbaum, Peter was sleeping peacefully, his arms wrapped around Lizbeth's plump form.

When he finally awoke, Peter made no immediate move to get out of bed. Although the draperies were closed, a thin ribbon of sunshine angled sharply through a slight part in the center. It looked like a golden sword. A good omen, Peter thought, smiling now. Before the sun rose again, Catherine would be gone. He tried to imagine what her plain little face would look like when he told her he was sending her to a nunnery for the rest of her life. Oh, how he hoped she would beg him to change his mind.

'Beg all you want, you miserable slut,' he muttered under his breath so as not to awaken Lizbeth. 'I shall not relent.'

For yet a while longer, Peter lay there, savoring what promised to be the happiest day of his life. At last he turned over and nuzzled the fleshy neck of his still-slumbering mistress.

Lizbeth opened her eyes and gave a mighty yawn. Then she remembered what had taken place at the supper table the night before, and her eyes grew bright with anticipation. Catherine was to be packed off to a convent. Of course, the chancellor had once again tried to dissuade Peter; this time, however, the tsar had turned a deaf ear.

'You won't forget your promise?' Lizbeth asked, putting her arms around Peter's neck.

'No, no,' he assured with a chuckle. 'It shall be as I said: You will be at my side when I rid myself of my harlot wife.'

Lizbeth sighed contentedly. In the not too distant future she would be a tsarina.

Peter gently disengaged her arms from around his neck, then reached for the bell cord.

After a hearty breakfast they departed for Peterhof in the imperial carriage. Behind them, another carriage held Chancellor Vorontsov, Alexander Shuvalov, and General Munnich.

As they drew up to the front entrance, Peter took a deep breath of satisfaction. 'For years she has played me for a fool,' he said to Lizbeth. 'But today she will learn who is in command. Today she will learn of her fate.'

Peter was laughing joyously as they entered the palace. Inside the large foyer, Peter motioned to the nearest servant and issued a command that Catherine be brought to him immediately.

For a moment the man stared at his tsar with a blank expression.

'Fetch her!' Peter yelled, annoyed by the hesitation.

'Your – Your Majesty,' the man stammered, 'the tsarina is not here ...'

Garbed in his blue Holstein uniform, Peter glared fiercely at the cringing servants. 'She *is* here! She must be.' His voice rose to a shrill screech, but no one dared wince at the sound of it. 'We have commanded her to stay at Peterhof. She would not dare disobey.' Reaching out, he roughly grabbed the collar of the servant who was still standing in front of him, squeezing so tightly that the man's face turned a deep shade of crimson.

Thoroughly terrorized, the man could only stammer again that the tsarina was not at Peterhof.

To the side, Alexander Shuvalov exchanged sharp, worried glances with Chancellor Voronstov and General Von Munnich. As yet, however, their concern was no more than superficial.

'Lies! You are telling us lies,' Peter screamed. His eyes were no more than slits. 'She is here, and we will find her,' he declared. Motioning to the servants, he ordered them to follow him.

Upstairs, he went from room to room, his commands heated. He watched closely as servants probed wardrobes, crawled beneath beds, threw aside draperies.

Peter had not yet completed his search when a servant of Shuvalov's arrived from the city with the disquieting news of the events that had occurred only hours before. Both Shuvalov and Munnich proceeded to question the man closely, becoming more and more fearful as the tale unfolded.

Peter, however, was annoyed and angry. 'Ridiculous!' he bellowed at them all when he was told. 'And when we return to the city tomorrow, we will have them all shot. Catherine will be the first to receive that honor.'

Disbelieving, General Munnich faced his tsar, his mouth, behind his thick white beard, agape. 'When?' he asked, not certain that he had heard correctly. 'Your Majesty, you can't wait until tomorrow,' he cried out. His hands moved frantically as he clutched at Peter's sleeve. 'We must act now.' Foolish, he was thinking, to underestimate that woman. His hand fell away and he tried to speak in a calmer voice. 'From all accounts, your wife has usurped your throne.'

Frightened by the general's tone, Lizbeth put a trembling hand on Peter's arm. 'He's right,' she exclaimed. 'You cannot allow her to act in such manner.'

'Nor do I intend to,' Peter replied blithely, patting her hand. Then he smiled broadly, remembering the golden sword of sunshine. A good omen, indeed. Now no one would condemn him for doing away with Catherine. The silly fool had played right into his hands. It was no longer necessary to send her to a convent. For this he would send her to her death! The idea so pleased him that he laughed out loud, causing Shuvalov and Munnich to eye him with despair.

For the rest of that day, ignoring the urgings of his chancellor, Peter refused to leave Peterhof.

'We have planned a day's hunting and see no cause to have it interrupted,' he announced, leaving little room for argument in his tone. Time enough, he thought, to deal with his harlot wife. He would give her all the rope she needed to hang herself.

As the group rode away in the direction of the wooded area not too far distant, General Munnich watched moodily from the window. Beside him, Alexander Shuvalov fidgeted nervously. Seated in a chair, Vorontsov seemed stunned.

With a sigh, Munnich turned toward Shuvalov, whose expression was as grim as his own. 'Can it be, Shuvalov, that all the people, all the army, all the imperial guards have betrayed their sovereign?' He gave his companion an earnest, imploring look, wishing with all his heart that Shuvalov would contradict him.

But the man turned away.

Feeling the need to act, Munnich took it upon himself to dispatch one of his own servants to the city. 'Return swiftly,' he commanded. 'Tell me of all you see and hear.'

Then the general sat down to wait. There was nothing else he could do.

Shuvalov paced about, restless and worried, his gaunt face growing more taut and sharp with each passing minute. He didn't need to be told what Catherine was like. Damn it, he thought savagely, why couldn't she have been an ordinary wench like the Vorontsova?

The hours passed, and his worry grew. Perhaps, he thought uneasily, noting the passing time, he should go to St. Petersburg and declare himself before it was too late. If Catherine had indeed played out a successful coup, then he would have to face her sooner or later.

Finally, clearing his throat, he regarded the general and then Vorontsov, who was still slumped in a chair.

'I think it would be a good idea for me to go to Petersburg,' he announced, ignoring the old general's knowing, cynical glance. Before he received any argument, Shuvalov hastily called for his horse and rode off at top speed toward the city.

Munnich made no move to stop him. His own loyalties were firm, and he had no intention of disgracing himself by deserting his tsar.

Peter and Lizbeth returned in time for the evening meal. Searching the tsar's face with great care, Munnich was astonished to see that little, if any, concern traced the disfigured features. The tsar was in a jovial mood as he sat down to eat.

Before the meal had ended Munnich's servant returned. The army, the imperial guard, even the people themselves had taken the oath for Catherine, he reported gravely.

Vorontsov got up out of his chair so quickly, it toppled over. 'Surely not all regiments,' he cried out, unable to believe what he was hearing. A monstrous joke! It had to be a monstrous joke!

The servant nodded. 'All,' he confirmed.

A first twinge of alarm shot through Peter. He fell silent, his appetite suddenly gone.

'There is still the navy,' Munnich mused, unwilling to admit defeat. 'With them and the Holsteiners you have at Oranienbaum we still have a chance. From Oranienbaum we can sail to Kronstadt in less than an hour.'

Peter shook his head. He felt as if he had been set adrift in a sea of doubt.

'The general is right, Peter,' Lizbeth cried out in a pleading voice, by now thoroughly frightened. 'We have perhaps delayed too long as it is. This must go no further. Once you show yourself, they will all remember who is their sovereign.' With the exception of Peter, Lizbeth, more than any of them, knew the tsarina's strength. Her fear began to melt into a terror that made her legs wobble.

'No, no ... she will listen to reason.' Peter jumped up

and grabbed Chancellor Vorontsov's arm. 'Return to the
city. Go to see Catherine. Tell her –' He began to sob, and
wavered on his feet as if he were about to fall down in a
faint. A servant rushed forward with a glass of wine, and
Peter drank it down before he again spoke. 'Tell her,' he
went on, 'that we will share the crown, as God intended
we should. I will not stand in her way ...'

The chancellor shuddered. If all this was true, he could
be relieved of his head for speaking such words.

'Go!' Peter shouted, appearing to lose control of himself.
He was shaking now and had to grasp the back of a chair
to steady himself.

Vorontsov only nodded as he backed toward the door,
alarmed by the tsar's crazed look.

It was almost four o'clock in the morning when the
chancellor arrived in St. Petersburg, and another hour
passed before he was able to gain audience with
Catherine, who had not been to bed yet.

Approaching the chair in which she was seated,
Vorontsov bowed low. The audience chamber was
crowded, despite the early hour. With his appearance, a
hush had fallen.

Voronstov cleared his throat. 'Your Majesty, I am here
by order of the tsar ...' He fell silent as she narrowed her
eyes.

'Who?'

The chancellor began to tremble and an irritating thread
of perspiration wended its way down his spine. 'Your ...
husband.' He wet his lips, aware that everyone in the
room – not a few of whom were his own kinsmen – was
staring at him. 'He feels it should be of great benefit to all
concerned if he were to ... share his crown with you.'

For a long, uneasy moment there was a deadly silence.

Suddenly, throwing her head back, Catherine began to
laugh. In only seconds the chamber echoed with the
sound as, one by one, everyone joined in. When their
Sovereign Majesty laughed, so did they.

Terrified now, Vorontsov fell to his knees and bowed his head until his forehead rested on the cool tile. Though he doubted it could be heard above the continual sounds of merriment, he fervently swore his allegiance.

At Peterhof, Munnich was growing more and more dismayed with each passing hour.

'Vorontsov should have been back by now,' he finally said to Peter. 'We cannot wait any longer.'

Peter was sitting in a chair, looking dazed. On a divan, Lizbeth was stretched out, fast asleep.

'Please, your Majesty,' Munnich pressed, alarmed by the hesitancy he was seeing. 'We must leave right now. The chancellor is not coming back. It would be foolhardly to wait any longer.' His voice had risen, and Lizbeth, awake now, sat up.

Peter looked at the general for a long moment, still wavering with uncertainty. In the back of his mind he knew that not once had he ever faced his wife in a dispute and won. He sighed, and the sound poured forth like a sob. 'Very well,' he said at last, but his voice was weak and without conviction. 'Ready the horses. We'll ride to Oranienbaum.'

Less than two hours later Peter stood at the prow of the imperial yacht, straining his eyes for the towers of Kronstadt, only a few miles distant.

At last they approached the channel, but despite the fact that the colors were raised high, the bridge remained down, barring their way.

In a hoarse voice, Peter shouted to the guard. 'Clear the way! It is your tsar who commands you.'

After only a short silence, the gruff voice of the guard came clear: 'There is no tsar. I take orders only from my empress!'

'We will have you shot,' Peter screamed at him.

'Move away or we will send your vessel to the bottom of the sea!'

Panicky now, Peter backed away and almost stumbled

down the narrow steps to the cabin where he collapsed in Lizbeth's arms.

Munnich was on deck when the yacht pulled up to the wooden pier at Oranienbaum. A surge of hope flared as he saw the imperial guards. Surely they had come to save the tsar!

Before the boat had been secured, however, Munnich realized he'd made a grave error. Turning, he viewed Peter and Lizbeth, who had both come to stand at his side.

Peter was staring at his Holsteiners, the small army of men he had brought here from his homeland. Disarmed, they were sitting on the grass in utter dejection, not a few of them sporting ugly bruises from their brief encounter with the imperial regiments.

'You and the Vorontsova are to come with me.'

Startled, Peter turned to look at Captain Alexei Orlov, who had boarded the vessel with two armed guards.

'Peter!' Lizbeth wailed.

Peter gripped her trembling hand in his own but had no reassuring words to offer. Once again Catherine had bested him. With a slow step, he followed Alexei as they made their way ashore.

Russian guards were everywhere, their bearded faces looking fierce and triumphant at the same time. There was a proud and arrogant bearing to their step that had long been missing. With contemptuous eyes they scrutinized the blue uniform Peter was wearing, remembering the sight of their empress dressed in the uniform of the Preobrazhensky Guard. Bitter and condemning murmurs erupted from them, wafting across the breeze like muted thunder announcing the approach of a summer storm.

His pale eyes darting frantically about the sun-drenched yard, Peter seemed to shrivel as his whole body slumped. Strangely, now that he was confronted with the inevitable, fear seemed to lessen, leaving only resignation in its wake. For a brief time he had been free, had toyed with power and found it to be as satisfying as a high blaze on a cold winter's night. Now there was nothing left but ashes.

Alighting from the yacht, Munnich just stood on the wooden pier in helpless despair, watching as Peter and Lizbeth headed for the palace under Alexei Orlov's granite stare.

When they reached the front door, Lizbeth was taken away by a guard. Orlov then escorted Peter into the drawing room, where Count Panin was waiting for him.

'It is my duty to inform you, sir,' Count Panin recited in a flat, unemotional voice, 'that you are a prisoner of her Majesty, the Empress Catherine II.' Dressed in a brown velvet jacket over a white lace shirt, loose trousers tucked into soft leather boots, Panin was emotionless as he viewed the man in the hated blue uniform who stood before the desk looking like a puppet that had lost its strings.

Peter turned ashen. His pale lips quivered with the sob that could not be held back. Even though the words had been expected, they echoed with a frightening finality that tied Peter's stomach in knots.

'What are you going to do with me?' he whimpered from a throat that felt dry and parched. He swallowed as if it pained him to do so.

'You will be taken to Ropsha,' Panin stated in the same flat voice. Although he spoke without rancor, he felt no pity for the broken man before him. He blamed Peter for the fate of the tsarevich. Paul would never wear the crown that was rightfully his until Catherine died, if then. Paul was still a crown prince, but he could be shunted aside any time Catherine took a mind to alter the succession. And Panin knew better than anyone that the relationship between Paul and his mother was not good.

Peter sighed, relaxing a bit. The country residence mentioned by Panin was comfortable enough. 'Lizbeth ...' he began, but Panin shook his head firmly.

'She will not be allowed to accompany you.' He drew forth an official-looking document from the top drawer.

Motioning for Peter to come closer, he laid it on the desk. Then he picked up a quill and extended it to Peter, who took it in numb fingers.

Only a glance told Peter that he was looking at an act of abdication. Trembling visibly, he affixed his signature to it without comment, dropping the quill beside it when he was through.

Panin now rose and came around the desk. Without speaking, he relieved Peter of his sword and placed the weapon on the desk.

'Will I be allowed to stay at Ropsha?' Peter inquired in a pleading voice, making no effort to resist as Panin proceeded to remove the many decorations from his blue jacket.

Panin answered with a short nod, not finding it necessary to inform him that he would eventually be sent to Schlüsselburg.

A desperate gleam came into Peter's pale eyes. 'What will happen to Lizbeth?' He clutched at Panin's lapels, and the count took a step back, frowning.

'She's being returned to the house of her father. She will not be harmed. The Vorontsovs have already taken the oath for the empress.' He saw the bitter expression that settled upon the fallen tsar's disfigured face, but he made no response to it.

Twenty-Four

The next few days sped by. Catherine made certain that the initial changes she made served to endear her further to her subjects. Everything that Peter had done to anger them, she now reversed. On the day the Holsteiners were sent home the citizenry turned out en masse, jeering and ridiculing the departing soldiers. Churchmen breathed sighs of relief and held special masses when the empress removed the hated regulations imposed by Peter. Bestuzhev was summoned home and all his confiscated estates and wealth returned to him. And a baby boy by the name of Alexis Gregorovich Bobrinsky was returned to the palace and installed in the royal nursery.

But the week was not yet over when a courier, breathless from his labored ride, delivered a sealed message from Ropsha.

Catherine was in her sitting room. Dressed in a morning gown of blue silk worked with gold thread, she had just completed a light breakfast of fruit and tea when she received the letter. After breaking the seal, she read it slowly. As the meaning of the words sunk in, the paper began to flutter and blur in her trembling hand.

Peter was dead!

Sitting as if she were frozen in her chair, Catherine read the shakily penned confession of Alexei Orlov, who admitted having committed the act in a fit of anger.

From across the room where she was refilling the china cup with tea from the large copper samovar on the

253

sideboard, Anya glanced at her mistress, alarmed by the sudden pallor she was seeing.

After getting up, Catherine began to pace nervously back and forth, hands clasped tightly at her waist, pondering her alternatives to this unexpected turn of events.

If the confession became public knowledge, Alexei would not only have to stand trial for murder, he would most assuredly be convicted and executed. How could she let that happen after all he had done for her?

She halted abruptly at an even more horrifying thought. Blessed Jesus, there would even be those who would think that she had ordered it done!

At last she ceased her aimless prowling and stared at Anya, who was still standing by the sideboard, cup in hand.

'Send for Count Panin,' Catherine instructed in a tight voice. 'We wish to see him immediately.' She observed her ladies. 'Leave us,' she commanded.

Her decision having been made, Catherine walked hurriedly to her writing table in the study. With a key, she unlocked the bottom drawer. Then, pursing her lips in thought, she rose and went to her dressing table in the next room. After picking up a small jeweled casket, she carelessly dumped the gems inside it onto the top of the table, then returned to her desk.

Her hand trembled slightly as she folded Alexei's letter and stuffed it into the casket. Then she closed the cover. She turned the little key on the outside, which she then removed. After placing the jeweled receptacle in the bottom drawer, she then locked that, too.

She had just time enough to safely hide the keys when Panin was announced. When she turned to face him, her manner was serene and composed.

'You sent for me, your Majesty?' Panin murmured, coming toward her.

Catherine nodded briefly, not inviting him to be seated.

'We have just received word that Peter Feodorovich died only hours ago.'

Panin's usual benign expression deserted him. His face, above a frothy white lace jabot, was a study in startled confusion. 'Died?' he repeated in a voice that matched his expression.

Catherine sat very still, her violet eyes never leaving Panin's round face, her tranquil composure never betraying the lie she spoke. 'The death was a natural one,' she stated quietly. 'He suffered an acute attack of colic that proved fatal.'

Panin continued to stare at her, his thoughts racing every which way as he tried to digest the unexpected news he had just been fed.

Without waiting for him to speak, Catherine went on. 'We wish for you to prepare a formal announcement to this effect, after which you will make suitable arrangements for the funeral.' She continued to regard him with a level look that gave no indication of her taut nerves.

Panin inclined his head, trying to gather his wits. Colic! he was thinking. Whatever Peter had died of, he would wager all he owned that it was nothing as prosaic as an attack of colic.

Finally, into the void of silence that had descended, Panin moistened his lips. 'How ... do you wish him dressed, your Majesty?' he asked.

Catherine's face held no smile as she replied. 'Dress him in the blue uniform of Holstein.'

As Panin made his way to the door, Catherine's voice again reached him. He paused, hand on the knob.

'I trust you will also inform the boy,' she said slowly, 'in as gentle a manner as is possible. He was, I know, fond of his ... father.'

Murmuring an appropriate reply, Panin bowed.

Alone again, Catherine stared at the closed door and issued a weary sigh. She tried to summon up some feeling for the man who had been her husband for more than seventeen years. But there was nothing. Their relationship had been a travesty from the start. Looking back, Catherine realized that they had both been only children when they had been thrust into the marriage bed.

Still, she had eventually grown and matured while Peter ... She shook her head and sighed again. No, there was nothing.

The week before the official coronation was to take place, Count Panin assisted the empress in a myriad of administrative details. Among these was the problem of the imprisoned Ivan.

They were in a small room that Catherine planned to use as a study and office because of its close proximity to her own bedchamber. She had risen every morning at five o'clock to begin work, and she planned to continue this routine.

Leaning back in her chair, she regarded Panin with a solemn expression. This was one problem that seemed to have no end.

'I've made inquiry, your Majesty,' Panin was saying. 'The ... young man is in excellent health, despite his lengthy confinement.'

Catherine eyed him wearily. 'Are you suggesting that we alter that state?'

'No, madame,' Count Panin replied hastily. 'It's just that ...' He fell silent a moment. Actually he was thinking about Paul. Alive, that wretched young man in Schlüsselburg would continue to be a threat to anyone who reigned. 'You understand, madame,' he went on carefully, 'that he will be a definite asset to anyone who may think to ... challenge your position.'

Catherine sighed deeply. 'Still ...'

Panin raised his brows and regarded her thoughtfully. 'Something must be done, your Majesty, for your own protection.' And that of Paul's, he added to himself silently.

'We will not have him killed,' Catherine stated firmly. 'This situation has existed for twenty years; there's no reason to suppose that it cannot continue for another twenty years.' She looked closely at Panin, curiosity getting the better of her. 'You said you have made inquiry?'

'I ... have seen him, your Majesty. He wasn't aware of who I was, of course,' he added quickly.

'You said you found him in good health. What of the state of his mind?'

Again, as he had been often in these past weeks, Panin was struck by the astuteness of the empress. She had, in a sense, gotten down to the one vital issue. Asset though he might be, no one would be stupid enough to release a witless man and put a crown on his head.

'That is difficult to answer,' he replied at last. 'One minute he seems sane, aware. The next' – he shook his head, – 'he shouts gibberish.'

Catherine looked away, her fingers drumming absently on the arm of her chair. Finally she turned to Panin again. 'If you have any suggestions,' she said quietly, 'we will listen.'

'In view of the fact that he will be allowed to live, there is only one thing to do,' he replied, fumbling within the pocket of his jacket. He brought forth a folded parchment and laid it before her. 'I've taken the liberty of drafting a *ukaze* for your Majesty's signature.'

She took hold of the document and unfolded it, but did not immediately read it. 'Does he know who he is?' she asked.

Panin cleared his throat. 'I believe he does, madame.' At her questioning look, he nodded. 'I admit I was amazed by his awareness. He was not yet three when he was confined. No one was supposed to converse with the child. But I suspect that, over the years, that's exactly what happened.'

She was silent a moment, then observed: 'Perhaps he has been given books.'

But Panin shook his head. 'He cannot read. I myself have tested him for that. There are neither books nor writing materials in his cell. There is, in fact, little of anything.'

Catherine winced, repressing a shudder. 'How can he have lived all these years and never fallen ill?'

'If he has any sickness, I saw no signs of it. His skin is clear and unblemished. He's apparently been well fed,' he added.

Catherine took a deep breath. Conscious that she was still holding the document, she studied it with care. When she was through reading it, she read it again. It was blunt and to the point: If anyone made an attempt to release him, Ivan was to be executed immediately by his guards. She glanced at Panin. 'What of his guards?'

'There are four, madame. They've been on duty for a number of years and are entirely dependable. They're very well paid.' Seeing her hesitation, Panin continued in an earnest manner. 'It was, I regret to say, madame, very easy for me to gain access to his cell. Had I been there for another purpose ...' He gestured and fell silent.

For long minutes, Catherine sat motionless. Then she viewed Panin. 'Summon my carriage. You will accompany me to Kexholm.'

Panin hesitated, not liking the idea, but having no way to deter her. Due to the fact that Peter would have soon made his home there, Ivan had been moved from Schlüsselburg recently and imprisoned in the fortress of Kexholm. Two tsars incarcerated in the same prison would have been foolhardy, to say the least.

Getting slowly to his feet, Panin instructed a servant to ready the imperial carriage.

A while later they arrived at the gray-stoned fortress of Kexholm. The guard who opened the door fell to his knees at the sight of Catherine, who motioned impatiently for him to rise.

In a low voice, Panin instructed the man to take them to Ivan's cell. After reaching up, the guard removed one of the torches from a wall sconce, then proceeded down the corridor. At the very end was a staircase that led to the lower level. The walls were damp and slippery with mold. Catherine drew her cloak closer about her.

Finally the guard halted. He handed Panin the torch. Then, using both hands, he raised the heavy bolt that was affixed to the outside of the door, after which he produced a key from his pocket and unlocked it.

As the iron door swung out, Panin hastily stepped in front of Catherine in order to shield her.

'Please, madame. Take care.' He held the torch high so that it threw some of its light into the cell.

Catherine stepped forward only far enough to cross the threshold. There were no chairs or tables, only a straw mattress flung carelessly in a corner. The one small window set high in the wall was barred, its panes painted so that not even a ray of sunshine could penetrate.

In some curiosity, Catherine viewed the sole inhabitant of the cell. His clothes were tattered and hung in dirty, ragged ribbons about his thin frame. He was walking in circles, his bare feet sliding with a whispering sound over the stone floor. For several minutes Catherine watched as the young man shuffled round and round. She knew he was twenty-two, but she could have been looking at an old man. His beard was unkempt. His hair was long and just as tattered as his clothing.

Abruptly he paused and stared at Catherine as if he had never in his life seen a woman. A wild look came into his eyes. Raising his arm, he pointed a finger at her.

'Kneel!' he screamed. 'Kneel before your tsar!'

Catherine gasped and took a step back. The young man began to shout at her, unintelligible words from which she could glean no meaning.

Quickly Panin ushered her out into the corridor again. 'Lock it!' he ordered, motioning to the guard.

Catherine was shaken but in control of herself when they reached her study once more. The young man she had just seen was the nephew of Peter the Great, the son of that great tsar's brother. His claim to the throne was strong – certainly stronger than her own, considering the fact that she had not even been born in this country.

The thought produced an unwelcome jolt of fear that left her feeling weak. 'The people ...' she managed at last. 'Are they aware of his existence?'

Panin offered a solemn nod of affirmation. 'A thing like this cannot be kept secret indefinitely, madame. They call him Ivanushka.' He sighed. 'No doubt they think of him as a romantic figure.'

Catherine made a face. The man she had seen could be termed many things, including tragic; but romantic, never. She rubbed her forehead with her fingertips. Good God, she thought, feeling chilled. Here was a greater menace to her than Peter had ever been. Mad or not, Ivan was a prince of the royal blood – a prince who had been officially named successor!

'You were right,' she said to Panin. 'Incredible as it seems, he does know who he is.' Her mouth compressed into a thin, hard line. She must allow no loose ends. She could not afford to have her position challenged now or at a later date. She reached for the quill and hurriedly affixed her signature to the document Panin had prepared, after which she returned it to him without comment.

He took the *ukaze*, pocketed it, then regarded Catherine thoughtfully. 'There is one other matter, your Majesty ...' He fell silent and coughed delicately.

Catherine waited a moment, but saw that her newly appointed minister was hestitant. 'Speak as you will,' she said quietly.

He shifted uneasily. 'There have been rumors that perhaps your Majesty might be considering marriage. One involving your ... lord chamberlain.' His normal aplomb deserted him as Panin groped for the proper words. He credited the new high lord chamberlain, Gregory Orlov, with the brains of a rutting bull.

Catherine's face was expressionless as she inquired: 'And you would not approve?'

Panin flushed deeply and raised a hand. 'Whatever your Majesty does has my approval,' he stated quickly and emphatically, then continued slowly, as if he weighed each word. 'That is not to say that I would advise such a step,' he added cautiously, still feeling uncomfortable.

Catherine wasn't at all surprised to hear of these rumors, for Gregory himself had been pressuring her in that direction. That she loved him, she could not deny. But she was no longer a foolish young girl in the throes of her first passion.

Catherine straightened in her chair, and the core of implacability, born so long ago, hardened about her heart. Her emotions must never again rule practicality.

'You may lay the rumors to rest, Panin,' she stated at last in a brisk tone. 'We have no intention of marrying, now or in the future. Now we suggest that you busy yourself with the preparations for our coming coronation.'

Visibly relieved, her minister rose, bowed, and went to carry out his instructions.

It was on the thirteenth day of September in the year 1762 that the former German princess made her state entry into the imperial city to be welcomed by the Muscovites, whose support she so dearly desired. Here, in the ancient and revered city of Moscow, the people cheered and wept, as they had in St. Petersburg, as she made her way through the streets to Uspensky Cathedral, situated in the heart of the Kremlin.

Catherine had seen larger cathedrals, but none more magnificent. Upon her entrance she gazed with shining eyes at the high altar and caught her breath at the sight of the jeweled medieval cross that had been brought here from Constantinople more than a hundred years ago.

During the lengthy ceremony, culminated by her anointment at the hands of the Metropolitan of Novgorod, Catherine prayed to be worthy of the task she had set for herself. She would always listen to advice, she promised herself, but she would rule alone. And she would do it well, she vowed as she knelt on the crimson cushions.

When she at last got to her feet, feeling the weight of the jeweled crown on her dark curls, Catherine raised her head and listened with equal satisfaction to the cheers of her subjects and the joyous pealing of the bells.

After a week of festivities, she returned to St. Petersburg.

The very next morning, Empress Catherine II faced her Senate. The men were standing around the large oval table, eyeing her with awed respect.

She paused for a moment, regarding each of the men in turn. Then she sat down at the head of the table. When she spoke her voice rang with a clear authority that was not to be questioned.

'Gentlemen,' she said. 'Let us begin.'

Epilogue

Catherine II, known to history as the Great, ruled Russia until her death on November 6, 1796.

A devotee of the Enlightenment, Catherine continued with the westernization of her empire, first begun by Peter the Great. Even though borders were augmented and territories gained during her rule, the institution of serfdom was also expanded, due to her practice of rewarding her nobles.

Catherine had no sooner been proclaimed empress when the first of five rebels claiming to be her husband, Tsar Peter, appeared on her distant horizons. Of these, Emelian Pugachev posed the greatest threat.

Pugachev, though a simple cossack, had been gifted with a persuasive tongue that would have done credit to Rasputin. As time passed, he had managed to gather an army, a motley crew of escaped serfs, fellow cossacks, and brigands. His credo was simple: Freedom! Beginning in the Urals and spreading out across the land like some self-proclaimed liberator, Pugachev's army eventually swelled to a horde that for three years ravaged and raped everyone in their path; even children did not escape the slaughter, but were savagely cut down without mercy.

When he was at last captured in 1775, Pugachev was brought to St. Petersburg for execution. Though many, including her son Paul, demanded the traitor's death for the Pretender, Catherine, never deliberately cruel or sadistic, ordered that he die by beheading. The traitor's death, being quartered, then decapitated, was one that Catherine had abolished.

The tragic young tsar Ivan VI, who had been imprisoned by Empress Elizabeth while still a child, lived out his shadowy existence in Schlüsselburg until July 1764. On the night of the fourth, what Panin had feared might take place occurred. A man named Basil Mirovich, a disillusioned lieutenant who had visions of furthering his fortunes, sought to effect the release of Prisoner Number One. Faithful to their instructions, Ivan's guards assassinated their captive before Mirovich could enter the cell. Mirovich was beheaded for instigating the failed coup d'etat.

The animosity, pronounced even early on, between Catherine and her son, Paul Petrovich, grew more so with each passing year. Deprived of her children during their formative years, Catherine gave vent to her maternal feeling by lavishing all her love and attention on her grandchildren. Ironically, she removed her first two grandsons from the care of their parents in much the same manner as Empress Elizabeth had spirited away her own two children.

Much has been said about Catherine's sensual exploits during her reign, but it would be a mistake to describe her as a woman mired in vice. A tireless worker and a prodigious letter-writer, it was Catherine's lust for life that was insatiable. Whether it was politics, art, or love, she desired to drain the cup, savoring everything life had to offer.

Gregory Orlov continued as Catherine's favorite for ten years, though during the last two years of this association Catherine began to display a noticeable waning of interest. Despite his physical attributes, Orlov was never on an intellectual level with Catherine. Although he made a valiant effort to share her interest in the arts, and even tried to offer political advice, Orlov failed in both these endeavors.

As Catherine became more and more involved in politics, in the war with Turkey, and in the expansion of her empire, Gregory became more and more of an encumbrance. At last she had to send him away.

In 1783 Gregory Orlov died, having sunk into madness. Panin, who remained loyal to Catherine all his life, also died in that same year.

Orlov's place was taken for a time by an insipid young man named Alexander Vassilchikov, whose fawning docility soon bored the empress. Catherine needed a strong man, one who could in effect be her right arm. She found him in Grigory Potemkin.

At first glance, Potemkin would seem to be an odd choice for a new favorite. At thirty-five, he was a giant of a man, with swarthy skin and only one good eye, which occasioned his detractors to refer to him as the cyclops. One day, having heard Potemkin express his admiration for the empress in very warm terms, Alexei Orlov took violent exception and provoked the fight that caused Potemkin to lose an eye. Potemkin was a forceful, dynamic man, something of a mystic, given to bouts of melancholy. He was, and had been for years, desperately in love with his empress. Acutely aware of her ongoing affair with Gregory Orlov, Potemkin suffered the torments of unrequited love, going so far as to once consider becoming a monk.

Catherine summoned this passionate, intense man to court in 1774, having long been aware of his devotion. When he arrived, Potemkin found Vassilchikov still very much in evidence. In despair, he actually did retire to a monastery. If he could not have the woman he wanted, he would have no other.

Suitably impressed by the sincerity of his feelings, Catherine recalled Potemkin to court and installed him as her new favorite.

At last Catherine had found a man equal to her in both a physical and mental capacity. That she grew to love him as passionately as he loved her there is no doubt. And as with most relations of this sort, jealousy reared its ugly head time and again. If Catherine so much as looked at another man, Potemkin would fly into a rage. The empress, for the moment submerged beneath the woman, would pacify and reassure her darling Grisha, as she called him.

In time, Potemkin's position at court was second only to that of the empress. The physical passion between them was so intense, however, that perhaps it is not surprising that after two years it burned itself out.

It has been said that Catherine was so enamoured of Potemkin that she secretly married him. No hard evidence – no legal document – has surfaced to substantiate this; yet in her letters Catherine did address him as 'my dearest husband.'

Be that as it may, the time did come when Potemkin took leave of her bed – though not her heart, and most certainly not her mind. Catherine now did something she had never done before: She began to discuss matters of state and even foreign policy with him. And she came more and more to rely on his advice, particularly in her territorial expansionist policy.

Now began an even more curious relationship between these two impassioned people.

It was Potemkin who chose his own successor, insofar as warming the empress's bed was concerned. Catherine was pleased with the choice, a young Ukrainian named Peter Zavadovsky.

When it became apparent that the empress had a new lover, the court reasoned that Potemkin was out of favor. He was not. When Potemkin decided that Zavadovsky had spent enough time in his post of 'aide-de-camp,' he promptly selected another. Then another.

These men, some of whom were young enough to be Catherine's grandsons, were first 'tested' by one of two countesses. Subsequently these trusted ladies reported to the empress on their sexual abilities. If the reports were satisfactory, Catherine would then admit the young man to her bed.

This situation continued until 1789 when a twenty-two-year-old lieutenant of the Guard named Plato Zubov appeared on the scene. Ambitious and incredibly handsome, Plato deliberately set out to convince the empress that he had fallen in love with her. One might have supposed that at sixty years of age, Catherine would have been skeptical. But Plato was a seducer par excellence. Before too long a time had passed, Catherine fell in love with her new aide-de-camp.

When the time came for Potemkin to make a change – something he did at roughly two-year intervals – Catherine flatly refused to give up her beloved Plato.

In desperation, Potemkin set about preparing a banquet at his residence, the Tauris Palace, the likes of which had never before been seen. Potemkin's only thought was to impress Catherine, to win back her love. And he went about it on a grand scale. Everything had to be perfect, and he began with the lighting of his extravaganza. Having purchased every candle in St. Petersburg, Potemkin decided that would not be enough. He sent to Moscow for more. No expense was spared.

Tropical plants, imported by the thousands, were placed at intervals along the marble walls of the Tauris Palace. There were plays, ballets, and fireworks. In the garden was a newly constructed temple. In it was housed a marble statue of Catherine. Every flower had been transformed into a glittering splendor never contemplated by nature. Each lush blossom held a precious gem that had been carefully placed in its center.

As intended, Catherine was dazzled. But the magnificent display did not change her mind. Plato was to stay.

Defeated, Potemkin retired from court to indulge himself in a round of debauchery that led to his death five months later.

Upon hearing the news, Catherine collapsed and was for weeks in the grip of a shattering grief. Zubov remained close to her side, and Catherine was more than ever convinced that the handsome young man was the great love of her life.

Potemkin was not the only man who remained faithful to Catherine under trying circumstances.

With the backing of Frederick of Prussia, Catherine installed her former lover, Stanislaus Poniatowski, on the throne of Poland.

Stanis, however, while well intentioned, proved to be too indecisive to be a strong ruler. As a price for his weakness, he was forced to witness the partitioning of his country in 1772. Twenty-five percent of Poland was divided between Prussia, Austria, and Russia. In 1793 yet another partition of Poland occurred. This time two-thirds of the remaining area was seized and once again divided between those three countries. These acquired territories greatly added to Catherine's domain. (Yet a third partition was in progress at the time of Catherine's demise. The result was the virtual abolishment of the state of Poland, which then came under foreign rule for more than a century.)

Through it all, incredibly, Stanis remained loyal to the empress, still in the grip of a love for her that seemed without end.

Being unable to come to terms with the fact that Gregory Orlov was Catherine's lover, the fiery princess Katrina Dashkova fled to Paris soon after Catherine was proclaimed empress, where she lived in self-imposed exile until 1783. Upon her return, Catherine gave her a job to do. She appointed Katrina Director of the Academy, the first Russian woman to hold that post. Katrina settled down to work, taking upon herself the monumental task of overseeing the first dictionary of the Russian langauge.

Alexis Bobrinsky was eventually made a count. When he completed his education he took the Grand Tour, then settled in Paris, where he lived with his wife and family for many years. He did not return to Russia until after Catherine's death.

Meanwhile, Paul Petrovich grew more and more unstable. Married in 1773 to Natalia Alexeievna, the former Wilhelmina of Hesse-Darmstadt, Paul at last found someone to love. Natalia, however, was not of a like mind. Before the year was gone, she had taken as a lover one of Paul's own equerries, Andrei Razumovsky, a situation of which Paul remained blissfully ignorant. It was not until her death during childbirth three years later that Paul discovered the liaison. Even then he might not have, had Catherine not had the grand duchess's papers collected and brought to her upon the latter's death. Among the papers were a series of love letters that Natalia had imprudently saved. Anxious for Paul to remarry quickly so that he could produce the grandchildren she so desperately wanted, Catherine gave the letters to him, whose grief was overshadowed by rage at being so deceived by the only human being he had ever loved.

The ploy worked, and five months later Paul married another German princess, this time Sophia of Württemberg, who became Grand Duchess Maria Feodorovna. This union produced ten children, the eldest of whom was destined to become Tsar Alexander I.

Catherine saw to it that Paul was excluded from state affairs and policies, and all of Europe was aware of the break between mother and son. Part of the problem was that Paul idolized his father, Peter III, and was convinced that his mother was responsible for his murder. As time went on, Paul began to emulate his father, preferring military uniforms to court attire and displaying a marked preference for all things Prussian.

With Paul's full maturity, Catherine began to have the disconcerting feeling that she was once again in the presence of her detested husband. For years Catherine had tried to convince herself that Paul's resemblance to

Peter was mere imitation. Now, viewing the adult man, she knew that was not so. She had not, as she had once thought, ended the Romanov dynasty; she had only perpetuated it. She decided to put some distance between them. Catherine deeded the lovely estate of Gatchina, which originally belonged to Gregory Orlov, to her son. Within a year Paul had transformed it into a dismal military establishment where, like Peter before him, he paraded and berated his soldiers by the hour.

Horrified at the thought that her son would destroy everything she had worked for and would attempt to turn the whole country into an armed camp when the time came, Catherine sought to change the succession in favor of her eldest grandson, Alexander. At first, this effort took the form of trying to convince Paul to abdicate. Catherine fully realized that to bypass the heir was to invite bloodshed. Paul, however, was adamant in his resistance.

Paul had long suspected that his mother was of a mind to place the crown on Alexander's head. After all, his reasoning went, she had ousted his father, torn the crown from his head, and murdered him! What would stop her from doing the same thing to her son?

Paul's hatred grew in proportion to his fear. His mental state became such that even his wife was alarmed for his sanity. He could not sleep without being visited by nightmares that left him trembling with fragmented visions of his own death or imprisonment.

There is some speculation that Catherine may have actually penned her wishes with regard to this change in the succession. That document, however, never came to light. Even so, had her wishes been expressed even orally before she died, the succession would have been altered.

It was with a mixture of terror and relief that Paul greeted the news of his mother's imminent death. In great haste, he hurried from Gatchina to St. Petersburg. His mother was unconscious, and she was dying. But what would happen if she recovered her senses before she died? What words would she speak?

Among those in attendance at the bedside of the mortally stricken empress was Leo Narishkin. He was almost seventy years old, and had spent close to fifty of them loving the woman who now lay dying. Though never lovers, their friendship had endured.

Many men had loved the fascinating Catherine: the woman who had captured a nation with her charisma, the woman who had endured a loveless marriage and the threat of imminent banishment or worse during her young years, but her husband and her son cannot be counted among them. They were, perhaps, too close to withstand her strength of character.

Paul's vigil lasted through the night and into the following day, each moment marked by an apprehension that she might open those violet eyes and change his birthright forever.

Catherine never regained consciousness.

When the last breath of Catherine II had been expelled, her son commanded that the body of Peter Feodorovich be disinterred and brought back to the palace. With full ceremony and much tears, Paul then returned the crown to what remained of his long-dead father. And with some peculiar sense of final justice, Paul ended this bizarre ritual by entombing his mother and his father side by side.

Not content with effecting this macabre rendezvous, Paul gave orders for the coffin of Grigory Potemkin to be exhumed, instructing that the contents to be scattered in the wilderness as food for the wolves. Though his hatred for Potemkin – who had lost no opportunity to ridicule him when the occasion presented itself – was still fierce enough for Paul to attempt vengeance even after that man's death, he took no action against Zubov, save to expel him from his exalted place at court.

The country then came under the heavy hand of its new emperor, Paul the First. As Catherine had feared, her son was quick to transform the glittering elegance she had brought to her court into a military establishment that quickly terrorized everyone who had to be a part of it. He reversed all of his mother's policies. What she wanted, he did not. Four years later, on the night of March 11, 1801, Alexander overthrew his father.

Paul was murdered on that night, probably with the knowledge, if not the consent, of his son. Among his assassins was Plato Zubov.

And so it came about that even after her death, the wishes of the German princess who became one of Russia's greatest rulers prevailed.